BURY ME
IN SHADOWS

Praise for Greg Herren

Lake Thirteen

"*Lake Thirteen* is a nice, fun, young adult type of ghost story....I'd recommend the book to anyone looking for a good m/m YA ghost story/mystery."—*Love Bytes: LGBTQ Book Reviews*

Dark Tide

"I highly recommend [*Dark Tide*] to anyone looking for a good m/m related mystery. There isn't any direct sex in the book, so if that is important to you, you should move on, but otherwise, give it a shot. I think you'll love it like I did!"—*Love Bytes: Same Sex Book Reviews*

Sleeping Angel

Sleeping Angel "will probably be put on the young adult (YA) shelf, but the fact is that it's a cracking good mystery that general readers will enjoy as well. It just happens to be about teens...A unique viewpoint, a solid mystery and good characterization all conspire to make *Sleeping Angel* a welcome addition to any shelf, no matter where the bookstores stock it."—Jerry Wheeler, *Out in Print*

"This fast-paced mystery is skillfully crafted. Red herrings abound and will keep readers on their toes until the very end. Before the accident, few readers would care about Eric, but his loss of memory gives him a chance to experience dramatic growth, and the end result is a sympathetic character embroiled in a dangerous quest for truth."—*VOYA*

Soliloquy Titles by Greg Herren

Sleeping Angel

Sara

Timothy

Lake Thirteen

Dark Tide

Bury Me in Shadows

Visit us at www.boldstrokesbooks.com

Bury Me
in Shadows

by
Greg Herren

2021

CREDITS
EDITOR: RUTH STERNGLANTZ
PRODUCTION DESIGN: STACIA SEAMAN
COVER DESIGN BY JEANINE HENNING

Acknowledgments

Bury Me in Shadows was a long time coming. When I was a child, my paternal grandmother used to tell me stories about the histories of the families I am descended from. They were wonderful, highly entertaining stories—complete with ghosts and witches and murders, disappearing boys, and of course, Civil War lore. I always wanted to write those stories, adapting them from my memories but also basing them in actual history; the reality rather than just the entertaining stories I was told. But as I got older, and started reading actual history, I began to realize most of the stories she told me were just that: stories, some of them plagiarized from novels and movies I hadn't seen at the time so just took as gospel truths. But the one story I never could quite shake from my head was the story of the Lost Boys, and finally decided that I would try to tell the story, which became *Bury Me in Shadows*.

I need to, as always, thank everyone at Bold Strokes Books for putting up with me and my eccentricities, and my inability to grasp technology or read instructions or keep deadlines. My editor, Ruth Sternglantz, is also a dear friend; any errors or problems in this book lie entirely at my feet—editing me is a Herculean task, and yet one from which she never flinches. Thank you, Ruthie, now and forever and always.

Sandy Lowe keeps the ship running and somehow also manages to find the time to write her own books. Thanks for all you do, Sandy—not the least of which is put up with my craziness.

Cindy Cresap also somehow always manages to keep me in line with the production side of things—whatever she is paid, it isn't enough. She also doesn't mind me replying to her emails with "which book is this?"

Carsen Taite—Lady H—my favorite partner in crime! I miss you and we need to share our burgers again sometime soon.

A big thanks and grilled mac'n'cheese sandwich for Dana Cameron, for all her help with the archaeological aspects of the story. Any errors or mistakes are all on me.

Victoria Brownworth and I have been friends for over twenty years now, and she's been pushing me to write this book for over fifteen years. I FINALLY DID IT, VICTORIA, so you can stop asking me about it.

Jean Redmann, Joey Olsen, Blayke d'Ambrosio, Cullen Hunter, Diane Murray, Leon Harrison, Dereck Alexander, Bryson Richards, Kyle Mills, Chris Daunis, Nadia Eskilden, Jeremy Schroeder, Foster Noone, Jordan Probst, Jasmine Davis, Tucker Barker, Allison Dejan, and Ashton George III make my day job an always pleasurable experience. Thanks, everyone!

And my friends—where would I be without you? Michael Ledet, Pat Brady, Gillian Rodger, Wendy Corsi Staub, Lou Berney, Chris and Katrina Niidas Holm (OUTER BANKS forever!), Bryon Quertermous, Michael Carruth, John Angelico, Harriet Campbell Young, Errol and Peggy Scott Laborde, Bill Loefhelm, Gabino Iglesias, Sumiko Saulson, Steve Driscoll, Rob Tocci, Stuart Wamsley, Beau Braddock, Jake Rickoll, Mark Drake, Josh Drake, Michael Thomas Ford, Catriona McPherson, Sherry Harris, Ellen Byron, Erica Ruth Neubauer, Jamanii Brown, Susanna Calkins, Alex Segura Jr, Elizabeth Little, Kellye Garrett, Laurie R. King, Lawrence Light, Alafair Burke, Nell Stark, Trinity Tam, Lynda Sandoval, Niner Baxter, 'Nathan Smith, Donna Andrews, Barb Goffman, Jeffrey Ricker, Rob Byrnes, Shawn A. Cosby, Sara J. Henry, Sarah Weinman, Ali Vali, Cheryl Head, Michael Nava, Jess Lourey, Linda Joffe Hull, Martin Strickland, Meghan Davidson, Jacob Chavitz, Anne Laughlin, Susan Larson, John and Matt McDougall, Candace Huber, McKenna Jordan, and so many, many more…thank you all for supporting me and being present.

And of course, thank you to Paul J. Willis, for putting up with me and loving me anyway.

This is for BEAU BRADDOCK
Thanks for letting me name a character after you!

"And nothing is concealed up which will not be revealed, nor hidden which will not be known."

—Luke 12:2

Chapter One

W as this an accident, or did you do it on purpose?"
I opened my eyes to see my mother standing at the foot
of my hospital bed, her heart-shaped face unreadable as always. The
strap of her Louis Vuitton limited edition purse was hooked into the
crook of her left arm. Her right hand was fidgeting, meaning she
was craving one of the cigarettes she allowed herself from time to
time—never more than two in a single day. Her dove-gray skirt suit,
complete with matching jacket over a coral silk blouse, looked more
rumpled than usual. Her shoulder-length bob, recently touched up
as there were no discernible gray roots in her rigid part, was also a
bit disheveled. She wasn't tall, just a few inches over five feet, and
always wore low heels because she preferred being underestimated.
Regular yoga and Pilates classes kept her figure slim. She never
wore a lot of makeup, just highlights here and there to make her
cheekbones seem more prominent or to make her eyes pop. No one
would ever guess by just looking at her that she was one of the top
criminal attorneys in the country, whose criminal law classes at the
University of Chicago were in high demand.

I could tell she was unnerved because I could hear her Alabama
accent, and it was strong. She'd worked long and hard to get rid of
that accent while in law school. "No one would take me seriously
after they heard me speak," she'd explained to me once, "or they
thought I was stupid." Now she used it only when she *wanted*
someone to feel superior to her.

It also came out when she'd been drinking or was upset.

And worked like a charm getting her out of speeding tickets.

I'd been neither asleep nor awake, hovering in that weird in-between state where I'd been living for the last three or four or however many days it had been since I woke up here.

"It wasn't on purpose." I croaked out the words. My throat was still raw and sore from the stomach pumping. My lips were chapped, and my eyes still burned from the aftermath of the insane drug-and-alcohol binge I'd gone on after the big breakup with fucking Tradd Chisholm. "It was an accident." I shifted in the hospital bed, trying to sit up more, the IV swinging wildly. That last and final fight with Tradd flashed through my head.

Why are you so fucking needy? he'd screamed at me. *I can't fucking breathe!*

Fucking Tradd, anyway. Why had I let him get under my skin the way I did?

Why had I let him isolate me from my friends?

Why, why, why.

He wasn't worth this—that was for sure.

Heels clacking on the linoleum floor, she moved to the chair beside my bed.

She peered at me with her big, emotionless gray eyes. "Given your history, you understand why I had to insist they put you on a seventy-two-hour hold, once they called me?"

I closed my eyes.

My history.

Tired of the nonstop bullying at St. Sebastian's, the elite prep school she'd said would set me up for the rest of my life, I'd slit my wrists at fifteen. The therapist she sent me to afterward was convinced it was more a cry for attention than anything else, and I had to agree with that assessment. I hadn't followed the vein up my arm with the X-Acto knife, after all, instead cutting across—so the wounds clotted long before any significant blood loss. I'd taken a handful of her Xanax, thinking it would make the razor slicing my skin hurt less.

It didn't.

I passed out in the bathwater from the Xanax, not from blood loss.

Put yourself in her shoes, Jake, Dr. Mendelssohn said, earning her seven hundred and fifty dollars per hour. *Imagine coming home from a long day in court, exhausted, and finding your only child unconscious in a bathtub full of bloody water, a bloody razor blade on the bath mat. That's an image she's not likely to ever forget. No parent would.*

"Yes, Mom, I understand," I replied, keeping my eyes closed. My throat still ached, and I had a headache. The doctor said it would take another day or so before I started feeling physically better. It had already been twenty-four hours. Forty-eight more to go before I could go home to my cute little apartment on Napoleon Avenue.

Not that I wanted to go back there.

The memories of the fight and Tradd storming out were still too fresh. Had we ever been happy? I wasn't sure. We must have been at some point. There must be good memories, too—I just couldn't remember them right now.

I'm not responsible for your feelings! he'd screamed at me. *You're too possessive! You won't let me breathe! I can't take it anymore!* And finally, the finishing touch: *You're just not worth all this drama.*

He'd slammed the door behind him.

I'd stood there, shaking, grabbed my phone, before remembering there wasn't anyone for me to call. Tradd hadn't liked my friends, and I'd chosen him over them. Our friends were *his* friends.

Without him, I was alone.

Instead, I'd gone into my little kitchenette, my hands shaking as I reached for the bottle of Grey Goose in the cabinet over the stove. I poured myself a glass, added some ice, and started drinking. I don't remember heading to the Quarter, whether I took a Lyft or the streetcar or called a cab or how I got there.

All that mattered was that I did get there.

I do remember deciding, somewhere between the second and third glass of vodka on the rocks, that the easiest way for me to feel better was a lot of drugs and liquor and a lot of sex with strangers. Most of the days between Thursday night and Sunday morning were a blur.

At some point I must have run into a dealer I knew and started snorting anything I could buy.

So. Many. Blanks.

The last thing I remembered was being on the dance floor at Oz, my shirt off and my heart racing and sweat pouring out of my body, the little packet of crystal meth I'd just scored from someone—the last of I don't know how many—clutched in my hand as I moved to the endless thump of the music, some total stranger dancing close behind me, grinding on me, dry-humping me on the dance floor. I remember dipping my apartment key into the baggie and inhaling up both nostrils.

According to the doctor who'd spoken to me when I came to in the emergency room, I'd collapsed on the dance floor around five in the morning on Sunday. The ambulance arrived at Oz around five thirty and brought me to University Medical Center. They'd pumped my stomach, given me something to counteract the meth, stuck an IV in my arm, and called my mother.

And once she told them about the suicide attempt when I was fifteen, they agreed I should be watched for seventy-two hours.

And here she was.

"I won't ask why you didn't call me." She sounded tired. She probably was—she was consulting on a case in Los Angeles and must have taken a red-eye flight in. "I know I've not been the best mother, Jake, and maybe it's my fault you're so messed up. Maybe I shouldn't have been a mother. God knows I can't make a marriage last. Oh, that reminds me, I've kicked Brock out and filed for divorce—" Brock was only ten years older than me and a tennis instructor. I hadn't thought it would last, but he was gorgeous, had a great body, and was nice enough, if not particularly smart. I didn't blame her for marrying someone for great sex after three failed marriages. "—but I've done my best, the best I knew how to do." Her right hand was twitching again. I was tempted to tell her to just go have the damned cigarette. "And I know I've not been around much because of my career but…" She shook her head. "Your father says you don't talk to him either."

I was so young when my parents divorced that I had no memories of them being married. He'd remarried and moved out to the Chicago suburbs with his second wife. They had three kids together and lived a very *Leave It to Beaver* existence. Cecily, my stepmother, always tried to make me feel like I was part of their family, which just made me feel even more out of place in the suburbs.

"So I guess we failed you as parents. Maybe you shut me out because you think I'm not there for you, have never been there for you. But I am your mother, and I wish you'd call me when you're in trouble." Her voice shook on the last words, the accent softening the *r*'s and drawing out the vowels, but she took a moment to compose herself. I watched her turn back into the high-powered, highly sought after criminal defense attorney who rarely lost a case and ambitious law students wanted to learn from. "I took the liberty of stopping by your apartment on the way here." She hesitated. "You tore up all the pictures of Tradd and burned them in the sink. And since he's not here, it's safe to assume he's what this was all about?"

"I don't—I don't want to talk about Tradd." I closed my eyes. I felt numb but was afraid the pain would come back.

"All right." She leaned forward in the chair. "You don't have to talk about it if you don't want to—I'm not going to make you." She got up out of the chair and walked over to the window, looking out through the blinds at the traffic on Tulane Avenue. "I've already talked to the dean, and they've agreed to withdraw you from this semester, even though it's so close to finals, given the circumstances. I think you need to get out of New Orleans for a while."

"Mom—"

"Don't argue with me, Jake." She began tapping her foot. "I've also spoken to your landlord and will pay your rent through September, so you can keep the place and come back here to go to school again this fall. But you need to get away from New Orleans, at least for a little while. I don't think this is the healthiest environment for you to be in while…while you're this fragile."

After the suicide attempt, she'd threatened to put me into a psychiatric facility. We compromised on Dr. Mendelsohn. "I'm not going to a treatment center."

"Dr. Benoit said you were inhaling the drugs, so while it's still possible you're addicted, at least you aren't injecting."

Thank heaven for small miracles, right?

"I'm not addicted to anything, Mom."

"I'll take your word for it." She hesitated. "But admitting you have a problem is the first step—"

I cut her off. "It was stupid, but that's all, Mom. I reacted badly."

I sat up farther in the bed, wincing as my head throbbed. "I smoke a little weed here and there, and yeah, I get drunk sometimes, and every once in a great while maybe I'll do something else—"

Always tell the truth, just not the whole truth.

"—but I don't *need* to do anything. Right now, just thinking about drinking again makes me sick."

"That'll pass." She turned back to look at me, her arms crossed. "You can't come home to Chicago because I'm consulting on a case in Los Angeles and will be gone most of the summer. I don't imagine you want to stay with your father—"

"No!"

"—and there really are few other options." She cracked a smile. "I never thought I would say this, but I know the perfect solution. It solves two problems, actually. You remember when I called you about your grandmother's stroke?"

I gaped at her.

She couldn't be serious.

Her mother, who only answered to Miss Sarah or Mrs. Donelson, had suffered a massive stroke back during Carnival. She hadn't been expected to live, but she'd grimly held on to life in a hospital in Birmingham. Mom had stopped taking me with her on the annual duty trips down to Alabama to visit her mother when I was about eight, so my memories of Miss Sarah were kind of vague. Mom always refused to talk about her mother—or any of her childhood in the country—and her younger brother, Dewey, never did either. Dewey lived in Birmingham with his wife and kids. They visited us in Chicago every couple of years or so. He seemed like a good guy and his wife nice. Their kids were a little spoiled—he was an investment banker—but no more so than my half-siblings out in their Mayberry-like suburb.

"You're going to send me to *Alabama?*" I stared at her. "For the *summer?*"

"She's getting out of the hospital," she replied calmly. "She wants to die at home, and Dewey and I are arranging for nurses to come in—one during the day and one at night, twelve-hour shifts. But those nurses are going to need to take breaks sometimes, and we can't trust that Donovan kid to spell them."

"What Donovan kid?"

"I've told you about Kelly Donovan." She furrowed her brow. I racked my brain. "No, you haven't."

"Of course I did—you just weren't paying attention." The *like always* was implied. She let out an exasperated breath. "His mother was a distant cousin—I'm not sure how we're related, to be honest, nor do I care, but his mother died last summer, and Miss Sarah took him in. He's some big-deal athlete, has a scholarship to play football at Troy this fall. But he's not family, and while I certainly couldn't stop her from taking him in, I don't trust him alone in the house with her and the nurses." She waved a hand. "It's bad enough he's had the run of the place since she went into the hospital, but Dewey—" Her face twisted, and she sighed. "He's been there the whole time, and Dewey thinks we can't very well kick him out—I really didn't like him staying there alone in the house while she was in the hospital—because he has nowhere to go, and Dewey certainly can't move there to stay while we wait for her to…" She stopped.

"Wait for her to die?"

"Well, yes." She nodded. "I don't know why it's always so hard to talk honestly about family things. Yes, while we wait for her to die. The doctors don't know how much longer she'll last. She could last for months, weeks, years—or she could die tomorrow. I know I'd feel better if you were there in the house. Not just because of this"—she gestured around the room, and I felt my own face turning red—"but to know a family member is there in the house with her. She can't really get out of bed—you don't have to worry about any of the personal hygiene things, that's what we're paying the nurses for—and she's not able to talk much. And you won't have to spend much time with her, except to give the nurses a break to have dinner or a cigarette or to stretch their legs or something." She sat back down in the chair. "And don't say you'll be bored. There's a satellite dish, so there's Wi-Fi and a big screen television Dewey bought her, and"—her eyes gleamed—"since she's dying, we might as well get a jump on things that'll need to be done once she's gone. You can start clearing out the place. No one has ever thrown a damned thing away since the Great Depression. The attic…the attic looks like something from one of those awful shows about hoarders. Lord, that place is a mess, filled with old furniture and boxes of things. Maybe some of that garbage is worth something, can be sold or donated somewhere it can do some good. You can take inventory."

"That sounds like a lot of fun."

"At least you haven't lost what you think is your sense of humor." She tilted her head and her eyes narrowed. "But if you'd rather spend the summer at a facility…"

"No, no, of course not." My heart was sinking. Awful as it sounded, a summer in rural Alabama was better than a summer in a rehab center and going to group therapy, knowing you don't belong there in the first place only making it worse.

And getting away, even to Alabama, didn't sound like such a bad idea. Maybe by the time I came back in August, I'd be over Tradd for good.

Thinking about him caused a pang. The numbness was fading.

"And of course, I'll pay you for the work," she went on. "You'll have your credit cards, and I'll double the monthly deposit into your bank account. Does that sound fair?"

I nodded.

"And you can also keep an eye on those archaeologists."

"Archaeologists?" I stared at her. "What are you talking about?"

"You really don't listen to me when I talk, do you?" She shook her head. "An archaeologist from the University of Alabama—Dr. Brady, I think is his name—has been after us for years to allow him to excavate the ruins. Miss Sarah, of course, would have none of it, but after the stroke, for some reason known only to him, Dewey gave his permission. You'll probably never see them—they're using the old road to the ruins, they've cleared it all out—but Miss Sarah doesn't know they're there and you're not going to tell her. Kelly has been warned about telling her—I am not as squeamish as Dewey about throwing him out. If she gets upset or angry…" She cleared her throat. "There's no need to tell her anything that might…well, finish her off. And she's just mean enough to go on living so she can cause trouble for both me and Dewey."

"But if she's bedridden—"

"I know my mother." Her voice became cold and steely. "She may be bedridden, but as long as she's breathing, she can still cause trouble. I think Dewey should have told them to clear out once she decided to come home to die, frankly, but he's the son and has the power of attorney, and so what I think doesn't matter." Her voice was bitter. "I'm just the *daughter*."

"What are they looking for at the ruins? The Lost Boys?"

Mom may not talk much about her childhood, but she *had* told me some stories about the family history. The Blackwoods had been among the original settlers of Corinth County, back when Alabama was still a territory. The legend of the Lost Boys was one of the stories she'd told me, while also letting me know that it was probably just a romantic fairy tale.

Before the Civil War, the Blackwood plantation had been one of the largest plantations in the state. The Blackwood family had also been one of the most prominent enslavers in Alabama—the original land grant made up most of what was now western Corinth County. When Alabama seceded and war broke out, Ezekiel Blackwood and his two oldest sons had gone to fight in Virginia, leaving behind his wife and the two younger sons. Ezekiel died at Gettysburg, the oldest son at Malvern Hill. When the younger son returned in 1865, all he found was the ruins of a burned house. The enslaved people, his mother, and two younger brothers were gone. "The story was that a Yankee soldier—maybe a deserter—had robbed the place, killed the family, and burned the house down." She had shrugged. "But that story—you hear it everywhere. It's not even original. Hell, even Margaret Mitchell used it in *Gone with the Wind*."

The mystery of Mrs. Blackwood, his mother, was cleared up when he found her wooden headstone in the family burial plot, but no trace of his two younger brothers had ever been found. The surviving son married one of the county girls and wound up losing most of the property, but his son Samuel had slowly built back up the family fortune. He built a huge Victorian house closer to the county road than the ruins of the old plantation house. But his descendants squandered the money, losing even more of the land, and the big house had started falling into ruin. Miss Sarah's father had been a farmer, barely scratching out an existence from the red dirt. The woods had grown back up, and the ruins were about a twenty-minute walk from the newer house, hidden from sight by towering pines.

One of the few memories I had of visiting Alabama as a child was a trip back to the ruins of the old house. I can still remember the columns on the porch and the chimneys at either end covered with moss—but you could still see where the fire had burned them black.

Mom raised me to not take pride in the fact my ancestors enslaved people. "Slavery was disgusting, Jake. The root of every racial problem we still have in this country is built on the foundation of slavery. We shouldn't forget the history, but we shouldn't take pride in the fact our ancestors owned people and were *traitors*. The heritage *is* hate, never forget that."

I never had.

"I should hope not, since he has an excellent reputation as a scholar," she said with a look of distaste. "Apparently, he told Dewey the ruins of Blackwood Hall are one of the few antebellum plantation sites in the state that haven't been excavated, so this Dr. Brady—don't worry, I did a thorough background check on him once Dewey told me about all of this—is more interested in finding how they lived and documenting the history than in any of the romantic family legends." A faint smile crossed her lips, and she arched one of her perfectly sculpted eyebrows. "Believe it or not, the Blackwoods of Corinth County haven't exactly been the subject of a lot of historical research. But Corinth County was a backwater even then, so I doubt he'll find anything of major significance there." She covered my hand with hers. "Is there anything you need that I haven't already taken care of?"

I closed my eyes. "No, Mom, as always—you've thought of everything."

CHAPTER TWO

Mom took me back to my apartment in a Lyft the morning I was released. She was staying in a suite at the Ritz-Carlton on Canal Street.

She'd also cleaned my place at some point, because I was certain I hadn't left it looking that neat and tidy. I suspected I wouldn't find any liquor in the place, either, when I checked for it.

But I didn't care if I ever took another drink again, and I sure as hell wasn't going to ever do drugs again—well, other than smoking some weed. When she wasn't paying attention, I checked for my stash in my locked center desk drawer.

It was still there.

But I wasn't about to smoke any before she got on a plane.

The week before her flight back to Los Angeles passed in a blur. She was tireless, checking things off her seemingly endless *get Jake ready for Alabama* list. All bills payable online? Check. Clean out refrigerator? Check. Hold on cable bill? Check. Oil change and tune-up for Jake's car? Check.

Check, check, check.

We ate in restaurants—neither of us were capable of much in the kitchen—and of course, she had another checklist of all the places she wanted to try. It felt sometimes like she was afraid to let me out of her sight, like, if given the chance I'd slip down to the Quarter to start another binge.

The thought of alcohol still turned my stomach. I might not ever drink again.

Of course, I never heard from Tradd. He was finished with me. He hadn't blocked me on social media—that would have been a kindness. He wanted me to see how well he was doing without me in his life. I finally hid him on all my social media because whenever his smiling face, having a great time with his friends, popped up, it felt like my heart was being ripped out of my chest again.

But the more it became clear Tradd didn't give a shit about me, the hurt began fading.

We'd met at a fraternity party, of all places. Beta Kappa. They were notorious on campus for their wild parties. My best friend— well, *former* best friend—Kayla dragged me there. Kayla was blond, blue-eyed, and running up student loan debt she'd never be able to pay off with her Public Health degree. She was interested in one of the Beta Kappa brothers, it was a Friday night, and I had nothing better to do. I was a loner by habit—all the kids at St. Sebastian's had avoided the fag, and after the suicide attempt it was like I'd grown a second head—and never learned how to start talking to a stranger, how to turn someone I'd just met into a friend, let alone a boyfriend. I'd tried the gay bars down in the Quarter with the fake ID Kayla had gotten me but not once had ever managed to drum up the nerve to talk to a stranger.

The dating app experiences were even worse—furtive, hurried hookups that left me feeling dirty and ashamed of myself.

Kayla and I met in an Econ class when we were both new to Tulane and New Orleans. Unlike me, she had the confidence to talk to anyone, and we'd gone from study buddies to friends.

We could hear the thumping of the bass from the party as we walked toward the house. The front porch and yard of the Beta Kappa house was crowded with people laughing and drinking and getting wasted. We wove through the drunks, and she vanished once we were through the front doors. I was going to spend the night standing by myself in a corner sipping a beer waiting for her to find me and release me from drive-drunk-Kayla-home duty because she was hooking up with a guy.

Tradd Chisholm approached me after I filled a red cup at the keg and wandered back out onto the front gallery of the house. I found a secluded corner and sat on the railing, watching some drunk frat boys playing boccie for drinks on the front lawn. I saw him approaching and figured he'd join one of the clusters of people out there, but instead he walked right up to me and smiled.

He was gorgeous, with curly brown hair pulled back into a man-bun and a tight T-shirt and skinny jeans sculpted to his body. He was a few inches taller than me, close to six feet. An expensive watch adorned his left wrist. When he smiled at me, his thick sensual lips pulled back over impossibly perfect white teeth, and his brown eyes twinkled as he stuck out his hand and introduced himself.

Like Kayla, he was on a mission and wasn't about to let my shyness keep him from what he wanted that night, which was to take my clothes off and run his tongue all over my body... When he asked if we could go back to my place and get to know each other better, I texted her that I was going home.

I couldn't believe my luck.

"Someone," he teased me in the morning while he waited for his Lyft, "needs to teach you how to be gay."

That was how it started.

I'd been such a fool, so dazzled and bewitched that I got lost in an obsessive love for him. It was my first time falling in love, my first time having a boyfriend...and he was so experienced and savvy about being out and proud. I couldn't believe how lucky I was, to somehow land someone so smart and funny and clever and sexy. I was so involved with Tradd that I let my own friends—the few I had—drift away.

And now that he was gone, I couldn't just call or text them and expect them to be there for me.

Yes, much as I hated the thought of burying myself in Alabama for the summer, it was better than being lonely in New Orleans, with temptation not that far away.

I got up early Monday morning to take Mom to the airport. I'd packed my car the night before, so I could head east after dropping her off. I was ready. The directions were loaded into the map app on my phone. The gas tank was full. I'd made several playlists to listen to on the drive.

Mom's flight was at nine, and she was waiting out on the sidewalk in front of the Ritz-Carlton, her rolling suitcases stacked neatly by her side, idly tapping her foot while scrolling through her phone.

Once we were on the highway heading for the airport, she reached over and touched my right hand. "You're—you're going to be all right, aren't you?"

"Why wouldn't I be?" I replied, surprised. She's rarely, if ever, sentimental.

"I don't like to talk about what it was like growing up for me." She typed something on her phone, hit send, and looked back over at me. "Not even with my therapist. My mother…she's unemotional, kind of cold. I can't remember her ever hugging me or telling me she loved me. I used to think it was something I did, there was some reason she didn't like me and preferred Dewey…but I think she just didn't know what to do with a daughter." She laughed. "And it's not like Dewey had it much better than I did. But now she's dying… I'm glad you're doing this." She mumbled something I didn't quite catch.

"Are you going to come see her before—before she dies?"

"If she gets worse, of course I'll come. Dewey says she's stabilized some." She rubbed her eyes. "God, I've not had enough coffee. But you're going to be all right, aren't you? You've got your prescription?"

They'd given me my own Xanax prescription when I left the hospital. "Yes, it's in my laptop bag. And I won't abuse them, don't worry."

"But you'll call me, right, if…" Her voice trailed off.

"Mom. It's okay. I'll just be bored. And I have my phone and my iPad and my laptop. And my textbooks." That had been her suggestion—*Since you're retaking the same classes this fall, you should take your textbooks with you and study when you're bored.* I smiled at her. "Mom, I'll be fine."

I pulled up at the curb at the terminal. "Yeah." She blinked rapidly, and I realized she had tears in her eyes. She held me longer than her usual drive-by hugs. "Call me if you need anything," she said. She let go of me, straightened her glasses, and the moment of being a mom passed. She was again Glynis Chapman, attorney-at-law. "And no trouble, okay?"

I switched from my Taylor Swift playlist to Adele as I crossed the state line into Mississippi.

Mississippi was so deserted it seemed like the state was empty, like a zombie apocalypse or something had happened without me knowing about it. Other cars were few and far between, mostly on the other side going south, the pine trees lined up like soldiers along each side of the highway. I kept expecting tumbleweeds to blow across the road, or a herd of zombies to come out of the brush alongside the highway.

I saw my first Confederate flag before reaching Hattiesburg. It was a decal on the rear bumper of a slow-moving, battered old pickup truck that hadn't been washed since the turn of the century. By the time I'd passed through Hattiesburg, I'd lost count of how many I'd seen—flags flying from antennas, bumper stickers, license plate frames. The Lost Cause was still venerated in this part of the country.

As I kept driving north on the lonely highway, memories kept bubbling up, a witches' brew of good times and bad. Tradd was right—I *had* been clingy and smothering. Those memories made me wince with embarrassment—Jesus, Jake, how about a little self-respect—but he also gaslit me, set me up so he could berate me, keeping me off-balance, never sure how he felt about me. His friends were always polite, but distant, like they didn't want to get too close, and I always worried what he said to them about me.

Remember that time they left you on the dance floor during Southern Decadence?

Tradd said it was an accident, but it happened more than once, didn't it?

I needed gas, and my stomach was growling, when I saw an off-ramp with a sign for a gas station and an Arby's. The exit was for a town called Toomsuba. I was close to the Alabama state line, at most maybe another hour. I filled the tank and parked the car over by some trees on the edge of the parking lot. I checked my phone as I went inside to order, and there was a text from Kelly Donovan.

How's the drive?

Kelly and I had emailed and texted a few times since Uncle Dewey sent me his contact info. He seemed nice enough—but he couldn't spell nor grasp the rudimentary rules of English grammar. I'd googled him a couple of times. Mom was right about him being a jock—and a good-looking one, at that. We started following each other on Instagram and friended each other on Facebook, but he

wasn't very active on social media. He usually just posted links to
newspaper write-ups about his athletic successes and occasionally
was tagged in a picture by one of his friends. He was blond, with big
gym-worked muscles and a flat, rippling stomach. He didn't seem
capable of taking a picture without looking drop dead gorgeous.
Dimples and golden skin and white-blond hair and thick muscles on
top of his muscles and a big smile with big white even teeth and...

He was a lot better looking than Tradd.

I replied, *So far so good—in Toomsuba MS getting gas and some
food.*

And he texted back, *Almost to the state line then. See you in a
couple of hours.*

I sat in a booth and ate my lunch, feeling the pinch of anxiety
starting up. I was going to be sharing a house with a stranger. I had
trouble talking to strangers.

He probably wouldn't be around the house much, anyway.
He'd told me he was staying in shape by playing on a baseball team
in Corinth and going to the gym every day, and he also had a part-
time job at the Hardee's in Corinth.

Another text from Kelly: *There's not much to do around here but
I'll show you around.*

I finished eating, emptied my tray into the trash, and walked
back out in the heat and humidity.

As I headed down the on-ramp to the highway, my mind
wandered back into forbidden territory again.

Tradd wasn't the first guy I ever had sex with, but I'd fallen
madly, head over heels, crazy in love with him—emphasis on *crazy*.
He was serious about teaching me how to be gay, too—advising
me what to eat and what not to, taking me to the gym and showing
me what to do to get my body to look its best, the ins and outs
of hooking up with guys on the so-called dating apps. "Some guys
might want a date," he told me one night as we got ready to go out
dancing, mixing me a vodka tonic in my apartment and wearing
just his black underwear. He winked at me. "But most guys are just
looking to get laid. Never mistake fucking for dating, Jake. Biggest
gay mistake ever. Never get attached."

Never get attached.

I hadn't known at the time how right he was.

Maybe he'd been warning me.

I swallowed my jealousy when he flirted with other guys, when he kissed them on the dance floor. Play it cool play it cool play it cool. He's the type to not like possessiveness.

I'd been such a fool.

He'd never cared about me.

He was never my boyfriend.

I wanted to pound my head on the steering wheel.

I crossed the state line and there was the sign: *Welcome to Alabama the Beautiful.*

It wasn't just a slogan, either—Alabama *was* beautiful. As I drove farther northeast into Alabama, the lower hills began gradually getting steeper and higher. The forests of towering pines were deep and thick, and as my turn off on the parkway— "There will be tolls," the map app had told me—got nearer, the highway had been blasted through hills rather than built over them. Towering orange half-moon-shaped slopes of dirt and solid rock rose on either side of the ribbon of pavement, crowned with more pine trees, followed by rolling fields breaking into the monotony of the forest. I drove across bridges over streams and creeks and small rivers stained brownish-orange. Some of the hollows—*hollers*, Mom may have worked on losing her accent but she still said *holler* instead of *hollow*—were filled with kudzu, that enormous green leafy vine originally imported from Japan as landcover that quickly got out of control, now taking over the South. The enormous vines of kudzu looked like leafy green suds, covering poles and trees and abandoned buildings and hiding them from sight, turning them into mysterious shapes carved out of green leaves, jutting up toward the sky.

If you're not careful, the kudzu will come through the window and get you while you sleep.

Goose bumps came up on my arms as the words faded in my head.

Someone said that to me when I was a kid.

I didn't remember much from coming to visit when I was a kid. I vaguely remembered my grandmother's house was tucked away from the paved county road behind a slope, facing a gravel road leading down into a hollow, and the big dark woods not far behind the house's back porch.

I always thought of the house as being dark for some reason.

And I remembered being afraid of my grandmother.

I couldn't remember why.

I began to slow for the exit to the parkway. This route bypassed both Tuscaloosa and Corinth.

I'd lost count of the Confederate bumper stickers and flags I'd seen.

Stop that, I scolded myself as I took the exit. It's not like I was wearing a sign screaming GAY to the world, and besides, not everyone in Alabama is a bigot.

Occasionally, I'd see a tractor out in the fields. Small country houses, sometimes with older women in cotton housedresses with a basin in their laps sitting on the porch in a swing or a chair. The road kept weaving up and down and sometimes through hills, erosion marks carved into the orange earth where water from rain found its way down. The white line on the side of the road was stained orange from the red dirt.

After about another hour the map app warned me I was approaching an intersection where I'd turn right. I slowed the car. There was an enormous signpost on the side of the road, reaching up about twenty feet, with an arm reached out over the road and on it big red squares with white letters etched on them: *Stop.*

I turned right. The corner to my left was a wide expanse of pavement, with weeds breaking through here and there. An abandoned cinder block building stood behind an enormous cracked paved area. There were two parallel rises of concrete where gas pumps had once stood.

Fowler's Four Corners, I remembered.

The Fowlers had been murdered when Mom was a little girl.

They got robbed for less than twenty dollars in the till. The killers were out drinking and joyriding and shot them both dead. Their brains and blood were splattered all over the bread and the canned goods, a voice whispered in my head.

I shivered.

I started climbing another hill. To my right, forest ran alongside the road, but on the other side was a railing and a steep, sharp drop. I put my window down a little bit and breathed in the scent of fresh pine. I remembered this road from when I was a child, and sure enough, the side road was right where I remembered it being, but there was a trailer parked on blocks where I could have sworn a house used to be. I went around a sharp turn and met a filthy pickup truck, covered in dried red mud, going the other way. I got a quick glimpse of a man in a flannel-looking shirt with a trucker cap with the Confederate flag perched on his head. Another steep slope, then another straightaway, then another slope. A sign warned me of an approaching S curve. I got around the first part of the curve, and there was the dirt road I vaguely remembered up ahead where the pavement curved left and uphill again. I remembered the dirt road, mostly unused, had small trees growing up from the orange dirt. It was now cleared, and the red dirt ruts were all churned up by tire treads—the road to the ruins. I went around the sharp left turn, and up ahead I could see the mailbox on the side of the road, right where another gravel road met the pavement. On the left, that gravel road climbed farther up the mountain and into the forests. I slowed down and turned on my signal, made the sharp turn, and there it was, in a small hollow on the other side of the high hill.

The rickety old white four room house Miss Sarah used to rent out was on the left side of the dirt road, practically a ruin with its roof collapsed, and on the other side of the gravel road stood the enormous house built around the turn of the twentieth century, when fortune had again smiled upon the Blackwoods.

I shivered.

It looked…it looked *haunted.*

My stomach clenched as I turned my car into the gravel parking area next to the house. There was the little wellhouse, just to the left of the big silver tank for propane gas.

I could hear my heart thumping in my ears.

I'd remembered that the porch wrapped around the entire house. The left front corner of the house had a kind of a turret bulging out from the straight lines, and on both the first and second floors the turret was all windows. Up on the top floor, the attic, the turret was open to the sun and wind, and crowned with a witch's hat. A brick chimney broke the sloping line of the roof, along with a gable in the direct center. The porch railing had intricately carved wooden designs mounted between the posts. The house had been painted green and yellow once, but the paint was peeling away with gray wood exposed. The front yard gently sloped down to the gravel road. The rose bushes I remembered were still there, and the four o'clocks in front of the porch.

I heard my grandmother's voice, harsh, low, saying, *They bloom every day at four o'clock, but only at four o'clock, for an hour, and then the blooms close for another day. That's why they're called four o'clocks.*

It looked smaller than I remembered—as a kid, it seemed to tower over me and blot out the sun. But it was still a big house. The forest was also closer to the back of the house than I remembered. The back yard was nothing more than a patchy spread of dark green grass with bare spots that looked like someone had scraped the grass off the dirt. The house sat on a wide ledge, or plateau, extending about twenty yards to the left side of the house, where it started sloping down to yet another ledge, overgrown now, that used to be my grandmother's garden. I remembered following her through the rows as she carried a wicker basket plucking ears of corn off towering stalks. She'd grown beans and okra and watermelon and peppers and black-eyed peas and tomatoes and green onions. The corn stalks were still there, amongst the weeds and slender reeds of young pine trees. At the far side of the garden there was about a five-foot drop to the creek running along the bottom of the hollow—the *holler*. On the other side of the creek—the *crick*—the slope was covered with weeds and grasses and bushes and young trees as it rose gradually to where the towering pines of the forest reached up to scratch at the sky. Out at the back edge of the garden I could see the graying, rotting wood of the old outhouse, covered with ivy and moss.

The house looked tired and defeated. The shingles on the roof had turned gray from long exposure to the brutal summer sun. Some were missing in places, others cracked and broken. Some windows were open, faded curtains moving in the slight breeze. Window air-conditioning units, dripping with condensation, chugged away in others. The front door was closed. The aluminum screen door looked battered, the screen bowed out with holes in some places, the green paint on the front door blistered and peeling. Some of the shutters hung crookedly like the next strong wind would blow them off away into the woods.

Despite all that, the house seemed...*alive.*

I shivered despite the thick muggy air and the broiling heat of the sun.

I shouldn't have come danced through my head as goose bumps came up on my skin.

I just sat there, staring at the house, unable to move.

Memories flooded through my head, and I experienced emotions ranging from anger to fear to absolute terror. The hairs on my arms and the back of my neck stood on end. My skin felt like it was trying to crawl off my body.

In my head I heard a loud noise, and somehow, I was inside, running, terrified, through a darkened hallway.

Must get away must get away don't want to die oh my God I don't want to die...

A dark green Subaru Forrester and enormous black Chevrolet pickup truck with the ubiquitous Confederate flag decal were parked in the gravel alongside the house. There was a gun rack inside the cab of the truck, and there was also one of those *From my cold dead hands* bumper stickers on the opposite side of the bumper from the Confederate flag.

I pulled up next to the truck and turned off my engine. I opened the door and scrambled out, staring up at the house.

My grandmother's house might be many things, but I doubted I'd ever think of it as home.

I don't feel safe here I shouldn't be here I need to get out of here—

CHAPTER THREE

The spell was broken by the slamming of the screen door. Someone emerged from the house and came out to the corner of the porch. "Jake? That you?" he drawled. The accent was so thick I could cut it with a knife.

His smile was even more dazzling in person, his thick red lips and big perfect white teeth, enormous eyes such a deep blue I could get lost in them forever if I didn't look away.

He hopped over the railing while I just stood there in the gravel, gawking and sweating. He was well over six feet tall and, well, *golden*. White-gold hair cascading in waves around his head, his eyebrows and eyelashes white gold, his eyes sapphire blue. His shoulders were broad, and his waist almost impossibly narrow. He was wearing cutoff denim overalls with no shirt underneath. His skin was tanned golden brown, his arms and chest covered in that same fine white-gold hair. The muscles of his arms were enormous, road-mapped with bulging veins.

He—he almost glowed in the sunlight.

He was almost obscenely attractive. *No gay guy would wear such faded and worn-out overalls in public*, I could hear Tradd sneering in my head. *Even at home.*

But *maybe* gays in Alabama were different?

They did look sexy on him, and wasn't that the most important thing?

I wondered if he knew I was gay, and if I should tell him. But if he'd ever looked at any of my social media, he *had* to know.

He held out an enormous hand for me to shake. His hand was

strong and calloused. "Welcome, I guess. You need help with your stuff?"

Yew need hay-ulp wit yuh stuff?

There was something—*something* about him.

I felt drawn to him in a way I'd never reacted to another guy before, like we were connected together somehow…

I shook myself out of the trance.

I'm sure the fact that he was the sexiest human being I'd ever seen had nothing to do with it.

That was just crazy, wasn't it?

And whatever it was I was feeling—*felt*—he clearly wasn't.

"Are you okay?" I heard Kelly asking from what seemed like a million miles away. "Jake? You tired from the drive?" *Yew tahd frum thuh drahv?*

Another mosquito landed on my cheek, and I swatted it away.

"Yeah, no, I'm fine," I said, taking another drink from my water. "The house…looks bad."

"Miss Sarah don't have the money to keep it up." Kelly opened the hatch of my car and grabbed the bigger suitcase, swinging it out effortlessly, the muscles in his shoulder and back flexing beneath that golden tanned skin. "I know Dewey offered to pay for it, but she told him no last summer."

"Why?" I slapped at another mosquito, leaving a bloody smear on my forearm. "She prefers to have the house fall down around her?"

Kelly shrugged. "She don't like to be beholden to no one."

"But Dewey—Mom—they're family."

"They don't act like it," he said, the golden eyebrows coming together over the bridge of his aquiline nose. "Dewey never comes out here to see her, and your mom? Once a year, maybe. And she told me she hadn't seen you since you were a baby."

Horseflies buzzed, and bees circled the rosebushes, and the wind whispered and nickered through the trees behind the house. Cicadas and crickets hummed and sang.

"I was eight," I said, feeling my face starting to flush. "Mom never wanted me to come with her."

I never really tried, though, did I? Did I ever ask?

I grabbed my other suitcase. The handle was hot, so I dropped it as Kelly carried the heavier one over the flagstones and tossed it up onto the porch with ease. He walked back and picked up the other one with a sly smirk, almost as if to say *Here, let me do it since you're so weak.*

I tried not to notice the way his muscles bulged as they worked, the veins standing out against the skin like they were trying to escape. *Stop staring*, I scolded myself. The other strap slipped down past his shoulder, and his overalls sagged a little bit, exposing the tan line just above where his buttocks started to curve out. I walked across the sloping, almost-terraced lawn, stepping from flagstone to flagstone until I reached the three sagging wooden steps to the porch. There was little paint left on them. Kelly just athletically leaped over them, landing like a cat on the sagging porch.

I heard a vehicle slowing down and turned back to look. A black pickup truck traveled past on the gravel road. The driver waved, and Kelly waved back. "That was Jimmy Tucker," he said casually. "The Tuckers live in the holler over that ridge. You don't want to go down there, ever." Kelly held the screen door open for me.

"Why not?"

"You just don't."

I stepped out of the heat into the muggy thickness inside.

I gagged.

The house smelled rank.

There was a musty, moldy smell, like damp, rotting wood. There was probably toxic black mold inside the walls, and I was breathing it in.

Coming here was a huge mistake.

The air was so heavy and thick and hot I could barely breathe, and I sneezed as dust went up my nose. My eyes didn't adjust to the dark right away. I could hear a window unit chugging away in one of the nearby rooms. I remembered there was a hallway to the back of the house as Kelly switched on a lamp, and I blinked at first as my eyes adjusted again.

A couple of ceiling fans began turning overhead, one of them squeaking loudly.

The hallway floor was covered with faded, yellowed linoleum tiles, some of the corners curling up, loose in places. It looked like it might have been white at one time, possibly with a green and gold mosaic pattern. There was dust everywhere, a fine layer of it covering almost everything from tabletops to light bulbs. Cobwebs hung from the corners of the ceiling and across the tops of the ceiling fans. The blades of the fans were covered in thick black grime, and the floor really needed sweeping. The flocked wallpaper was faded and water-stained, peeling back at the seams, and there were more water stains up on the ceiling.

The entire house smelled like it needed a good airing out, like the windows hadn't been opened since the Vietnam War.

The front hallway ran through the house, straight from the front door to the back porch.

The sun was shining through the big stained-glass window that made up most of the back door.

I recoiled from it, my stomach twisting into knots.

The window was one of the most gruesome depictions of the crucifixion I'd seen, and I'd gone to a Catholic school. St. Sebastian's had been filled with gory religious images, of the sacred heart of Jesus and the blood and suffering of the holy martyrs. Everywhere you looked at St. Sebastian's, really, just try getting away from the gore of the martyrs, and good luck with that.

But nothing at St. Sebastian's came close to this image for nightmare potential.

Blood spurted in vivid red from the hands and feet, from the wound in His side. The sunlight streaming through the picture painted colors on the floor, and the vivid red looked like puddles of blood on the linoleum. So much agony was etched on the face, the big eyes cast up toward the sky, imploring *My God, my God, why hast thou forsaken me?*

I closed my eyes and could hear my grandmother's voice, low and growling, saying, *Jesus is our Lord and Savior, He died to take away our sins, you need to ask Him for forgiveness.*

I could feel her hand on my shoulder, pushing me down to my knees in front of that window, the sun shining through it and turning my skin those colors.

It was a miracle that window didn't give me nightmares.

I took a deep breath.

The back porch was beyond that door, I remembered, and the steps down to the back lawn, sloping slightly downward toward the woods behind the house.

"I know, it's dirty," Kelly was saying as he rolled my suitcase to the staircase. "But Miss Sarah's room is clean, and so is the kitchen. It's just too much work for one person, but Miss Sarah won't allow no one to come in to clean." He shrugged in a *what are you gonna do* kind of way. "And I don't got time."

She really needs to get over that, I thought, saying out loud, "She also didn't want the archaeologists messing around at the ruins, either." I felt the soft wood beneath the tiled floor give almost imperceptibly beneath my weight as I followed him to the stairs. "And that's going on, isn't it? I don't see how she could stop you or Dewey from having a cleaning crew come in."

He looked back at me over his shoulder. "That's easier to hide because they don't come into the house like cleaners would," he replied. "And the idea is not to upset her—don't you get that? She's come home to die. She didn't want to die in a hospital, and I don't blame her for that, can you? She wants to die in the house she was born in." He pointed in the general direction of the back of the house. "If the door to her room is closed, then she's sleeping or doesn't want company. Don't go in there if the door is closed, you understand?"

I realized Kelly must have been the one who found her after the strokes. He picked up a suitcase in each hand and started up the stairs, which groaned under his weight.

I swallowed, and I could feel my cheeks reddening. She took him in and gave him a home when he was orphaned and alone in the world. No matter how weird my memories were, no matter how my mother felt about the old woman, there had to be some good in my grandmother if she could take in a homeless teenager, a stranger, a distant relative she barely knew. She didn't have to do it—she didn't owe him anything.

"Her room is the one across from the kitchen. I don't know if you remember that or not," Kelly went on, climbing up the sagging stairs. "Good thing she always stayed on the first floor, since it's easier for the nurses, and if we have to get EMTs in, you know"—his voice broke a little—"if there's an emergency, you know. But it takes them a good while to get here from town, you know? It's a miracle she didn't die last time." The stairs groaned under his weight, and the wood felt soft under my shoes.

Yes, he was definitely the one who found her, poor guy.

I followed, a little embarrassed I was letting him lug my suitcases without even offering to help.

But hey, he was strong and might as well get some use from those muscles, right?

And I wasn't feeling so good. The air was thick, close, and hot, as I went up the stairs. The railing wobbled a little bit when I put my hand on it. I've always been afraid of heights, and this house... these stairs didn't seem stable. I knew the high ceilings were meant to help keep it cooler inside, but the stairs seemed to go up forever. I was sweating and slightly out of breath when I reached the top. Kelly opened a door at the far end of the hallway. He turned and looked back at me. "I put you in your mom's old room," he said. "I thought that would be nice."

Nice.

I wiped the sweat from my face and tried catching my breath. I felt like I was in a steam room, the air too thick and heavy to breathe. The window at the end of the hallway was open, but the curtains didn't move. There was no breeze, nothing. But when I reached the door, I felt a delicious blast of delightfully cold air from inside.

And that was when it happened.

At last! flashed through my brain.

I felt a burst of joy, exhilaration. Happiness flooded through me like...I couldn't remember feeling this delighted, thrilled, excited, and joyous about anything before in my life, and *relieved*, at the same time, like electricity was flowing through my body, almost—*almost* like I'd taken another bump of something, coke or Tina or Ecstasy or *something*, and—

"Are you okay?" Kelly was giving me a funny look.

And just like that, it was gone, poof, like it never happened. I shook my head. Weird. "Fine. This air feels amazing."

"Dewey had a new air conditioner delivered yesterday," Kelly said. He swung my suitcases effortlessly onto the bed. "I also put new sheets and blankets and stuff on the bed for you. It smelled kind of musty in here." He shrugged his shoulder straps back up, hiding his muscular chest and big pink nipples behind the denim bib again. "I aired it out overnight, so it shouldn't be so bad." He made a face. "Probably not as nice as what you're used to, sorry." His face looked like he was expecting me to say something rude.

I decided to disappoint him.

"Thank you. I appreciate it." I sat down in an old vinyl armchair with a hideous green, yellow, and orange floral pattern on it. I drained the rest of the water and tossed the empty bottle into a little metal waste can.

The wall next to the hall door was hidden behind an enormous armoire with greenish-looking copper handles on the three doors. "The bathroom's the door at the top of the stairs. We got to share—it's the only one on this floor." His voice was slightly mocking.

The house didn't have indoor plumbing, I remembered Mom telling me, until the late 1960s. I walked over to one of the windows. From here, I had a great view of the hollow—the *holler*—and the stream. It looked stagnant, but there wasn't any scum on the surface of the orange-brown water. On the other side of the dirt road I could see a rusted tin roof peeking out from the pine trees, which had to be the old barn—yes, there was rusty barbed wire running along in front of the tree line, almost completely hidden by brush. Deep in the woods I could see leafy kudzu covering trees like greenish lather.

I heard my grandmother's voice whispering to me, *The kudzu can't be stopped, Jacob, and maybe one of these nights it'll climb through the window and choke you, too.*

I shivered.

It felt so real. I could almost smell her perfume—lily of the valley, she preferred lily of the valley—feel her breath in my ear as she whispered the words.

"Are you sure you're okay?" Kelly was staring at me. He wiped sweat from his forehead, and I could see his damp underarm hair, the beads of water on his forearms.

"Just tired from the trip." I shook it off. "Yeah, well, and it's just been a while since I've been here. I'm—remembering things." I walked across the room to the window with the air conditioner resting on the sill. I parted the green curtains and looked back at the woods. The roof for the porch wasn't there anymore. "What happened to the back porch?"

"Tore it down a while back, rotted out and it was starting to collapse," Kelly replied. "Took me a few days."

The woods looked darker and thicker and more malevolent than I remembered. There was the opening for the path back through the woods to the ruins, disappearing down into the trees and brush—almost as though the forest closed up again behind the opening. I shivered again and turned the air conditioner down a bit. "The woods are so thick. Clearing out that road to the ruins must have been a lot of work."

Kelly's face twisted. "It was. They cut down some trees and pulled up the stumps, cleaned out the underbrush and stuff." His voice sounded angry. "They did it almost right after she went into the hospital. Dewey thought she was good as dead, I guess."

Another memory flashed through my head. My mother and I, walking along the path through the trees. My mother was holding my hand. Hers was sweaty and hot. Just off the path and down a slight slope was a pile of garbage shaded by the trees—rusting cans, buzzing flies, a pile of stinking rot and refuse. She told me to stay put and not to move as she carried a garbage can down the incline, emptied it, and came back up. She carried me back out of the woods.

"Is the garbage dump still back there?"

He looked at me like I'd lost my mind. "No," he replied. "There's a service that comes out from Corinth once a week. We roll the cans out to the mailbox. The dump was cleaned out years ago." He made a face. "Health hazard, you know."

That made sense. "Okay."

"I'm running into town to get some groceries," he said. "Anything you want specifically?"

"Just Cokes and bottled water."

"I'll get us pizza for dinner, too. Anything you won't eat?"

"Anchovies, black olives, Canadian bacon, pineapple. Anything else is fine."

"Hope Pizza Hut is okay."

He closed the door. I heard him walking down the hallway back to the stairs. I climbed onto the bed and lay down, my head on the pillow. The mattress was soft yet firm, and I wondered how old it was.

The battery in my phone was getting low, so I plugged the

charger into the wall and set the phone on the nightstand. I knew I
should unpack but felt tired—the drive, the heat, the weird memories.
I started to shove the suitcases off the bed but remembered I should
probably go check in on my grandmother before taking a nap. I got
off the bed and walked across the room. I didn't want to go back out
into the oven of the hallway. Why didn't she ever put in central air?
I took a deep breath and opened the door.

My shirt was stuck to my back with sweat by the time I got
downstairs. I tried to remember the layout of the first floor and
couldn't. It was so dark in the house, hot and stuffy and that awful
smell…I gagged a bit and walked down the hallway. I knew the last
two doors on the right were the parlor and the kitchen. There was a
mudroom off the kitchen, with a door out to the back porch, which
wasn't there now.

Kelly had said the last shut door on the left was where the
nurse and my grandmother were.

Closed or not, I couldn't just not let her know I was here.

I knocked on the door softly and turned the knob. I stuck my
head in.

I shivered as the cold air escaped. A hospital bed was set up
in the center of the room. My grandmother was lying in the bed,
and in the slight light from a reading lamp I could see her eyes
were closed. The nurse, an older Black woman, was sitting in a chair
reading a Mary Higgins Clark novel. She smiled at me, got to her
feet, and whispered, "You must be Jake. I'm Geneva, the day nurse."
She glanced at the bed, then gestured to the hallway. I nodded and
stepped back away from the doorframe.

She shut the door behind her softly. "Your uncle has told you
about her condition?"

I nodded. "Can she talk at all?"

Geneva nodded. "She can. Sometimes it's easier for her to just
write things down, so she has a pad and paper. It's just a matter of
time at this point." She looked over her shoulder at the closed door.
"She'd probably be better off in a facility, but I don't blame her for
wanting to die at home. Why don't you come back in a little bit, say
an hour?"

"Okay."

She nodded, opening and closing the door behind her silently. I heard her footsteps across the wooden floor, the sound of her sitting back down. I turned to go back to the stairs, but instead I examined the stained-glass window more closely.

Up close, it was even more gruesome than I remembered it being. But awful as it was, whoever made this window was clearly an artist. I'd never seen such good art in stained glass before...but still. The bright vivid blood and gore, the agony on the face—the detail was amazing. It must have cost a fortune.

I noticed something outside move at the forest line but couldn't tell what it was through the colors of the window.

I opened the door, and the miserable humidity and heat slapped me in the face.

With the porch gone, three concrete steps led down to the scarred back lawn. Some of the short brick columns that used to support the back porch were still there. Some partial support beams still stuck out of the back of the house, sawed down almost all the way, with maybe about an inch or so of jagged wood jutting out.

Given the general state of disrepair of the rest of the house, I couldn't imagine how bad the porch must have been to warrant tearing it down.

For a moment I saw the porch as it used to be, through a foggy haze—but then it was gone again.

Thunder roared in the distance.

I saw a white flash out past the tree line, too far back in the woods for me to quite see what it was.

I started to call out but remembered my grandmother sleeping. I walked down the rickety stairs to the red dirt. I slapped at mosquitoes and fleas and gnats as I walked over the patchy grass down the slope to where the path went into the woods.

"Hello?" I called tentatively into the woods.

The only response was the chattering of birds.

Something rustled in the forest.

It could be anything—a wolf, a raccoon, a skunk.

The path sloped downward and curved off to the left about fifty yards deep into the woods. The path itself was carpeted in dead pine needles with weeds poking out here and there. Yellow wet dandelions bloomed in the shadows. The bed of the forest was also covered in dead brown pine needles. There were snakes,

I remembered, as I started making my way down the path. I was sweating and worrying about snakes and mosquitoes and raccoons and possums and all the other things I could remember my mother told me about when I was a kid, warning me away from the woods.

They're haunted, I heard her voice in my head again, and a memory flashed—

The history of this county, of this family, is written in blood.
You have to stay away from the woods, she was saying to me, tears in her eyes, her voice shaking as she gripped my little arms with both hands, and I was scared because she was scared and my mommy was never afraid of anything, she was my mommy and she protected me from everything, and she was shaking me a little, and saying, asking, demanding I promise her I won't ever go near the woods without an adult.

Why was she so afraid?

I kept walking, sweat running down my back and trickling down inside my shorts. I heard sounds from up ahead, but the path curved back around to the right, and I was walking past where the garbage dump had once been. I keep walking, wondering about ticks and Lyme disease and the million other dangerous things that could be in the woods, but now I could hear voices and music playing, the sounds of shovels, someone shouting excitedly, and I came around the corner into a clearing—

And everything changed.
The house was standing there, complete and undamaged, like it must have looked in its heyday, before the war, and as I looked around, the woods were gone, all I could see was yards and yards of tilled fields, cotton blooming on stalks like popcorn, and I saw them, Black men, bent over the rows and pulling off the cotton and putting it into sacks strapped around their bodies. They're wearing little more than rags, and I heard the crack of a whip—

"Hey!"

I blinked, back in the present, in the woods. The house wasn't there anymore, just the raised platform of the ruins, blackened columns still reaching for the sky running along the front, wide stairs leading up to the wreckage.

What the hell had that been? Was I losing my mind?

Was it a drug flashback? God only knew what all I took…

There was a young man walking toward me, his face flushed, wearing a pith helmet and long khaki shorts. His Alabama Crimson Tide T-shirt had sweat spots under the arms. He was slender, with big round green eyes and olive tanned skin, shiny and slick with sweat. A few pimples decorated his chin and forehead.

"You can't be here." He looked and sounded angry, stopping a few feet away from me, hands on his hips. "This is a working archaeological dig, and you're trespassing. I don't know—"

"My name is Jake Chapman, and this is my grandmother's property."

His sweaty face turned beet red. "Oh, I'm so sorry, I didn't know. I mean, I knew Mrs. Donelson's grandson was coming to stay, but I mean, I didn't know—"

"It's okay." I shivered, despite the heat. "I thought I—" I stopped myself. No sense in sharing my craziness with a stranger. "Never mind."

"If you'd like a tour…" He hesitated. "I'm sorry, my name is Beau Hackworth. I'm an intern." He looked dubious. "Dr. Brady isn't here. I mean, I'm sure it would be okay to show you around…"

I held up my hand. "It's cool, Beau. Nice to meet you. When will Dr. Brady be here?"

"He had to drive into Tuscaloosa for a meeting." He looked back at the campsite. "He won't be back until tomorrow."

"And you all are camping out here?"

"No." He shook his head. "Some nights, sure, but most nights we stay at the Best Western over in Corinth." He looked at me, confused. "Are you…are you okay?"

"Yes. Why?"

"You just look a little…green."

"I'm fine." I turned and walked back into the woods.

"Hey!" he called after me.

I ignored him and kept walking.

CHAPTER FOUR

*S*omething is after me.
  It wants to hurt me.
  It wants to KILL me, whatever it is.
  I can hear it breathing, and it wants to hurt me, do bad things to me, and finish by killing me.
  But it wants to have fun with me first.
  I start running, the stairs creaking beneath my feet as lightning flashes and thunder roars, the sound of rain pounding on the house, on the porch roof, hitting the windows and splashing into the yard as it gushes out of the gutters. The house is dark, and things seem to move in the shadows as I run up the stairs. I've never been so frightened. My heart is pounding, and I can barely breathe as I run, the dust flying up from my feet with each step, and I can hear whoever it is that wants to hurt me coming up the stairs behind me, and then I reach the second floor and run around, down the hallway to the door at the end of the hallway where the stairs up to the attic are and as I head up the even creakier stairs which are even scarier because it's closed off and no one ever comes up here anymore but I have to get away, I have to because I don't want to die and I don't want to die in this house I don't want anything to do with this house I just want out I want to be free and is that so wrong is that such a sin and why and I reach the attic and lightning flashes and I can see the shapes and mounds of things covered in sheets or piles of boxes and it smells like death up here, and I am not safe here, not even here, and then the lightning fades and it's darker and mustier and dirtier up here, and I can hear the footsteps coming up the attic stairs, over the rain and the other noise, which is ever so much louder up here, so much louder up here it's like being inside a drum, and if I stay

here I'm going to die, and I don't want to die, but I don't know that there's another way out, and then I think about the dormer windows—maybe I could get out onto the roof and slide down one of the drainpipes—

I sat up in bed, gasping for air, my heartbeat pounding in my ears, as a lightning flash brightened a room I didn't recognize.

As thunder shook the entire house, I remembered where I was.

My teeth were chattering. It felt colder than it should, even though the air conditioner was running on high. I could hear the metallic pinging of the rain striking it. My heart slowed a bit, but the goose bumps remained on my arms, and I couldn't stop shivering. My phone glowed in the darkness on the nightstand. It was just after three in the morning.

The rain was coming down so hard I wondered about flooding as I reached for my sweatpants and T-shirt from where I'd left them on the floor.

This seemed like, after all, the kind of rain that filled the streets of New Orleans with water.

I switched on the bedside lamp.

It was just a nightmare, but it felt so *real*, like I'd really been running through the house trying to get away from someone— *something*—that wanted to hurt me.

It was so real it was…it was almost like *memory*, and as my heart began slowing down to a normal pace and my breathing slowed…

I could still feel the fear.

But it *had* to be a dream. It *couldn't* be memory.

I would remember if that had ever happened to me, wouldn't I?

I got out of the bed and turned the air conditioner down to its lowest setting. It coughed before slowing. I glanced out the window and could see nothing outside the glow from the light in my room. Beyond the reach of the light, it was just black as pitch.

The woods, the yard…nothing.

Even at its darkest, the nights in Chicago or New Orleans were never this dark.

The night seemed to press against the edge of the light, trying to get its fingers inside and around my throat.

Stop that, I commanded my brain.

I shivered again, wrapping my arms around myself.

The air conditioner continued to hum and tick.

Lightning flashed again, thunder rattled the windows, the rain kept falling.

I was thirsty. I'd eaten too much of the pizza Kelly brought home—three large Meat Lover's pizzas. I'd had three or four slices while he methodically ate one entire pizza and half of another. There was still a whole pizza in the refrigerator, and I suspected it wouldn't be there in the morning.

It took a lot of fuel to run that big body, apparently.

I picked up my phone because I didn't know where the light switches in the hallway were. I needed a glass of water. I heard a toilet flushing when I reached the bedroom door. I'm not the only one awake in the middle of the night, I thought, opening the door and scrolling through the apps on my phone to find the flashlight.

I opened my bedroom door and bathed in the heat and humidity.

The bathroom door opened, and lightning flashed again. It wasn't Kelly, after all. It was a girl, short, with long brown hair, wearing an Alabama football jersey that barely covered her bare white backside. She didn't see me. I palmed my phone and watched her shadowy form move hurriedly down the hallway and open the door to Kelly's room.

So Mr. Football Star wasn't so perfect after all, I thought, shaking my head. I doubted Miss Sarah would approve of him having girls sleeping over.

Another memory flashed through my mind as the bedroom door closed behind her.

She wouldn't let either Dewey or me date in high school. Mom's voice, slurring slightly in my head again. *No makeup or short skirts.* Like every time she ever talked about her mother, she'd been drinking wine that night. *Told me only whores wanted to be cheerleaders, girls who wanted attention. Be glad I never made you go to church.* She'd shuddered. *You've no idea how awful it is to go to a church that's a small step above snake handling and speaking in tongues.*

The old woman would not approve of Kelly having a girl spend the night.

I aimed my flashlight down the hallway and walked to the stairs. I was sweating. Between the freezing cold in the rooms with air conditioners and the hot wetness of the rest of the house, I'd be lucky to make it out of here without getting pneumonia—hot cold hot cold hot cold couldn't be good for me. I started down the stairs, putting one hand on the railing and keeping the other pointing the phone's light down the stairs, which seemed steeper than they had during the day. The banister wobbled slightly. The stairs groaned. I mopped sweat off my forehead with the tail of my T-shirt. Finally, I reached the bottom step as another bolt of lightning flashed.

The thunder followed almost immediately.

This house was so damned creepy, even in daylight, little wonder I'd had a nightmare.

The memory of the nightmare was fading. The realness, the emotion…I don't think I'd ever forget that feeling of absolute terror.

There was a soft light coming from under my grandmother's door. I'd met the night nurse, Geoffrey, when he came on to relieve Geneva around seven. He seemed nice enough, slightly overweight but friendly, curly hair and bright blue eyes and just good energy.

He commuted from Tuscaloosa, about an hour in each direction. Geneva lived in Corinth, so her commute wasn't quite so bad.

I switched on the kitchen light. At least it was cool in the kitchen, the window unit working overtime. Soon I was shivering again, wishing I'd put on a sweatshirt. My eyes readjusted to the light.

I got a bottle of water from the refrigerator. The Pizza Hut box was sitting on the top shelf, freckled with grease spots. I lifted one end to see that there were only three slices left. I smiled. Kelly was a nonstop eating machine. I debated grabbing another slice while gulping down the cold water. I closed the refrigerator door and walked into the mudroom. The light from my bedroom window shone on the wet grass. I looked out into the inky darkness beyond the half circle of light.

There was a white flash out in the woods, gone as fast as it appeared, so quickly I wasn't sure I'd seen anything at all.

"What the hell?" I muttered. The backyard light switch was there by the outside door. I flipped the switch up and the backyard filled with enough light to reach the tree line.

But the rain was coming down so hard I couldn't see much. The yard was filling with muddy water. The pine trees were weaving back and forth in the wind, the light disappearing into the trees, sucked into the greedy darkness.

I couldn't see anything out there.

What had I seen? My overactive imagination playing tricks again?

I continued looking, squinting, but there was no sign of whatever it was now.

If there had been anything there to begin with.

You don't get flashbacks from coke or Tina. Had I taken acid? I couldn't remember.

I should poke around out there in the daylight, I thought, flipping the light back off.

I stepped back into the kitchen, marveling again at the difference in temperature.

She wouldn't even let us have window units, I heard my mother saying as I closed the door to the mudroom, flipping the dead bolt. *She always said air-conditioning was why Yankees could stand living in the South, and she wouldn't have it in her house.*

Window units weren't enough. A house this big needed central air. The constant variance in temperature between rooms couldn't have been good for her, either, old as she was.

She certainly had a window unit in *her* bedroom now.

The floor gave a little under my feet as I walked back to the refrigerator. I grabbed a slice, finished my water, grabbed another bottle, and sat down at the cheap plywood table with fake wood finish, which wobbled on its metal legs when I put my elbows on it.

All the furniture needed to go, best as I could tell. Not even a broke college student would want any of it. The whole place needed to be gutted and renovated from floor to roof. It would cost a fortune.

I munched on the cold pizza.

The dark pressed against the windows. It was full dark out there, no moon. If the kitchen light wasn't on, I wouldn't be able to even see the screen.

What was that flash of white out in the woods? It was like someone had turned a flashlight on, then turned it back off.

I closed my eyes and thought.

I'd seen it during the daytime, too, hadn't I?

No one would be out there in the woods after three in the morning.

Especially not on a night like this.

When I finished the pizza slice, I headed back to the stairs.

Just when I reached the stairs, the front windows lit up for a moment. I blinked, startled and confused, until I realized it was the headlights of a car, flashing on the front of the house as it turned off the paved county road onto the dirt road in front of the house.

I walked to the front door and peered through the blinds. I could see the headlights illuminating the rain as the car headed down the slope, but it was so dark and raining too hard for me to see anything about the vehicle other than it was large—SUV size, or maybe an enormous pickup truck. The taillights were barely visible as it climbed up the slope on the other side of the hollow.

The house was enormous and eerily silent. When I get to the top of the stairs, I glanced down the hallway at Kelly's door. That end of the hallway was all darkness.

I wondered what time he was planning on sneaking her out.

I closed my bedroom door and got into bed, falling asleep almost immediately.

It was bright and sunny the next morning when I woke up. I looked out the window. Birds were flying, insects buzzing around, a cloud of gnats circling the opening in the forest for the path. The forest was teeming with life. I didn't see anything out of the ordinary. I tried to remember exactly where I saw the white flash but couldn't be sure.

In the daylight, it was easy to think I imagined it all.

Just my mind, playing tricks on me. I thought I saw something yesterday afternoon and so I thought I saw something again last night.

Kelly was scrambling eggs and frying bacon when I walked into the kitchen.

"I didn't hear you come in last night," I said, pouring myself a cup of coffee. I was curious to see if he'd mention his overnight visitor.

"I try to be quiet," he said without looking up from the stove. "You like scrambled eggs and bacon?"

"Sure." So he wasn't going to bring it up—meaning she hadn't seen me.

He dumped the eggs into a bowl and placed bacon on a paper towel to drain. "Good, because I didn't want to eat this all myself." He patted his flat stomach. "I could eat it all, but I shouldn't. I'm going to go work out in a little while if you want to come with."

Dude, you ate a pizza and a half yesterday in one sitting. "Thanks." I helped myself. I've never been a big breakfast person but didn't want to be rude.

We sat down at the table. "How long have you been staying here?" I asked, taking another drink of my coffee. It was good and strong.

"It'll be a year since Mom died in July," he replied between bites. He narrowed his eyes, his forehead wrinkling as he thought. "And I moved in here in August, right before football practice started."

"And you didn't have to go to the country high school?" Mom and Uncle Dewey both had gone there. That was what they both called it—the country high school. Its name was Kenilworth High for some obscure reason. There wasn't a town or anything in the county called Kenilworth.

"Nah, Coach pulled some strings with the school board to keep me at Corinth County High." He mopped up some bacon and egg juice with a piece of toast. "I just had a longer drive than I used to have. Mom and me used to rent a place up near Hackworth Holler." He said this like it's a place I should know, and it came out *holler*. He cleared his throat. "Speaking of—you remember I told you yesterday you don't want to ever go too far down the road?" He gestured to the front of the house with his fork.

"I got up in the middle of the night to get some water, and a car was driving by," I replied. "It was after three in the morning. Is that normal?"

"Did you notice a lot of cars driving up and down last night?"

"Just the one."

He smiled. "That's why I put you in the back of the house." He shook his head. "There's traffic up and down that road all night long."

"Why?" I was confused. "You said I shouldn't go down there—"

"Like I said, the Tuckers live down there, and dude, you do not want to fuck with the Tuckers," he said with a frown. "It's called Blackwood Holler because that's what it's always been called, but it's all Tuckers down there now. You need to stay away from there—the Tuckers are bad news. They've got a meth lab and a moonshine still and God knows what else down there."

"Seriously." Mom had sent me out here to the boondocks to get me away from drugs and alcohol, and they were just on the other side of the ridge.

"Yeah, and they'll shoot you just as soon as look at you." He got up and rinsed his plate before putting it in the dishwasher. "Sheriff Poteet knows all about it. The Tuckers pay him off."

"That's…not reassuring."

"As long as you stay away from them, you ain't got nothing to worry about." Kelly leaned back against the counter, crossing his arms across his big chest. "But it's best to just stay away. Don't go over the hill and down into the holler."

"I won't."

"I'm going to mow the lawn before the gym, while it's still cool—if the ground isn't too soft from the rain."

I glanced out the window. The dirt was a dark, wet-looking orange.

"What are you going to do today?" he asked.

I yawned and stretched. "Maybe I'll get started on the attic."

He scowled. "It's going to be hotter than hell up there in the attic. You're going to need to take some fans up there. There's some in the hall closet upstairs. It's the door next to my room."

I nodded. "Thanks."

I went back upstairs. There was no point, I figured, in taking a shower before I was done in the attic. I was just going to get dirty and sweaty all over again. I washed my face and wondered why I didn't ask him about the white flash I'd been seeing.

Maybe it had something to do with the Tuckers?

I got my laptop and headed down the hot hallway to the door hiding the attic stairs. It was just across the hall from Kelly's bedroom door, which was open. I couldn't resist glancing in and was rewarded with chaos. I closed the door. I found the closet with the fans—old, dusty, grimy, cheap box fans—and grabbed one by the handle. I was sweating again. How the hell did people live down here before air-conditioning? I wondered as I opened the door to the stairs. It was like opening an oven door. Hot, stale air swept over me like it had been waiting for someone to come along and set it free. I took a deep breath, wiped my face, and started climbing. The railing was loosely attached to the wall. I didn't trust it so didn't touch it. The paint on the walls was faded and yellowed and cracked, peeling in places. At the top of the stairs was another door. Sweat rolling down my face, I finally made it to the top. I opened the door, and another wave of stale, damp hot air slapped me like a wet blanket right out of the dryer.

I started to step across the threshold when a wave of nausea hit me so hard I had to sit down on the steps.

I spread my legs and lowered my head. In, out, in, out, breathing deeply until the nausea and dizziness passed.

It's this place, danced through my mind as I sat back up. There was something about this house that was wrong.

You're being ridiculous, I told myself, standing up again. But Kelly was right—one fan wasn't going to be enough.

I stepped over the threshold into the still quiet of the attic. The roof was peaked, and exposed wooden crossbeams ran from front to back. There were windows, covered with years of dirt and grime. I flipped a light switch and several bare bulbs hanging from the ceiling lit up. There was a door on the far side, which opened out onto the turret's balcony. I struggled with the bolt but got it open, hoping to get some fresh air moving up there. I went around opening windows. Finally, I set up the fan and plugged it into an outlet and took a look around.

There were boxes everywhere, piled up haphazardly, and old furniture shoved and stacked every which way. Everything had a thick coating of dust, and cobwebs hung in every corner. I could see dust motes floating in the sunlight. The dust on the bare wooden floor was undisturbed.

No one had been up here for years.

The entire attic smelled like damp, rotting wood. I'd need to clean up here before I got started.

As if on cue, dust went up my nose, and I sneezed.

I walked around, sweat rolling down my face and down my back. Anything could be inside these boxes including…

Spiders.

My mother hated spiders. I'm not afraid of them the way she is—she will run screaming out of a room if she sees even the tiniest spider—but I don't *love* them, either. I tried to remember if there were any deadly spiders in Alabama. Black widows? Brown recluses, like in New Orleans? Stop it, I told myself.

And like an idiot, I'd left my phone downstairs.

No, I was just looking for an excuse to get out of here, slam the door and lock it behind me, and never come back up. There was something horribly wrong up here.

I shook my head. Why was I having these weird creepy thoughts? Maybe the overdose messed up my brain? I pulled my T-shirt away from my chest. Soaked through, and even with the windows and balcony door open, it was still hard to breathe.

I should go back downstairs and get cleaned up, let it air out up here.

I dragged my foot through the dust on the hard, raw wood floor. The dust was about a quarter-inch thick.

Maybe a vacuum cleaner?

But it needed airing out first.

I heard a car coming up the road, and I walked out onto the balcony. A filthy, battered old green pickup truck was now passing the house. I heard the lawn mower start and—

I stumbled and fell against the railing.

It cracked, and for a brief, horrible moment it felt like it was going to give—

—and it was raining again and I was terrified, absolutely terrified, because they were going to throw me off the balcony and the lightning

flashed and my feet dangled, my hands grubbing on to the wood, slick with rain water, and I didn't know how long I could hold on—

—and it was gone.

I swallowed.

Maybe…maybe I should go back down to the dig and meet Dr. Brady.

I left the door open but went down the stairs very fast.

Chapter Five

I grabbed some clothes to change into after showering. My shirt was glued to my skin when I reached the bathroom door. Thank God the bathroom not only had a window unit blasting on high, but the ceiling fan was spinning so fast it looked like an airplane propeller. I turned on the shower and waited for the water to get hot.

I climbed in and washed off all the dried sweat. I needed an air conditioner up there, at least one, otherwise I'd suffocate…not to mention how bad it would be for my laptop.

Yeah, Dewey needed to have more window units delivered and installed.

Once I finished showering and toweling dry in the bathroom, I walked quickly back to my room, trying not to notice I was getting drenched in sweat again, negating the shower.

"I always dry off when I get back to my room," Kelly called from behind me. "It's easier that way. Keep some towels in your room."

I looked back as I opened my door. Kelly had a towel wrapped around his waist. The white-gold hairs on his chest and stomach were dark with sweat. With the sunlight coming through the window behind him, he looked like a Greek God—Apollo, glowing with light. He was handsomer and better built than Tradd could ever hope to be, but I didn't…I didn't feel attracted to him, even in the *he's so damned gorgeous* way I used to look at some of the guys at the gym or the shirtless frat jerks playing Frisbee on campus.

It was weird. I'd been attracted to straight boys before—a hot guy is a hot guy—yet despite his almost godlike beauty, I didn't feel anything when I looked at him. No stirrings of lust, no fantasies, no nothing.

"Smart," I replied.

He gave me a thumbs-up, which allowed the towel to slip a bit on the right side, showing the deep line from his hip bone downward where the leg attached to the torso.

Nothing. I felt nothing.

The bathroom door closed behind him.

It's this place, I thought as I gratefully closed my bedroom door behind me. This weird fucking place was messing with my brain.

Or did…did the overdose mess up my wiring somehow?

I sat down on the bed and took a deep breath. The Xanax prescription bottle was sitting on my nightstand, next to my charging phone. I hadn't felt the need to take one once since arriving here. That was kind of weird, wasn't it? I'd had nightmares, kept thinking I was seeing a light out in the woods, having weird reactions…and yet, no panic attacks. No anxiety.

I'd even forgotten I had the prescription.

I picked up my phone. I touched the home button with my index finger to unlock it.

I messaged Uncle Dewey, requesting the air conditioners. I hit send, and before I could put the phone down, he replied: *Will order them and have them delivered. Meant to do this before you arrived, sorry.*

I put my phone down.

Yeah, sorry.

I got dressed and headed downstairs. I could hear the shower running. My hand was slick with sweat on the railing as I went down the staircase.

As hot as it was inside, I was not prepared for how horrible it would be once I got outside.

Chicago and New Orleans both got hot and humid in the summertime, yes. But I'd never experienced anything like this. I went out the door with the stained-glass window and stepped down to the top step. The sky was cloud free, and the sun felt like a laser. I could feel my skin getting sunburned as I stood there, trying to breath in the thick, damp, hot air. I could feel heat coming through the souls of my shoes from the cement steps and leaped down into what I hoped would be the cooler grass. A mosquito landed on my arm, and I slapped it dead. The forest was alive with sounds—frogs croaking, birds squawking and singing, the almost constant *reeeeee* sound of cicadas. The ground still felt squishy under my feet as I walked toward the cool shade of the tree line. I walked around the mangy spots where the grass didn't grow because I could see the orange dirt was still dark and wet.

I'd reached the tree line and was wiping my face off with my shirt, wondering if I should have grabbed a bottle of water from the refrigerator, when I heard tires on gravel.

An ancient black pickup truck, raised on enormous tires with orange mud spattered all over the side, was heading down the road into the hollow, moving too fast, throwing up rocks and clods of mud.

How did Dewey not know what's going on in Tucker Holler?

I waved away a horsefly circling my head. A cloud of gnats was swarming just inside the forest, so I avoided that spot, peering into the woods approximately at the place where I thought I'd seen the white flashes.

There was nothing there now but moss and trees and underbrush.

I must have imagined it, I thought. A fat bee flew right in front of my face as I headed over to the path. Hornets and wasps and bees, so many unpleasant things in these woods. I started walking down the path toward the ruins. It was cooler once I was out of the direct sunlight, but the air was still thick and heavy. My skin was covered with a thin layer of sweat as I walked, trying not to lose my balance or trip over tree roots. Pine cones were scattered along the path and the forest floor. The woods were alive with insects, grasshoppers and bees and flies and moths, and birds. The underbrush rustled from time to time as I descended the steep slope.

I slapped at mosquitoes and gnats. Every so often a butterfly drifted lazily through the heavy air, fluttering its wings. As I made my way down the path, I kept glancing to my left, just in case I might see whatever that white flash was, but there was nothing. I turned my eyes back to the path and froze.

An enormous snake was slithering across the path only a few

feet in front of me. It was paying no attention to me, but I didn't dare breathe.

It was a cottonmouth.

Another memory flashed through my head.

There was a big snake in the front yard, slithering between the rosebushes, and someone was screaming. "Oh, for God's sake, Glynis, it's just a cottonmouth," my grandmother snapped. She pushed me aside as she went down the front steps, a hoe in her hands, and she swung it, cleanly slicing the head off the snake. "You forget your raising?" Miss Sarah picked up the snake's body and tossed it into the ditch alongside the dirt road. She kicked the head, and it rolled down the lawn.

I realized I was trembling and didn't—*couldn't*—move until the snake's tail disappeared into the underbrush. I took a few deep breaths and waited a few more moments before walking again, my eyes darting back and forth from one side of the path to the other.

I crossed the little rotting wooden bridge over the creek, slick and slippery with moss and wet, and started up the other side. I could hear digging sounds, voices talking, low music playing. I kept climbing.

When I came into the clearing, a lance of pain shot through my head, so awful and strong that I gasped and had to put my hand against the rough trunk of a pine tree. I stood there, gasping as the pain faded, trying to catch my breath. I felt nauseous, like I was going to throw up, and everything was dizzy and spinning, and I just felt this sense of sudden terror—

"Are you all right?" a male voice called over to me.

I looked up and saw the guy from yesterday. He was walking toward me, in his hiking boots with the socks folded down, khaki shorts, and yet another Crimson Tide T-shirt. His face was red and wet with sweat, beads of water glistening on his tan arms. I slapped at another mosquito on my leg.

"You need to use repellant," he said, his voice friendly as he walked up to me. "Keeps the ticks off, too." He shrugged. "There isn't much Lyme disease down here, but better safe than sorry."

"Thanks, I'll get some the next time I go into town."

"Here, you can use mine," he said, pulling a small can of insect repellant out of one of his pockets. He handed it to me, and I shook it before spraying my legs and arms and rubbing it in. I rubbed my hands over my face and gave the can back.

"Thanks."

"So, you're Mrs. Donelson's grandson?" he asked, pushing his glasses back up his nose, but they slid right back down. His voice was much friendlier than yesterday, and he was smiling.

He looked better smiling.

I nodded. "Sorry about yesterday and barging in on y'all like that. My name's Jake." I held out my hand. He took it. His hand was sweaty and warm, but his grip firm.

"I'm Beau Hackworth," he said, letting go of my hand. "I'm sorry I was rude yesterday. It's just Dr. Brady wasn't here, and I'm… I'm not comfortable letting strangers on the site if he's not here. I'm sorry." He hesitated. "We've had some…there's been some…" He made a face. "There's just been some…incidents."

"Incidents?"

"It's nothing." He smiled again. "Anyway, I'm sorry."

"It's fine." I smiled back at him. "How do you stand this heat?"

"You get used to it." He grinned back at me. "Don't you go to Tulane? This can't be hotter than New Orleans."

"I do go to Tulane, and it's about the same. I just don't spend that much time outdoors there." I looked around beyond him. There were some tents set up in front of the ruined house, some coolers, a barbecue grill. Voices were coming from around the back side of the house. "Is Dr. Brady here now?"

He nodded. "Do you want to meet him? Come on."

I followed him around the ruins to a large canvas open-air tent set up behind the rear of the structure. There were several large rectangular holes, the red clay-dirt sides looking wet and slippery. There were also several other areas marked off, with string running between pegs. I pointed to the holes. "Are those full of water?"

"We're going to pump the water out later this afternoon," Beau said. "But we can't really do much when the ground's wet. The earth is too much like clay when it's wet like this. Too dangerous, too easy to miss something. You can sift easier when it's dry—oh, Dr. Brady? This is Mrs. Donelson's grandson, Jake."

An older man standing at a large table staring at a geological map looked up at us. He was in his late fifties. A large belly hanging over the waist of his khakis strained his tan short-sleeved button-down shirt. There were dark splotches in the armpits. He looked up from the map and smiled. "Jacob? Your uncle Dewey let me know you'd be here for the next few weeks. Do you want me to show you around?" He laughed. "You probably know this place like the back of your hand."

"Actually, I don't," I replied. "I've not spent a lot of time here. I haven't been here since I was a kid—and my mom never let me come down here. She said there were snakes in the woods." I shivered. "I saw a cottonmouth on my way here."

"She's right, there are." He beamed at me. "If you get bit, come down to the dig. We've got antivenin. You can't be too careful in these woods."

"Thanks." I looked around. "I've never been to a dig before."

"We're trying to be careful"—he gestured to the back of the house—"not disturb too much. Of course, we had to widen the road and take some trees down. But your uncle pretty much gave us free rein."

"Thanks to Miss Sarah's stroke," I replied.

"Your grandmother could be…difficult. The first time I came to ask her about excavating the ruins, she ran me off with her shotgun." He laughed. "She's something, your grandmother. I think she respected me for coming back after that, to tell you the truth." He gestured for me to follow him. "Come on, I want to show you something."

"What are you hoping to find?" I asked as we walked to the closest hole.

"I'd be lying if I said I wasn't interested in finding the truth about what happened to the Lost Boys," Dr. Brady said, wiping sweat off his upper lip. "I first heard that story when I was a teenager, and it's been a kind of obsession for me ever since." He pointed down into the hole. "But our primary interest here is, of course, how the Blackwoods lived. This is one of the few antebellum sites in Alabama that hasn't been excavated."

"Or plowed over," Beau interjected.

"Or plowed over," Dr. Brady amended.

They showed me one of the holes, where they'd found some pre-Civil War cooking utensils. Dr. Brady tended to explain in such excruciating detail my mind began wandering. After my tour was complete, I asked about the house.

"We're saving that for last," Dr. Brady replied. "We may not get to it until next summer. The house is a much bigger project," he went on, something about money and hiring more crew and the dangers of the unstable basement and foundation and having to slowly take the ruins apart, bit by bit, to study. "I have a theory about the fire," he finally said as we walked back to the tent where I first saw him, "Just a theory, and I may never be able to prove it. But I had a friend out here who's a fire inspector for an insurance company, and from him just looking around the ruins, he doesn't think the story about the fire being set is true."

"No Yankee deserter?" I replied with a bit of a smile. "If there's no deserter, then the story of the Lost Boys can't be true, either."

"It was the burn pattern, but of course his theory was also just that—a theory." Dr. Brady laughed. "Usually when houses were burned during the war, they didn't just set a fire in a room—they set multiple fires. This fire, he seemed to think that it started in one room and then spread to the rest of the house. Of course, the evidence has been exposed to the elements for over a hundred and fifty years, and it was only a preliminary examination. Next summer, hopefully, I'll have the money and the staff to do a true investigation of the fire."

"Well, thank you for the tour," I said. I was hungry and wanted to get back to the house and maybe take another shower. "It was nice meeting you."

"Come back anytime, Jake."

Kelly's truck was still gone when I got back. As I stood over the kitchen sink, I looked back into the forest and again saw the white flash. All right, let's see what you are, I thought, heading for the back door again. But when I came out onto the mudroom, there was no sign of it. I took a drink from my sweating bottle of Coke. I sat down in a rusted old porch chair, which squeaked and rocked a little. I heard a car slowing down, then tires on gravel. The Tuckers clearly had a good business going.

I went back into the kitchen. There was some tuna salad in a plastic bowl in the fridge, so I made a couple of sandwiches and sat in the blessed cool at the table.

What on earth could that be?

While eating my sandwiches, I remembered the nausea and dizziness I felt when I got back to the ruins. I'd had the same experience going into the attic. I wasn't sick, so what caused that?

And there was that terrible nightmare, too.

Sweat was running down my face as I headed back up the attic stairs, but this time I felt nothing when I walked through the door. I took my shirt off and wiped my face with it. The fans were still running, and the moving air felt good. It wasn't nearly as stuffy and stale as it had been. The fans had stirred up some of the dust. I bent down and ran my finger through the dust on the floor. I was right—it was about a quarter inch thick and so old it was almost gummy. Surely Miss Sarah had a vacuum cleaner somewhere?

I finished my Coke on my way back down the stairs and found the vacuum in the hall closet on the first floor. I lugged it back upstairs and plugged it in. I started running it over the attic floor as another storm broke. The cool wind coming through the windows made it a little more bearable up there. I started pushing the vacuum around. The floor was unfinished wood—there were splinters, and it was rotted away in some places. I used the detachable hose to suck up dust and cobwebs from some of the boxes and kept working until it was not quite as disgusting.

I heard tires on gravel and looked out a window. It was Kelly. He got out of the truck as I watched. He wasn't wearing a shirt. There was a patch of golden white hair in the center of his thickly muscled chest, and a trail leading down from that to his navel. His shorts were hanging low off his hips, and I could see his white BVDs, wet and clinging to his body. I watched as he jogged over the mud and gravel around to the front of the house.

Why didn't I feel anything—lust, desire, anything I usually felt when I saw a hot boy?

It must be this place.

I turned abruptly, hitting a box and knocking it over.

It hit the floor, and the top flaps opened, spilling out odds and ends across the sort of clean floor.

"Damn it." I reached down for the item closest to me. It was a picture frame, old style, with a faded color photograph of two young boys with their hair slicked down, wearing dress shirts and ties and smiling big for the camera.

I caught my breath.

One of the boys was a dead ringer for me when I was ten—if I'd had blond hair.

The other boy looked how Kelly must have when he was twelve or thirteen.

CHAPTER SIX

"What is this?" Kelly asked.

I jumped. I hadn't heard him walk into the kitchen. "Jesus," I said, "don't sneak up on me like that." I turned off the stove burner. I slid my two grilled cheese sandwiches onto a plate.

"Didn't mean to scare you." He didn't sound sorry, though, and when I turned around, he was smirking, standing by the kitchen table. He was holding the picture frame in one of his big hands. A black tank top was draped over his left shoulder. He needed a shave, reddish-blond stubble visible on his cheeks, chin, and neck. There was a hickey at the base of his throat, and another one on his right pectoral, near the enormous pink nipple. His curly blond hair was damp from his post-workout shower. There was a long scab on his right shin and a purplish bruise just above the knee.

"I found it in the attic," I said.

He walked over to the counter next to me and set the picture down. He smelled clean, soap and deodorant over boy-musk. He tapped his index finger on the older, bigger boy. "This looks like me when I was a kid," he said, opening a cabinet and getting down the blender. He moved around me to the refrigerator. "Weird."

I sat down with my plate at the linoleum kitchen table, scarred with cigarette burns and the corners peeling up, and took a swig from my sweating glass of ice water while he made a protein shake. He dumped it into an enormous plastic cup with Roll Tide written in crimson on the side and sat down at the other side of the table. He was still holding the picture. He took a huge drink, leaving a frothy pinkish-orange mustache on his upper lip. Muscle fibers moved in his chest and shoulders as he put the cup back down and sighed. He frowned. "You found this in the attic?" He flipped it over and looked at the back.

I'd already checked it. There was nothing on the back—no notes identifying the boys, no sticker from the photographer, nothing.

"Yeah. It was in a box of junk," I replied, sprinkling salt on my sandwiches.

"It looks like it was taken at the Pig," he replied and smiled at my puzzled expression. "The Pig. The Piggly Wiggly in town? Back in the day, a photographer used to come down from Tuscaloosa a couple of times a year to make pictures for people, years ago." He tapped the glass. "That background. Almost every house in Corinth County has a picture of kids in front of that." He slid the picture across the table to me. "I've got some of my mom from when she was a kid with that same backdrop."

The backdrop was a sea scene, complete with white sand and palm trees. I could make out barely visible whitecaps in the sea. And now that I thought about it, a lot of the formal family pictures hanging in the living room had the same background.

"Nowadays, Ruth Collingsworth has a studio on Main Street," he said, taking another swig of his protein shake. "People don't have to save their money and wait." He shrugged.

"You wouldn't happen to know who they are, do you?" I asked, cutting the first grilled cheese in half.

He shook his head. "Well, Miz Collingsworth opened her studio about twenty years ago, so the picture's probably older than that." He peered at it. "Okay, one of them looks like me, but the other one—he kind of looks like you. You don't know who they are?"

"No, but I don't know much about the family," I replied. "Mom hardly ever talks about them."

"Well, your mom's some kind of a big shot lawyer, isn't she? I guess she's too busy to come home much," Kelly replied, finishing off the protein shake with an enormous gulp. "That's what Miss Sarah says—used to say, I guess. Dewey never came out too much before she got sick, either. Guess it's a family thing." He expelled a huge breath. "But I can't think who they could be. I mean, sure, there's lots of kin of some kind right here in the county. Maybe cousins of some kind? On your grandfather's side? Miss Sarah only had the one sister, and she died young."

"Are there Donelsons around?" My grandfather died when Mom and Dewey were kids. There were pictures of him on the family wall in the living room.

"No, he was from Mississippi," Kelly replied. "She never talked about him much. I guess she never got over him dying so young on her. He was younger than she was, you know. She was old when she got married. Almost thirty, and he was barely twenty."

"Really?"

Why had Mom never told me any of these stories?

I knew everything about my Chapman relatives on Dad's side—grandparents and cousins and aunts and uncles. The wall around the fireplace in the basement family room at my father's was covered with framed photos.

"I guess I can take it with me and ask Dewey Saturday night," I said.

I had a lot of questions for Dewey.

Better to ask him than Mom, obviously. He might tell me something instead of changing the subject.

Kelly scowled and pushed his chair back. "Yeah. Do that." He rinsed out the blender and his plastic cup before walking out. A few moments later I heard the stairs creaking under his feet.

I finished eating and washed out the pan and plate before putting both in the empty dishwasher.

Time to go back up to the attic and get back to work. I moaned and wondered about waiting for the air conditioners to arrive.

I should've asked Kelly to help—it would go faster with two people. I could split the money with him.

And I could ask him more questions about the family.

I didn't want to go back to the attic, but what else was there to do?

For the first time since I woke up in the hospital, I felt the need to be around people, to go out and listen to loud music and maybe have a beer or two.

And stalk Tradd?

A memory flashed into my head of a night a week or so before he dumped me for good. We were supposed to go out for his friend Kayden's birthday, and I'd gotten jealous about something and we'd had a fight. Finally, he told me I wasn't welcome at Kayden's birthday celebration and left my apartment, me shouting after him, *Good, I didn't want to go anyway!*

Within ten minutes my anger had faded and I texted him: *Sorry.* He didn't answer. When I called, it went to voice mail.

I spent the rest of the night calling and texting him, begging him over and over again to forgive me, weeping into the phone that I was sorry, so sorry, and to give me another chance, typing out apologetic text after text, knowing I should stop, knowing I should just leave him alone, that he wasn't going to answer until he was good and ready, that I was acting crazy and making things worse instead of better, and finally at two in the morning I couldn't take it anymore and got in my car. I parked across the street from his house, staring at his dark windows, ducking down whenever a car turned down the street.

He never came home, and when the sun came up, I'd driven home, ashamed and embarrassed and hating myself.

I got a bottle of water from the refrigerator. Miss Sarah's door was open, so I stuck my head inside. Geneva was sitting in her chair next to the bed, reading a Wendy Corsi Staub paperback. Miss Sarah's eyes were open, and she was looking up at the ceiling. Her breathing was raspy. There was a slight rattle of some kind in her lungs.

I took a tentative step into the room, unease growing, Geneva smiled at me over the top of the book—*Little Girl Lost*—and I said, "Hey, Miss Sarah," barely above a whisper. "Remember me? I'm Jacob, your grandson."

Her head slowly rolled over to look at me.

Her eyes widened and her mouth started moving.

She was *recoiling* from me.

Geneva put the book down and got to her feet as a croaking sound came from the cracked, thin lips of the old woman. She was trying to form words, trying to say something, but couldn't, but that face, the look on her face—

Geneva moved so her thick body was between me and Miss Sarah, gesturing behind her back for me to go.

I shrank back to the door.

"Juh-juh-juh—"

"Shh, now, don't get yourself all worked up." Her hand wagged furiously. *Go go go!*

"Juh-juh-juh—"

I stepped backward over the threshold into the hallway. I pulled the door closed.

She was trying to say my name.

I backed away from the door, gulping, the thick hot air pressing down on me, sweat running down my back. I started moving toward the staircase. My head was spinning. I ran up the stairs as quickly as I could. I was out of breath and sweating by the time I got to the second floor. I stopped and drank some blessedly cold water.

The sight of me *terrified* her.

What was that about?

I stood there, waiting for my heart to stop racing.

Kelly's door opened. He was wearing a Hardee's uniform, the shirt maybe a size too small, the brown polyester fabric pulled tight across his thick chest. "I'm off to work," he said, his heavy tread throwing up small clouds of dust from the carpeting, and I wondered crazily when the last time was that someone vacuumed upstairs. "Are you okay? You look like you've seen a ghost."

"I'm fine," I managed to say, swallowing more water. "The heat, the stairs…" I made a gesture with my free hand. "Takes some getting used to, I guess."

He smiled. "Well, be careful. You don't want to get heatstroke or something. I'll be home later—I'm closing, and Bonnie and I might go do something after work."

Bonnie. Her name was Bonnie.

I resisted asking him if doing something meant bringing her over to spend the night again.

"Okay, great," I replied.

I shut my bedroom door behind me.

I sat down on the bed.

Miss Sarah looked terrible. My childhood memories, from those rare visits here, were of an enormous woman, tall and stern with an angry face, her black eyebrows threaded with gray always knitted together in disapproval, the wiry muscles in her arms strong and swift. She was taller than my mother. Mom feared her mother…I remembered she always smelled of lilies of the valley over sweat, and how hot the house was back in those days when there were only box fans in the windows.

But now she was shrunken, her face collapsed in on itself. Well, there wasn't any point to her wearing her dentures now, and she'd never been fat—she was big-boned, big framed. But her muscles had wasted away, and—

Why would seeing me scare her?

Maybe I reminded her of someone. The kid in the picture, maybe? But why would that scare her?

Nothing scared the old woman.

I headed up to the attic. I got out my Sharpie and approached the first box, right there alongside the door to the staircase. I wrote a big one on it and opened the flaps.

Three hours later I was covered in dust and dirt and cobwebs and sweat. But I'd also gone through most of the boxes in that corner of the attic, listed their contents in the spreadsheet and labeled each box clearly. Almost everything I'd come across was junk—musty old clothes from a different time, shoes and light jackets, suits and dresses carefully packed away, reeking of mothballs. I didn't think anything had any value, but I made careful, neat notes on every item: size, color, label.

Maybe a vintage shop would take the stuff on consignment.

Stranger things had happened, after all. I'd have to check online to see if there were any in Birmingham. It was that or the Goodwill.

Or just take it out in the yard and burn it all.

The whole house should be burned to the ground.

I took my laptop back down to my room. The air-conditioning felt fantastic. I was peeling off my sweaty clothes when I again saw a white flash in the woods from the corner of my eye. Naked, I walked over to the window and stared into the dark green. It wasn't there now.

After my shower I checked my email and social media. I knew—I knew I shouldn't look at Tradd's Instagram, but I couldn't stop myself. He'd posted a video of himself at the gym after a workout. His short dark hair was damp, and he'd cut up the sweaty T-shirt he was wearing so you could see his arms and sides and the curving outside edges of his chest. He was grinning at the mirror, and when I touched the picture it started moving. He winked and flexed his free arm on a continual loop I couldn't look away from.

He was so good-looking.

He doesn't want anything to do with you anymore, Internet stalker. Do you blame him?

He wasn't the first guy I'd been obsessed with that didn't want me.

It wasn't easy being the only openly gay student at St. Sebastian's. Father O'Connor, the principal, didn't like it, but so long as I didn't cover myself in glitter and dance down the hallways wearing a Speedo, he didn't lecture me about sin or going to hell. Sister Mary Frances, my English teacher, scowled in disapproval at me all the time, but I was also her best student, so she wasn't sure what to do about it. It was hard hearing all the other boys talking about their girlfriends and going out on dates and all the locker room talk about boobs and asses and sex and how far some girls would go and how little others would do, and there I was, the gay kid still waiting for his first kiss. Maybe Hunter Boyce wasn't gay, but he never seemed to have a girlfriend and never went on dates— or at least he never talked about it—just listening to the other guys and smiling when they did their locker room boy-bullshitting.

And sometimes…sometimes he saw me looking at him and smiled at me.

Would he do that if he wasn't a little bit interested?

I didn't know.

I mean, I couldn't be the only gay boy in a school with over twelve hundred students, could I?

But if there was another one, they were so far in the closet I never found them.

Hunter was just a nice guy, that's all. He was nice to me because he felt sorry for me, the faggot, the lonely gay kid no one wanted to know, wanted to hang around with.

Hunter, so pretty with his mop of curly brown hair with reddish-gold hints, the big smile, the thick lips, and the hockey player's ass. Hunter, who I tried to sneak glances at in the locker room after gym, who I always watched walking away from me, who I never had the nerve to even say hello to or even send a friend request on social media, but whose Instagram and Facebook and Twitter and Snapchat I stalked, downloading pictures to stare at and masturbate to late at night in the quiet of my bedroom behind a locked door, Hunter who I'd been so obsessed with for so long, Hunter in his underwear in the locker room or playing basketball in the schoolyard with his shirt off and the sun glistening on his sweaty skin, Hunter and his big brown eyes and big round hard butt and—

I closed my laptop and went downstairs. I walked out onto the front porch and sat in the swing, which groaned just a little. The front porch was shaded and cool in the late afternoon. The four o'clocks had opened with their pink and white blossoms, and a bee buzzed around the enormous lilac bush behind me. I heard a car slowing down, and then a dirty red pickup truck turned on the gravel road and crested the rise in the dirt road before accelerating, throwing gravel and leaving a cloud of red dust behind it. I got a look at the guy driving—he looked older, his face reddened from the sun and a ball cap pulled down low over his forehead. I looked after the truck as it picked up speed on its way down the incline, straining up the other side before disappearing over the hill.

Kelly said the Tuckers were meth dealers.

I hoped we weren't in any danger from them.

"Hey."

I jumped. "Don't do that," I said, scowling at Beau.

"I knocked on the back door, but no one answered." He hopped up onto the porch and sat in a rusty iron chair. "I wanted to apologize again, for the other day. It's just that, well, Dr. Brady doesn't like having strangers at the site. We're still in the early days of the dig, you know, getting things set up, and with the rains and things—"

"It's not a big deal, Beau." I pushed at the peeling paint on the porch with my feet, and the swing started moving back and forth, the rusty metal links squealing. I glanced up at the hooks the swing hung from. They were rusty but seemed to be holding.

For now, at any rate.

"Yeah." He smiled at me. "But you can come down there at any time, you know."

"Do you really think you're going to find the Lost Boys?"

"I don't know. I mean, I've heard that story ever since I was a little boy—"

"So you're from Corinth County?"

He nodded. "Born and raised. How'd you know?"

"I can't imagine legends of Blackwood Hall are very well known outside the county," I replied. "I mean, I wrote a report about them for a class back in junior high school, but there wasn't much to find online. And there was just one book—*Civil War Legends of Alabama*—and that was only a very brief chapter. Most of it rumor and legend."

"Yes, my family has been in Corinth County since before the war." I didn't have to ask which war—there was only one down here. "We weren't quite the Blackwoods, though." He made a face. "We're what you'd call white trash."

"Well, if we weren't before the war"—I gestured at the crumbling porch—"we kind of are now."

"Your mom and your uncle are doing pretty well for themselves."

"They also got out of here."

"Fair point." He cleared his throat. "So, I was wondering…You must get pretty bored and so maybe you'd want to go see a movie in Tuscaloosa sometime?"

He was asking me out.

Or was he?

"You want to hang out, or is this a date?" I replied, feeling my own face start to color.

He cleared his throat. "I was kind of hoping a date? But if you're straight, we could just hang out or something."

"A date, then." I smiled at him. "I have to have dinner with my aunt and uncle Saturday night in Birmingham, but other than that, anytime you're free."

He grinned. "Terrific! I'll check my work schedule and get back to you." He took my phone and sent himself a text. "There. Now we have each other's numbers."

He jumped off the end of the porch onto the gravel and disappeared around the side of the house.

I smiled. Just went to show—who would have ever thought I'd get a date *here*?

Not me.

CHAPTER SEVEN

The air conditioners came the day after Beau asked me out.
Two men in a Sears delivery truck arrived from
Birmingham around ten. I was rinsing out the bowl I'd used for my
Honey Nut Cheerios when I heard a vehicle make the turn onto the
dirt. I didn't look up at first. I'd learned to ignore cars turning onto
the dirt road, since the Tuckers seemed to get business at all hours.
I'd just turned the water off when I heard it slow down and pull
up beside the house. It didn't even take them an hour to haul the
window units up to the attic, find windows with an outlet in reach
of the power cords, and mount them, sweating and swearing and
grunting the entire time.

Now that the window units were here, I saw no point in trying
to do any work until the attic was cool enough to be bearable, and
didn't it make more sense to drive into Corinth to hit the grocery
store and get a look around town?

It's quite beautiful here, I thought as I drove down the paved
county road that descended like wide stairs—a steep incline down to
the next spread of flat road, followed by another steep incline, with
the occasional hairpin turn. Towering pines reached for the blue sky,
giving way occasionally to exposed half-moons of eroded orange
dirt where the road had been cut through a hillside. Low aluminum
guards served more as a warning to not get close to the side of the
road, where the ground suddenly dropped away steeply a foot or
so beyond the orange-stained white line marking the edge of the
pavement. Dirt roads intersected the county road, curving up along

a hillside or coming up from a gorge, and there were mailboxes posted along driveways that curved up to the front of trailers or old, weathered houses. The sun glinted off tin-roofed barns, and I finally reached Fowler's Four Corners, where the murders happened so long ago.

The history of Corinth County is written in blood.

There were no other cars—I hadn't passed anyone on my way down, and the intersection was equally empty.

"Drive forward another ten miles," my map app instructed.

The land wasn't exactly flat now—there were still hills, but not nearly as extreme—and I was passing fields, symmetrical rows of growing things: corn stalks, watermelon vines, beans, peas, and tomatoes. Little iron bridges over orange-watered streams and creeks rattled beneath my wheels. The county seemed stuck in a past time—barns and houses with rusted tin roofs, rotting buildings that used to be country stores, with grass and weeds growing in front by the rusting gasoline pumps, ancient decaying old trucks or cars out in the middle of grassy green fields where cows moved around, heads down while they chewed cud.

There were also many hollows and fields consumed by kudzu.

Some night the kudzu will come through the window looking for you.

The county road dead-ended at a stop sign where I could only turn left or right onto a four-lane road. Two signs greeted me before I reached the stop—the uppermost one said *Corinth 5* with an arrow pointed left, the other *Winfield 20* with an arrow pointing right.

"Turn left on State Road 47," my phone instructed me, interrupting Taylor Swift's singing about holding a blank space.

After I waited for an enormous old farm truck with a bed filled with striped watermelons to trundle past, I made the left turn and side-eyed the red brick church with its unmistakable, large iron cross mounted on the front. I'd lost count of how many churches I passed on the drive so far. Corinth County was almost defiantly Christian. This one was Pentecostal, and I couldn't remember what exactly Pentecostals believed. My dad and his wife were Episcopalians but never forced me to go to church with them when I stayed with them. I'd gone a few times but always got bored, and my mind wandered during the sermons. I didn't know what Mom believed. She never talked about it, and we never went to church. What I knew of Christianity was what I'd learned at St. Sebastian's—so primarily Catholicism.

A vague memory tugged at my mind, of sitting in a hot room on a hard wooden bench while voices, many off-key, sang while hand fans fluttered, and I remembered. Miss Sarah went to church, always.

The green *Now Entering Corinth Population 4760* sign was littered with rusted bullet holes. Maybe I should count how many signs had been shot up. And how many churches there were.

God, guns, and—

I shivered as I drove past a few more churches: Baptist, Church of God, Presbyterian. I passed a sign for the Corinth Aquatic Center and a curbside open-air farmer's market, several pickup trucks and cars pulled up at forty-five degree angles to the curb, box fans whirring and big fat horseflies buzzing around the tired-looking housewives picking over the fresh fruit and vegetables.

I should check that place out, I thought, passing a patch of pine trees and an auto dealership. Fresh fruit and vegetables? Hell yeah!

There was a Sonic Drive-In just ahead. I pulled into one of the stalls, ordered from their meal menu—choosing a bacon double cheeseburger, Tater Tots, and a large Coke—and picked up my phone. I pulled up the map app while I waited for my food and checked the Corinth map. There were still more churches, and a Walmart superstore on the opposite side of town. There were hardware and paint stores, pharmacies and a public library, banks, a high school and an elementary school and a Christian academy and even a junior college, a McDonald's and a Pizza Hut and the Hardee's where Kelly worked, a YMCA and a country club.

Not bad for a small town, really.

I decided to go to the Piggly Wiggly instead of the Walmart. It was just off a town square that looked like something out of an old TV show, but you couldn't miss the three flagpoles flying the US flag, the Alabama flag, and the Confederate flag in front of the county courthouse. The little park in the center of the square had a statue of a Confederate hero—I could tell by the uniform.

The repudiation of a shared racist past hadn't reached Corinth yet.

It was cold inside the grocery store, and not crowded. The Piggly Wiggly looked tired—even the letters outside on the front of the store seemed to be drooping. There were three checkers of indeterminate age, scanning groceries and chatting away with the shoppers whose polite smiles looked forced, anxious to get their plastic bags stored into their carts and escape as soon as they could.

I grabbed a cart and started exploring the aisles, not really knowing what I wanted or needed. I couldn't spend the summer eating fast food or pizza—Tradd's voice snidely whispered in my mind, *No one will want you if you get fat*—so I lingered over the fruit and vegetables, getting ingredients for a big bowl of salad, then bagging oranges and apples, plums and pears, grapes and bananas.

My solo exploration ended in the snack aisle.

I heard her before I saw her.

"Sweet Jesus, but you *have* to be a Donelson!" The high-pitched, thickly drawling voice was dripping with sugar. "You are the *spitting* image of Jacob Donelson, as I live and breathe! You must be Glynnie's son!"

I looked up from the Doritos choices—did I want Nacho Cheese or Spicy Nacho? Cool Ranch?—to see a woman smiling at me. Her face and arms and neck were darkly tanned, the low neck of her blouse showing almost blue-white skin below the tan line. Her hair was pulled up tightly into a bun, gray streaks running through the mousy brown. She was wearing black cat-eye framed glasses with a rhinestone in the upper outside corners, attached to a chain around her neck. Her teeth were crooked and yellow, her faced lined with wrinkles and pockmarked. She was heavyset, a thick round belly bulging over wide hips and black stretch pants, and there was grime under her broken fingernails. She was wearing a worn pair of flip-flops, her toenails and feet also grimy. "I haven't seen you since you were a baby!"

Glynnie?

"I'm Jake Chapman," I said politely. "Glynis is my mom."

Her spotted hand went to the deep, wrinkled cleavage at the neck of her blouse. "I knew it. As soon as I saw you, I knew. I used to change your diapers, but I don't imagine you remember that. How's your grandmama?"

Grandmama.

I didn't have to think up the right response because she barreled on. "Lord have mercy, poor Kelly, having to find her that way. I found my daddy when he had his heart attack, and I will never forget that." She shuddered. "You tell her I'll be praying for her. Are you going to come to church? You tell Miss Sarah we all miss her."

"I—"

"Crossroads Church of Christ." She smiled again at me. "But I know you already know that. Glynnie always comes when she visits. I just can't get over how you've grown!"

I added two bags of Doritos to my cart and smiled.

She started pushing her cart away down the aisle, the right front wheel squeaking and wobbling, making her entire cart shake. "Oh, where are my manners?" she asked loudly, stopping and turning back. "I'm Lucy. Lucy Rutledge. Your mama knew me as Lucy Tucker. You be sure you tell her I said hey!"

"I—I will."

She pushed her glasses up closer to her eyes and peered at me through them. "You are your uncle all over again. I can't get over it."

"You knew him?"

"Didn't I go to the homecoming dance with him our junior year?" She laughed again, a high, cackling sound that set my teeth on edge. "I knew him well as anyone, I reckon. So sad the way he ran off, too. I guess he just didn't want to be around anymore after what happened to Dunk." Her eyes looked wistful. "Jacob always said he was going to go live in the big city when he was old enough. I guess after the wreck he didn't see any point in waiting anymore." She shook her head sadly. "Your poor grandmother sure has had her crosses to bear."

She wandered away down the aisle.

Tucker? Lucy Tucker?

All I wanted to do was get out of there. My head was swimming.

Could she tell I had no idea what she was talking about?

Who the hell were Jacob and Dunk Donelson? And what happened to Dunk?

Dunk turned out to be Duncan Donelson, according to Google. After loading the hatch with the groceries and with the air blowing full blast, I typed *Dunk Glynis Donelson Sarah Corinth County* and found an obituary from the *Corinth County Ledger* archive. The grainy picture was clearly his senior picture, and it was the boy from the picture I'd found. He still looked like Kelly, but his hair was cut short and darker, not curly at all. He'd been killed in a car accident, survived by his mother, his sister Glynis, and his two brothers, Jacob and Dewey.

Jacob. She said he ran away.

I called my mother and left a message on her voice mail, then drove back out to the country.

That night, Mom called me back while I was eating my salad. "Why didn't you ever tell me about Jacob and Duncan?"

She sighed tiredly. "I didn't really see any point. Jacob was gone and Duncan was dead."

"Jacob just ran away?"

"I was really young when it all happened, Jake. I barely remember. I'm sorry. How did you find out?"

"I ran into one of your old friends at the Piggly Wiggly. Lucy Rutledge. She said to tell you hello."

"Lucy Tucker? No friend of mine," she snapped. "How's Miss Sarah doing?"

"I haven't really seen much of her. She kind of freaked out when she saw me—I guess I look like too much like Jacob?"

"Maybe," she replied. "I named you for him…How's everything going?"

We chatted for a little while longer before she had to run, and as I went back to my salad, I thought, Why didn't you mention the picture?

I stumbled across a box of books in the attic the next afternoon. I've always loved to read. The books smelled a little musty. Some covers were torn, and the pages were yellowed. In some of them the glue in the spines had dried out, so pages fell out when I picked them up. Most were crime novels from the 1960s and 1970s, with a scantily clad woman, either nude or in lingerie, on the cover posing sexily with a gun, with a menacing-looking man in the lower right corner. Most were short, less than two hundred pages. I stacked some of them by the door to take down with me.

Every morning I would have coffee, go up to the attic, and start going through the junk, meticulously adding everything I found to the spreadsheet and labeling each box appropriately. Every night after dinner I went up to my room and read in bed. The sameness of the days was weirdly comforting.

I wasn't checking Tradd's and his friends' social media accounts as much anymore, and every time it seemed to hurt less and less.

After my first attempt to visit my grandmother, Geneva asked me to wait on stopping in to see her again. "Just for a little while," she said quietly. "She reacted that way because—well, she didn't know you were staying here. She needs to get used to the idea that she's not in control of her home anymore."

Saturday finally rolled around. I'd gotten so used to the sound of vehicles going up and down the dirt road I didn't even notice them anymore, or the way traffic on the dirt road picked up after the sun went down every night. I worked up in the attic until around five and realized, with no little satisfaction, that I'd gotten quite a bit of it done. Most of the boxes were filled with clothes and linens, and I decided to just trash it all.

I showered and got dressed. Kelly was gone, and Geoffrey had already taken over for Geneva when I got into the car. The route took me through Corinth again on a back way to Tuscaloosa, where I caught Highway 20 for a while before branching off onto I-459. I was streaming a Taylor Swift playlist through the car stereo, singing along and playing the drums on the steering wheel as I kept an eye on the cars and 18-wheelers sharing the highway with me.

The Mountain Brook exit rolled up before I knew it. I got into the right lane and exited the highway.

Mountain Brook was an exclusive and expensive suburb of Birmingham. I'd always known Dewey had done well for himself, but I hadn't realized how well until I started navigating the serpentine streets of Mountain Brook trying to find his home. The houses were all big and expensive looking, the lawns lush green velvet carpets of Saint Augustine grass. Some had circular driveways. Others had fountains bubbling in the front yards. Enormous bushes hid some houses from the road, while others were hidden behind enormous red brick fences. The streets were shaded by enormous pine trees, towering up into the sky.

Dewey's house was one of those hidden behind a brick fence. I missed it the first time and had to make a U-turn and come back. The gate was open when I turned into the drive. I stopped the car to take a good look at the house. It was like a cross between a Southern plantation house and a McMansion. It was enormous and tacky. The lawn was perfectly manicured, a deep green velvet. The curved driveway encircled a sloping patch of lawn with an iron fountain of three mermaids spouting water centered in it. The mailbox was a cairn of red bricks, with the name *Donelson* mounted on its side in wrought iron script, the *D* large and scrolling. As for the house…

It took me a moment to realize the house was a modern replica of Blackwood Hall as it must have looked before the fire, with hideous brick wings mounted on either side of the center. The wings didn't match the main part of the house with the big wide veranda, the round columns, and the wood painted white with crimson shutters at the windows and looked like the kind of add-ons modern people who grew up without money would put on a classic house to show off.

Wow, that was snobby of you, I thought as I pulled up to the front of the house.

The right wing of the house functioned as a four-car garage on the ground floor, with two stories above it. The left wing only had two stories, giving the house a lopsided look, like it was ready to tip over on the right, heavier side.

I could hear my mother saying *It's not mean if it's true* as I got out of the car. Our place in Lincoln Park was more of the modern style Mom preferred—she hated Dad's house out in the suburbs—and as I stared at the colonnaded gallery of Dewey's house, I wondered if her taste was a rejection of being raised down here. Most of the houses I'd seen in this suburb had gone with that *Gone with the Wind*, Tara-type theme.

Mom said once Dewey had all the bad taste one assumed came with the lack of imagination banking required, and his wife Tracy thought expensive meant classy.

Tracy and Dewey had been childhood sweethearts. Tracy graduated a few years ahead of Dewey—she was in my mom's high school class. She'd graduated from the University of Alabama and taught high school English after she graduated. Dewey went into the military for four years after high school and had been shot in the hip during the first Gulf War. The injury left him with a slight limp. Dewey was going to Alabama when they got married—Tracy and the GI Bill put him through college. After trying for years, Tracy had three children in slightly less than three years. The kids—named Ashleigh, Cael, and Brady—were nice kids, if a bit spoiled, and were eight, seven, and six years old.

I rang the doorbell and watched the lightning bugs floating around the lawn in the fading light. It was quiet here, almost too quiet for a suburb.

And the kudzu, creeping ever close to the house, inch by inch, every night an inch closer...

I pushed the thought away.

Aunt Tracy opened the front door. She'd always been pretty, and you'd never know she'd been working in the kitchen. She was wearing heels, a nicely tailored cotton dress, an apron, full makeup, pearls around her neck. There was a smudge of flour on her cheek.

Her face creased in a beaming smile lighting up her face and she threw her arms around me. "Oh, Jake, it's so good to see you. It's been too long!" Her accent was honey, thick and sugary. "Come here and let me hug your neck!"

Mom always said you should never trust a Southern woman. *They're used to killing you with sugar.*

Sometimes, the sugar was laced with rat poison.

I hugged her back and stepped inside. She shut the door behind me and started talking a mile a minute.

"Oh, did you have any trouble finding us? I was so worried you'd get lost that interchange at 20 and 459 is so confusing and I miss the turnoff all the time and then the roads here in Mountain Brook can be so confusing and I remembered you'd never been to this house before but Dewey said you're capable and almost an adult and I worry too much and I shouldn't think of you as a child anymore but I guess that's just how it's always going to be I am always going to see you as that cute little boy who caught the bouquet at our wedding do you remember that and it's just going to be the three of us tonight the kids are at my mama's she never gets to spend as much time with them as she would like so I thought I'd pack them off for a nice long visit but this big old house just gets so lonely without them here I made a pot roast for dinner you're not a vegetarian or a vegan are you oh good I don't really get a chance to cook very much and then of course I realized the pot roast I bought was just too big and you're going to have to take most of it home with you and how are things going with Kelly and do you spend any time with…"

The foyer was enormous, rising two or three stories, an enormous hideous black wrought iron chandelier hanging from the ceiling far above my head. There were huge windows, a hanging stair, and railings across the upper floor hallways looking down on the entryway. The floor was black and white tile, the walls painted a rosy shade of beige.

She kept talking as we walked. I wasn't sure I'd ever heard Tracy talk so much, her words and cadences charming with her thick Southern accent.

"…your grandmother the poor old dear it must be so horrible I can't imagine being trapped inside your body like that the doctors say she can see and hear every word but she can't respond or react—"

She reacted to me all right, I thought, remembering the look of terror on her face when she saw me.

"—and here we are. Do you want some iced tea?"

She led me into a man cave. The walls were covered with dark paneling, and the most enormous television I'd ever seen was mounted on the wall with two reclining chairs facing it. The entire room was done in early modern Alabama Crimson Tide. Framed posters proclaimed their football success, national championships, coaches hoisting crystal footballs as crimson and white streamers snowed down. Even the enormous mirror had the big crimson italic-looking *A* in the middle of it, with Roll Tide in crimson letters underneath it.

Dewey was standing at the sliding glass patio doors leading to the back veranda. There was a kidney-shaped swimming pool out back. The green lawn flowed down into the still, dark waters of a lake—a weathered-looking pier jutted out onto the water. A boat was tied to one of the posts. Dewey was holding a rocks glass with amber fluid in it. There was a bottle of Dewar's on the makeshift bar.

"I'll leave you two to it and finish dinner." Tracy stepped out of the room, closing the door softly behind her.

Dewey turned to me in the soft light of the fading sun and smiled. He offered me a Coke from the bar, gesturing for me to take a seat in one of the easy chairs. We talked about nothing for a little while—the kids, the house, his job and life in general—until I got the nerve to pull out my phone. I pulled up the scan I'd made of the picture I'd found in the attic. I held it out to him. "Who are these kids?" I asked.

"Where did you find that?"

"In the attic. I started up there with the inventory, because I figured the rest of the house would be easy after finishing up there," I replied.

He took off his glasses and rubbed his eyes. "That's my older brothers, your uncles, Duncan and Jacob." He pointed at the one who looked like me. "That's Jacob. Your mother named you after him, you know."

"Yeah, she told me." I stared at him. "Why have I never been told about them before?"

"They were a lot older than your mother and me," he said. "They were born right after our parents got married, a year apart. They were, I think, ten and eleven when your mother was born? About the age they are in that picture." He rubbed his eyes again. "Duncan was killed in a car accident when I was about five. I don't remember either of them very well, to be honest. Your mother might remember them more than I do. Jacob ran away that same summer, never came back. We never heard from him again." He got a faraway look in his eyes. "Mama took that picture down years ago—she got rid of all their pictures. She got rid of everything in the house that reminded her of them." He shook his head. "She seems like a cold, hard woman, Jake, but she's had a pretty rough life."

I stared at the picture. "But don't you think Duncan looks like Kelly?"

"Kelly *Donovan?*" Dewey started laughing. "No, son, no, I don't."

"Okay," I replied. If he said so.

How could he *not* see it?

"You're not getting too bored out there, are you?"

"A little," I admitted. I started telling him about the box of books and some of the other boxes I've gone through. The subject continued through the excellent dinner Tracy made.

After dessert Tracy tried to get me to spend the night and drive back in the morning—"after church"—but I made excuses. "I really don't want to lose a day's work," I said, not letting on that I actually had a date. Telling them would only lead to more questions, and I didn't know if Mom had told them I'm gay.

I wasn't in the mood to have that conversation with them.

Dewey walked me out to the car.

Before I shut my car door, Dewey said, "And if you find anything"—he paused, as though trying to find the right word—"*interesting*, be sure to call me right away."

As I headed back toward the state highway, I wondered what he considered interesting.

CHAPTER EIGHT

I'd always marveled at how dark New Orleans got at night, but it had nothing on rural Alabama.

There wasn't much traffic on either I-459 or I-20 as I drove back toward Tuscaloosa. Occasionally, an 18-wheeler would pass on my left, the drag from their size and speed rocking my little car. I probably could have driven faster, but every time the speedometer crept past the speed limit, I could hear Mom warning me about tickets and accidents and insurance costs, and I took my foot off the gas pedal. There was heavier traffic in Tuscaloosa—Saturday night in a college town, of course there was—but as soon as I left the city limits and exited onto the rural state road, it was like someone flipped a switch, plummeting the world into darkness.

Outside the car windows there was only inky bluish-black velvet darkness. Occasionally the red eyes of a dog or a wolf on the side of the road startled me, and once an animal darted across the pavement too quickly for me to see what it was. Roadside signs materialized out of the dark and vanished back into it as I passed by. Outside the pyramids of light thrown forward by the headlights, there was just nothingness stretching out to the almost shapeless forms of trees. The headlights exposed the pines, the ditch alongside the road, and how the red dirt crumbled away into nothingness. Bugs and insects materialized out of the darkness, moths and otherworldly-looking things with wings I didn't recognize, splatting against the windshield and spilling their guts across the glass. I had to keep spraying wiper fluid across the windshield, using the wipers to clean off the corpses from the mass suicide of bugs drawn to my headlights.

It was like one of the plagues of Egypt from *The Ten Command-ments*.

Maybe I *should* have spent the night in Mountain Brook.

Occasionally, in the distance I'd see the headlights of another car in the dark, clicking down to low beams as it got closer, passing me with a rushing whine of wind and engine and the bass line from a too-loud car stereo.

It was like being in one of those ridiculous documentary television shows, where someone has an encounter on a lonely road with aliens, slender silvery creatures with big heads, long fingers, and rounded black slits for eyes peering through the windshield.

I'm losing it, I reminded myself. *Stay calm and get your imagination under control.*

It would be so easy to get lost out here in the middle of nowhere. Why didn't I stay the night?

My hands on the steering wheel were slick with sweat, and I reached down to turn the air-conditioning up higher as more bugs splattered on the windshield. A doglike creature—maybe a wolf, probably a wolf, oh my God what if it's a werewolf—appeared on the side of the road, staring at me, eyes glowing red in my headlights. I swerved over the center line to make sure I didn't hit it, not wanting to think about what that would sound like, how it would feel, having to clean fur and blood and skin off the front of the car the next morning.

Get a grip, I reminded myself, wiping sweat from my forehead. There's nothing out here that would hurt me even if I did get lost. There's no such thing as werewolves.

And my phone wasn't going to let me get lost anyway.

What did people do before cell phones?

It felt like I'd been driving for hours, but the time glowing on my phone told me it hadn't even been forty-five minutes since I left Mountain Brook.

It couldn't be too much longer.

I took a deep breath and promised myself this was the last time I drove anywhere after dark for the rest of the summer.

Think pleasant thoughts. Think about your date with Beau tomorrow.

My first date since the whole Tradd disaster.

I heard Tradd's voice in my head: *You're smothering me! Why are you so needy? Why do you have to be jealous of everyone? What is wrong with you?*

I winced, remembering that last night when he stormed out, slamming the door behind him, the texts that went unanswered.

How stupid I'd been.

I'd learned from that and would be different with Beau. I'd take it easy and slow and wouldn't rush things. Besides, I would be gone by the end of the summer, and that would be the end of it.

"In one mile, turn right onto State Road 31," my phone's tinny, monotone female voice commanded through the speakers.

See? I was almost to the turnoff. Almost there.

I remembered the road to my grandmother's house climbing into the hills, the flimsy guardrails along the side that would never be able to stop a fast-moving car from plunging through and down the steep slopes, remembered how dizzying it felt to look out the car windows and over the side of the road, how little shoulder there was on those slopes. It terrified me in the daylight—one false move, one jerk of the wheel, and the car would be cartwheeling down the slope, over and over until coming to rest against a tree and—

I had to stop scaring myself.

If I just stayed on the left side of the white line on the side of the road, I'd be fine.

I thought about calling Kelly, asking him to meet me at Fowler's Four Corners, pulling over into the abandoned parking lot of the old store and waiting so I could at least follow him back up the road at a safe pace, watching the red taillights ahead of me.

Like he wasn't with his girlfriend. She was probably up in his room right now, and he wasn't going to stop what he was doing to come escort me home.

Grow up. I could do this.

"Turn right on State Road 31 in five hundred feet."

My headlights caught the big stop sign hanging over the road ahead.

My headlights danced across the brooding empty lot of the abandoned store.

"Mrs. Fowler's brains were splattered all over the Coca-Cola cooler," I remembered Mom saying. "They only had a daughter, and

BURY ME IN SHADOWS

seeing the crime scene caused her to have a breakdown, and when she got out of the hospital, she moved away. She hired some people to empty out the store, and now the place just sits there, rotting in the sun."

The history of Corinth County is written in blood.

I kept slowing down, and the car rolled to a stop right at the white line painted on the pavement. My turn signal was blinking. I sat there for a moment. My headlights caught the tall skeletal signpost, the concrete blocks where the gasoline pumps used to stand, the collapsing store building, the graying, rotting raised house with weeds surrounding it right before the woods begin again.

What must it have been like that night, I wondered, for their poor daughter? Did she hear the gunshots? Who found them?

My phone rang as I started making the turn, and I looked at the screen on the dashboard. Mom. I clicked to take the call. "I'm driving back from Dewey's," I said without the courtesy of hello. "Just passing Fowler's Four Corners."

"That horrible place," she said. There was a slight slur to her voice. She'd been drinking. How much earlier was it in Los Angeles? Two hours in time difference, so just past nine. "You better be on Bluetooth."

"Yes, of course I'm on Bluetooth," I snapped back.

"I always thought that place was haunted." Her voice sounded clearer. "They used to say sometimes at night you could hear Mrs. Fowler screaming and the gunshots sometimes."

"Jesus, Mom," I replied. "Have you been drinking?"

"A little. A martini or two with dinner. What about you? You're not drinking, are you? No drugs?"

I started accelerating up the steep incline, trying not to think about the sheer drop on the other side of the guardrails. "No, clean as a whistle," I replied. "And, you know, getting me away from New Orleans and sending me to live where there's a meth lab in the next hollow might not have been the best idea. But I've managed."

"The Tuckers sell meth now?" She sounded amused. "Well, they always made shine. Dewey never mentioned it. How do you know?"

"Kelly told me."

"Ah." She was silent for a few moments. "But you're okay?"

"I'm fine. I told you—I'm not an addict." I could hear her saying *but you wouldn't admit it if you were.*

"You sound better," she replied. "I noticed it the other day when we talked."

"I am doing better," I said, a little surprised. She didn't know I'd been seeing things or maybe hallucinating, though, but no need to make her worry. "How's it going there? How's the case coming along? You're not going to have to stay longer, are you?"

"I'm bored most of the time, to be honest. If it wasn't so damn far, I'd fly home for the weekends. And no, I don't think it's going to run long. If anything, I might be done sooner than I'd thought." Another animal vanished out of the headlights' cone as I got to the top of the slope and let up pressure on the gas pedal. How many climbs were there before home?

"Why didn't you ever tell me about your older brothers?"

For a moment there was silence, the only sound the car's engine as I reached the flat at the bottom of the slope and start up the next one—which was both higher and steeper.

"I didn't see much point," she finally replied. "I was a little girl then, you know. I barely remember either of them."

"But still, Mom, you named me after one of them. What else haven't you told me?"

"There's probably a lot I haven't told you." I heard ice being dropped in a glass. "I don't know, Jake. What was the point of telling you about two uncles you'd never meet?"

"I kind of look like Jacob."

"You think so? And before you ask, yes, I tried to find Jacob as soon as I could afford to hire a private eye." She sighed. "The detectives found no trace of him anywhere. He walked out of the house that night and just…vanished."

"But Mom, it's my history, too, you know."

"I know." I heard her pouring another drink, putting the bottle back down. "There never really seemed to be a good time, I don't know. I don't like to think about…" She paused. "Alabama. I don't have good memories from there. I've spent my entire adult life erasing Alabama from my life."

"But you sent me here for the summer."

Silence.

"You chose to go there instead of rehab," she reminded me. "It was *your* choice."

"Some choice."

"Nothing's…nothing's happened?"

"What do you mean?" I remembered the weird feelings, the white whatever-it-was I kept seeing in the woods, the strange joy when I'd arrived, the fear in the attic, the headaches at the ruins.

I couldn't tell her about that. She'd never believe I was sober.

"No, no, nothing's happened, everything's fine, I'm fine," I replied. "Kelly's okay, the nurses are pretty cool, and the people from the dig I've met—" I stopped myself from mentioning Beau. She'd think it was too soon for me to even think about dating.

"How's Miss Sarah?"

Her voice changed. I'd never realized how afraid of her mother she was.

She sent me here because she thought it would be safe, because her mother was dying and can't hurt me.

I remembered that look of horror on Sarah's face when she saw me, the way she recoiled from me. Maybe she thought she was seeing a ghost. "She's…well, she's immobile and can't really speak. The nurses are great. I—" I stopped because I didn't know what to say to her. "The stuff in the attic is…interesting. There's some stuff up there I think we might be able to sell, but most of it is just junk."

She laughed, and I heard her pouring another drink. The last time I saw her drunk was when my stepfather—the first one—moved out. I was eleven. I never knew if he'd left on his own or if she'd asked him to leave, but he was gone, and when I got home from a roller-skating party that Saturday night she was sitting in the kitchen, drinking by herself and incoherent. I had to help her to bed and wound up sleeping on the floor in her room, worried she'd choke on her own vomit.

For the record, never google *worst case scenarios with a drunk person.*

She was a grown woman, I reminded myself. She could take care of herself.

She laughed. "Don't spend too much time up there," she said, hiccupping. "Listen to me. I have been drinking too much…I was about to say it was a haunted place. There are ghosts everywhere you turn up there, Jake." She laughed. "The history of Corinth County is written in blood…and our family is cursed, always has been." Her laugh died away into a choked sob. "Maybe you should go home to New Orleans, temptations aside. I don't know."

"Are you sure you're okay?"

She mumbled something I couldn't really hear. The speakers made that three beep sound to let me know she was gone.

The entire car filled with light.

A gigantic pickup truck with enormous tires, its chassis sitting probably higher than the roof of my car, had come out of nowhere and was now behind me, following too close and weaving back and forth, crossing over the broken yellow line in the middle of the road. In the brief silence before my phone started streaming Taylor Swift through my speakers, I could hear the low thump of a loud bassline, in that register you feel in your nerves and your bones. The truck cab was too high for me to make out who was driving. I could just see weird dark shapes behind darkened glass, and the reflection of the high beams in my mirror was blinding. I flipped it up and could only see the truck in my side mirrors.

I felt the fear starting on the edge of my brain, the part that my Biology teacher at St. Sebastian's used to call the lizard part, offending the good Catholic boys in the class who didn't believe in evolution.

I gripped the steering wheel.

Why didn't he just pass me?

I pressed the gas pedal down to the floor.

The digital speedometer jumped, going from fifty-five to eighty before I came to my senses and eased off. I flipped the mirror down again and looked back. He was maintaining that same speed, still weaving back and forth—

I turned my eyes back to the road just in time to see the S curve sign in my headlights.

It was the last curve before the final slope.

I could see the dirt road leading back through the woods to where the ruins sat and thought for a moment about heading down it. But what if the truck followed me? It was an irrational fear, but I didn't want to be alone in the woods with whoever was driving that truck.

I took my foot off the gas pedal and remembered to not stomp on the brake, depressing it slowly as the curve came up on me way too fast.

I leaned as I spun the wheel to the left, still braking slightly, like leaning would help keep the car centered.

The tires screeched and squealed and complained but held.

And I breathed in relief. I was heading up the final incline.

I saw the mailbox up ahead.

And the truck was right behind me again.

I flipped the right turn signal on and continued slowing.

The truck swung out into the other lane and shot past me, honking the horn as he went by, and a beer can came flying out of the passenger window as he swung back in front of me again.

I winced as the can hit my hood and bounced over the car.

The truck, though, went up on two wheels as it took the turn onto the gravel road running past Miss Sarah's house.

The cloud of dust the truck kicked up was still thick when I reached the mailbox. I made the turn and parked.

I turned off the car and sat there, panting and shaking, for a moment before I got out of the car.

The truck was sitting on the downward slant of the dirt road about forty yards past the house.

As I climbed the front steps, the dust was still swirling around it, but I could see it was a Ford, dark, the cab had a back seat, and red mud was spattered all along the side.

When I put my key in the front door, the truck started moving down the road again slowly, picking up speed at the bottom of the hollow before climbing up the other side, leaving nothing but the cloud of red dust behind.

"I told you, the Tuckers have a meth lab," Kelly said from behind me, making me jump. "They still make moonshine, too."

I flipped on the hallway light. He was standing there at the foot of the stairs in just his underwear, tighty-whitie BVDs. His hair was flattened out on one side, and there were dark purple hickeys on his neck and chest. He scratched his ass and started climbing the steps.

"You didn't tell me they were crazy."

He paused halfway up the stairs. "You think meth heads are sane?" he said. "And it's never too safe out there on the roads, especially that one, on Saturday nights."

He reached the top of the stairs without looking back, turned right, and disappeared.

I locked the dead bolt and put the chain on the front door.

As I started up the stairs, I remember Mom mumbling before she hung up the phone.

I could swear she'd said, *It's a bad place.*

Chapter Nine

I woke up late Sunday morning.

I hadn't slept well, the vestiges of the nightmares I'd suffered through all night long leaving me uneasy as I opened my eyes and sat up in bed. The details—someone was chasing me, like always, sometimes in the house, sometimes through the attic, sometimes through the woods—faded as I yawned and stretched.

It was raining again. The light in my room was gray, and rain was spattering against the windows, the air-conditioning unit chugging away dutifully.

Did it ever not rain here? I thought, getting out of bed and wandering down the hall to the bathroom. My phone let me know it was almost ten. Kelly's bedroom door was shut—oh yes, he went to Bible study at ten at his church. He'd asked me if I wanted to go with him, but despite the look on his face when I said no, he didn't press the issue.

After brushing my teeth and washing my face, I went downstairs and made toast. There was already a pot of coffee made, and I was eating my toast when Geneva came into the kitchen to get another cup.

"Morning," she said. She sat down at the other end of the table from me, setting down the book she was carrying. It was a Bible.

She smiled faintly. "Miss Sarah sleeps a lot when it rains."

"How is she, really?" I swallowed some toast.

Geneva gave a little shrug. "She could go tomorrow, she could live another year or two," she replied. "Younger people, with therapy, can get better or make a recovery. Someone her age…" Her voice trailed off. "She's getting used to the idea of you being here. Maybe later today you could stop in and have a visit, read to her a bit while I take a break for lunch."

I could think of a lot of things I'd rather do, like eat a roach or jump off a bridge, but I nodded. "Are you missing church this morning?" I asked, pointing at her Bible.

"I go to evening services," she replied. She gave a little shrug. "I hope the Lord doesn't mind."

"If you want, I can cover for you on Sunday mornings, so you can go to church."

She smiled. "That's kind of you, Jake. Maybe I'll take you up on that next weekend. The deacon from Miss Sarah's church comes by some Sundays after services to visit and pray with her. If you want, you can join them. It would make her happy, I think."

"Well…"

"She is your grandmother," she said quietly. "And this summer—this might be the last summer."

"I know." I closed my eyes.

A flash of memory came to me.

I'm running down the hallway on the second floor, a big figure coming after me, and I'm terrified, scared to death, I can't let her catch me, and I keep running, stumbling on the steps as I run down the downstairs hallway to that damned door with the stained glass, and I pull it open and run out into the rain…

I shivered.

Geneva smiled at me. "Jacob, I'm from Corinth County. I know—we all know—what your grandmother is like, okay? But she is your grandmother, you know, and if you don't spend time with her now, you might regret it later in life."

"What do people say about her? I mean, what was she like, you know, before?" I got up and got another cup of coffee. "Mom doesn't talk about her much, and neither does Dewey."

"She's had a rough life." She gripped the coffee cup with both hands. "A lot harder than you probably know." She looked down into the cup. "She lost her first two boys only a few years after she lost her husband, you know. And she married late—most people reckoned she'd never marry. She was thirty-two when she married your grandfather, which was old for a woman not to be married back then."

"Really?" I sat back down. "I mean, it wasn't *that* long ago."

"This is the country, Jake." Geneva laughed. "Things are different in the country, you know. It takes us country folk a while to catch up. I was about ten when she lost the boys."

"What was my uncle Jacob like?"

She smiled. "He was smart and funny and liked to laugh. Everyone liked Jacob. He was a good singer, was in all the school plays and things, and he loved to read." She pointed at the book next to my plate, Erle Stanley Gardner's *The Case of the Calendar Girl*, with its scantily clad, long-legged blonde backed into a corner, being menaced by a shadow holding a gun. "He loved to read. Those are his books, I think, that you're reading."

"Why did he run away?"

Her forehead wrinkled. "I don't rightly know. It wasn't long after Duncan got killed in that car wreck. Miss Sarah never spoke of it, you know. She just closed herself off from everyone and stayed here, raising the young ones…" She pushed her chair back. "I should get back."

I got another cup of coffee and glanced out the window through the rain to see a shape coming out of the woods. I squinted as I watched the person struggle with an umbrella in the wind and splash their way through the orange current running from the parking area down the slope into the woods. Finally, he made it up to the flatter ground just as the wind turned his umbrella inside out, and he ran for the mud porch door. I walked back there and opened it just as Beau got to the top step. He was soaked through, his calves stained orange with mud, and his teeth were chattering.

"Stay here," I said, "and I'll get you a towel and some clothes to change into."

A few minutes later his clothes were in the dryer, he was wearing some of my sweats with a damp towel wrapped around his shoulders, and we were sitting on the front porch, watching the rain coming down in sheets, water pouring off the sides of the roof.

"Doesn't look like we'll get any work done today," Beau said. He was sitting in an old chair on the other side of the cast-iron table from me. "Driving out here was a waste of time today." He sighed. "Everything back at the site is just mud. I don't know if I'll be able to get my car out if it doesn't stop raining soon."

"If you still want to drive into Tuscaloosa to see a movie or something, we can take my car," I said. As long as we're back before it gets dark, I thought, remembering my drive home last night.

"Do you mind if we just kind of hang out here?" Beau asked, finishing his lemonade. I refilled his glass from the glass pitcher on the table. "I'd rather be around when the rain stops, to see if Dr. Brady needs me." He gave me a sad smile. "You must think I'm an idiot."

"My mother's a workaholic, so no, I don't." I took another drink from my glass. "And it's kind of your job, right? You're not getting paid, but you're getting credit for helping, right?"

Beau nodded. "Yes, it's an internship. I'm hoping to get to be Dr. Brady's graduate assistant once I finish my undergrad. He's going to help me get into grad school."

"You want to be an archaeologist?"

"I do. I love history." He nodded. "There aren't many Civil War sites left that haven't been excavated or plowed under. That's why Blackwood Hall is so important—why Dr. Brady was pushing your grandmother for so long to let him dig there." He gestured to the woods with his sweating glass. "Blackwood Hall has never been touched, really, since the fire. This house wasn't the original house on this site, you know. Zebulon Blackwood built a small house here after the war to be closer to the roads, and then of course his grandson built this house when he got rich from selling lumber to the paper mill over in Sparta."

"You know more about the Blackwoods than I do," I replied.

He smiled faintly. "Everyone in Corinth County knows a lot about the Blackwoods. These stories are all part of county lore, our shared history." He rolled his eyes. "And believe me, there are a lot of people around here who prefer to live in the past."

"So you're from the county?"

"Yup." He gestured down toward the hollow. "The Tuckers are distant kin to me—I'm not really sure exactly how. We used to go to the Tucker family reunion, until they went into the meth business." He looked at me. "You know about that, right?"

I remembered the truck from last night and shivered. "Yes, Kelly warned me."

"Good. They're dangerous people, especially Ma Tucker." His voice trailed off. "Hackworth Holler is on the other side of the county, close to town." He rolled his eyes. "And I'm sure there's some stills and meth labs back in our holler, too. The Tuckers don't have a monopoly on meth and moonshine in Corinth County."

"Wow. You grew up in Hackworth Holler?"

"No, I grew up in town. My dad works at the condom factory, and my mom is one of the lunch ladies at the grade school." He laughed. "We're Hackworth success stories."

"Really?"

"Yeah, we're just as much white trash as our Tucker kin." Beau cracked a sad smile at me. "My cousin Ricky was the first of us to go to college—well, more than 4Cs."

"4Cs?"

"Corinth County Community College. It's a junior college, more of a vo-tech training school." He smiled, holding up his palms. "Not many of us make it there, either. Most of us work at the condom factory or at the bakery, if we work at all."

"You shouldn't call yourself white trash," I said with a frown. "It's derogatory."

"It's true." He finished the rest of his lemonade. "I've always liked history, ever since I was a kid. So I read a lot of it, but when my fifth grade class took a trip to Moundville, I knew I wanted to be an archaeologist." He wiped sweat from his forehead as lightning temporarily blinded us both. The thunderclap came almost immediately afterward, rattling the house. "So, yeah, I know a lot about the Blackwoods. If you read county history, most of it is about them." He pointed down in the direction of the ruins. "And most of the legends and stories. Most have been handed down and repeated over the years and changed and exaggerated, as oral histories often are. I used to want to write down all the oral history of Corinth County."

"Why don't you anymore?"

"Because it's written in blood." He stood up, picked up his glass, and tossed his ice out into the rain. "Dr. Brady isn't going to be happy about this rain."

"Does the campsite flood?"

He shook his head. "No, the tents and everything are watertight and on higher ground, but that area all behind the ruins floods, and any holes fill up with water. And you can't drive in or out because the road floods or gets too muddy."

"Why would they put a plantation house up here?" I scowled out through the stream of water draining off the roof. "Especially if the land is swampy in places. Why didn't they put it down in the valley, or in the hollow?"

"You really don't know anything about your family history." Beau grinned at me as he sat down again. Another flash of lightning and thunder—but this time, the porch light flickered. The wind was picking up, spraying the rain farther up onto the porch. I grabbed my glass and the pitcher and gestured for Beau to follow me back into the kitchen.

The screen door slammed behind him, and for a moment I heard an angry voice shout in a drawl, *Jaaaaaaaa-cob! What have I told you about slammin' that door?*

I almost dropped my glass and set the pitcher down on the counter heavily. I held on to the counter for a moment, breathing hard. The air in the kitchen was cool, the rain beating a steady backbeat on the air conditioner chugging away in the window. For a moment, though, the kitchen was hot, the air was heavy with water and anger, a long strip of yellowed flypaper littered with the corpses of dead flies twisted lazily in the light breeze coming through the window over the sink, and I smelled *grease*, bacon grease, and that other smell—

"Jake? You okay?"

"Yeah." I shook my head, and the kitchen was cool again. There were goose bumps on my arms. I felt a little sick, not quite right—but *sick* wasn't the right word. It was the aftermath of fear, that slow adrenaline crash when the danger had passed, and I was safe again and… "I think I may need to sit down for a minute."

"Coming into the cold so fast from the hot." Beau nodded, straddling a chair and putting his elbows on the kitchen table.

"Maybe." I pulled out the chair across from him and slid into it, shaking my head. "I just had a dizzy moment, that's all."

Maybe something *was* wrong with me?

I heard Mom saying again, mumbling over the phone line, *It's a bad place.*

Places couldn't be bad, could they?

The history of Corinth County is written in blood.

"I've had some…odd experiences since I got here," I said slowly, putting my hands down flat on the table. The air conditioner continued to chug along in the window. The rain continued without sign of letup. More lightning, so close this time I could smell the ozone as the thunder rattled and shook the house. The lights flickered again.

"May lose power," Geneva said, walking into the kitchen. She walked over to the refrigerator, got a bottle of Diet Coke, twisted the cap off, and took a long drink.

"Does it stay out long?" Power failure had never occurred to me. But the lines came in from a pole out closer to the road. A fallen branch or a high wind could easily take the power out.

Geneva laughed. "It can go out for a good long spell." She gestured in the general direction of Miss Sarah's room. "But there's a portable generator in Miss Sarah's closet, if we need to power up anything in her room. And she's dealt with the heat for most of her life. It's not going to kill her now." She got another Diet Coke out of the refrigerator. She smiled at us both and walked back out of the kitchen.

"What else do you know about the Blackwood history?" I asked.

Beau grinned back at me. "Besides the Lost Boys? Did you know that the original Blackwood, Jeremiah, married a witch?"

"What?"

He laughed. "Jeremiah Blackwood was the original settler up here." Beau grinned at me. "He got a land grant that made up the original plantation—most of this little mountain, with all its hollers, and a lot of the flatland down at the bottom, pretty much all the land down to the banks of the Sipsey River. That was the boundary. His first wife died, and he went to New Orleans and brought home a wife. Everyone thought she was a witch—so the story goes. Poor thing was probably just a Catholic—but it's a hard kind of Christianity people believe in around here." He scratched his nose. "The story is a mob dragged her off and burned her at the stake, and she cursed them all from the flames, including her husband and his descendants."

"Seriously?"

"It's probably just a story—there's no record anywhere of any such thing happening. But when the boys disappeared...you see how these kinds of legends take root." Beau tugged on his ear. "Well, that's kind of what we're doing out at the ruins," he said slowly. "Part of what we're doing is trying to see if there's any truth to the legends and stories. The Yankee army never made it to Corinth County—the closest they came was Tuscaloosa." He scowled. "That's why we wonder about the story of the Yankee deserter being true. No other building in this county burned. And communication wasn't, you know, what it is today or even later in the nineteenth century. Are those stories true? Possibly. There's a couple of other Yankee deserter stories in the history." He ticked them off on his fingers. "The Lost Boys of Blackwood Hall. Blanche Fowler was supposedly raped and robbed, and Serena Collingsworth supposedly killed one." His smile got a little crooked. "The wicked Yankee deserter, looting and raping his way across the county, is an apocryphal story."

"One mothers scared their children into behaving with?"

"Exactly." Beau beamed at me. "The most famous is the one in *Gone with the Wind*, of course—the book sold a gazillion copies and everyone has seen the movie."

"And of course, by demonizing the enemy you make the Southern cause seem even more noble." I shook my head. "Are there other possibilities for the Lost Boys?"

"The last record of anything from Blackwood Hall before Zebulon returned was a typhus outbreak here," Beau went on. "It's actually in the Corinth paper from the time—warning people away from coming here. So it's logical to assume Louisa Blackwood died from typhus. Someone buried her, put up a headstone, even if it was just wood and not stone. Is it possible that the boys also died of typhus? What would the enslaved people have done in that case—if everyone in the family was gone, what would they do? What would you have done?"

"Run away," I replied promptly. "Especially if the entire family was dead." I shuddered. "There's no telling what would have been done to them."

"The problem is all the records of Blackwood Hall were actually in the main house here," Beau said. "There was no way of even trying to find the missing enslaved people, and from all accounts Zebulon was traumatized by the war. He lost his arm. I can't imagine how hard it must have been to come home to find everyone and everything gone..."

"Pardon me for not feeling bad for a slave owner," I replied. She might not have told me much of the family history, but Mom had made it clear that she wasn't proud of our heritage, and I shouldn't be, either. I quoted her to Beau, "There's nothing to be proud of in the Blackwood history before or during the war. They enslaved people, treated them like they were livestock, broke up families... Whatever happened to the Confederacy during and after the war was less than they deserved."

"No argument from me on that score." Beau held up his hands. "Peace."

"Sorry." I smiled back at him. "Mom's an attorney and has some pretty strong opinions about civil rights and the law..." I let my voice trail off.

"I'm just glad your mom and Mr. Donelson are letting us dig now."

I started to say something but heard something—something faint and distant. Someone calling. Over the downpour and the thunder and the lightning, I heard something. "Do you hear that?"

Beau cocked his head to one side. "It sounds like Dr. Brady."

He went out the kitchen door to the mud porch. I followed. Once we were out on the porch, the rain was even louder. It seemed like the rain was coming down harder, which didn't seem possible. The sheet of water draining off the porch roof was almost a solid curtain, and when the lightning came again, it was close. The thunder was so loud my ears rang.

Beau hesitated before going down the back stairs. He slipped in the slick grass, and he went down, sinking into the mud a little bit. I tried not to laugh but it was hard not to—his face and entire front were covered in orange mud. I went down to help him.

I was soaked within seconds. My teeth started chattering as I shouted, "Are you okay?"

He nodded and gestured with his head toward the road into the woods.

I glanced over and saw that the muddy streams were running fast downhill. I heard Dr. Brady again, and it sounded like he was calling for help.

Where was everyone else from the dig? I wondered as I followed Beau to the tree line. The edge there crumbled away under our feet, and Beau slipped again, going down hard on his backside, and he slid before I could grab him and was carried away by the rushing water.

"Beau!" I went after him, just as headlights turned into the carport. I caught him and grabbed him, pulled him up to his feet. Water was running down my face and into my eyes. My shirt and shorts were clinging to me—so were my socks and my shoes. I managed to keep following Beau, keeping my eyes on his wet back, the water running off him, my skin pruning before my eyes.

Onward we slogged, but once in the woods we were a little more protected from the rain. The ground was still soggy, and the water was still rushing down the hill, but it wasn't as bad. It seemed to take forever, but we finally reached the clearing. I put my hand up to shield my eyes from the rain, and Beau grabbed my arm and pointed.

Close to the back corner of the old mansion, I could see a yellow rain slicker being held aloft, being pelted by rain and pine needles. I splashed my way back there, my legs getting more and more tired each time I freed a foot from the goopy mud. I followed Beau around the side of the mansion to where Dr. Brady was holding up a yellow tarp.

"The rain," he shouted at us, over the roar of the deluge, "must have washed it free."

I followed his eyes and looked down at the ground at what he was trying to shield from the rain.

It was a human skeleton, half exposed in the red mud, the bones stained orange.

CHAPTER TEN

I couldn't stop staring at the skeleton.

I was getting drenched by the rain, but it didn't matter. I couldn't get wetter than I already was, my body and clothes reaching saturation point as the wind howled through the trees. Muddy water swirled around my ankles, rain running down my face, and lightning flashed again, very close, so close I could smell ozone and burnt water. I was blinded for a moment—

Oh my God I have to get away I don't want to die I'm too young to die I am sorry I am sooo sorry but

—and the thunder was so loud I could feel it in my teeth, in my spine, so loud it almost hurt.

I shook my head, and for a moment, the rain was gone, the moon was out, and I was running through the trees, slipping and stumbling trying to get away *I have to get away* and—

"Jacob!" Beau grabbed my shoulders and shook me. "Are you all right?"

I came back into myself.

Okay, that was just weird.

"I'm fine," I yelled back at him, but it was a lie. I was not fine. My heart was racing, and I was having trouble catching my breath, but I didn't want him to know, couldn't let him know, as shame washed over me, so much shame and guilt and—

I must have been having some kind of psychotic break.

Like Mr. Powell in the second grade. I'd noticed something was wrong because he looked worse every day, like he wasn't washing his hair and his clothes weren't clean and he smelled kind of funny and his glasses were smudged so bad I could see it from my desk in the front row and then that one day he just started breathing hard and panting and mumbling to himself in front of the room and started scratching at his face and his glasses flew off and one of the lenses cracked and we all stayed in our seats not able to move not able to say anything because we were just kids and he was our teacher and he was an adult and adults were always in charge they were supposed to watch out for us and I didn't know what to do what would Mom want me to do she'd want me to get him help and I slid out of my seat and he yelled at me and I ran, I ran for the door and I ran down the hallway to the principal's office and I never want to have that happen to me but—

"Are you okay?" he was practically shouting in my face, his glasses spattered with water. His teeth were chattering, his face was pale, his eyes wide open, and he looked terrified, he looked exactly like I felt and—

Just like that, it was gone.

Am I losing my mind?

"I'm fine," I shouted back at Beau, whose face relaxed and he stepped—sloshed—away from me a few steps.

"Dude, you scared me!" He rubbed his wet arms, his eyebrows together, still watching me through the wet glasses. "Don't do that again."

I gave him a weak smile.

"Boys, can you give me a hand?" Dr. Brady shouted. His hair was plastered to his head, and he'd shoved his glasses up to the top of his head. His tan shirt and shorts were dripping with water where they were exposed to the rain, his yellow slicker unbuttoned and untied, his face both excited and worried at the same time. He was standing right behind the skull, with Beau and me standing on either side of the skeleton. In just the short time we'd been here, the water had cleared away the mud from inside the ribcage and had exposed more of the spine.

"We have to secure the site," Dr. Brady shouted over the rain as lightning illuminated the skeleton again, the skull grinning at me. I shivered again and the thought *This is a bad place* ran through my mind...again. The running water washing the mud away was getting stronger the more rain kept falling, washing dirt and debris past my calves. Dr. Brady pointed vaguely to the front of the ruins. "Beau, get some of the two-by-fours from the supply tent!"

Beau nodded, splashing through the running water and disappeared into the grayness around the front corner of the ruined house.

And that's when it started.

This was different than the weirdness, the whatever-the-hell-that-was.

This was worse.

Much, much worse.

Every nerve in my body was tingling, the bumps rising on my skin again. My whole body was alert, alive, and I felt it, coming up my spine, like nothing I'd ever experienced before. This was so much worse, like a feather was lightly touching my skin, tracing slowly up my spine even though I knew there wasn't anything there, there couldn't be, not in this rain, so it couldn't be a fly or a mosquito or some kind of insect, but it was there, whatever it was, and my skin felt like it was rippling, resisting the touch, yes, that's what it was, a *touch* of some kind, and then it was up to my neck, and I could feel it going into my head, inside through my ears, trying to get into my mind…

My eyes, my head, turned back to the skeleton, to the empty eye sockets green eyes once looked from, *how could I know that*, and my vision starting to blur a little bit, but that might just have been the rain running down my face, water getting into my eyes, but that feather was there, inside my skull when I knew damned well that's impossible, there's nothing, nothing could be in there, but I could feel it, it was trying to push itself into my brain, my head, into who I was, *Make room for me, please*, and I was screaming inside my head, must…resist…But suddenly my stomach seized up, like someone had punched me really hard, and I doubled over, my head swimming, gasping for breath.

And every nerve end was on alert.

Evil…so much evil…this is a bad bad place…

And whatever it was stopped.

The knot in my stomach untied, my body went back to normal—if you can call standing in running muddy water getting drenched in a thunderstorm normal.

"Are you all right, son?" Dr. Brady shouted.

I nodded, biting my lower lip.

Was I losing my mind?

There'd been something going on in my head since I got here. Beau sloshed up, slipped, and dropped the armful of two-by-fours he was carrying. Dr. Brady grabbed one and shoved it into the ground lengthwise above the skull. Moving much faster than I thought he was capable, he created a wooden barrier around the skeleton by placing two more of the planks on either side. The running water now swirled around the board above the skull before running along the side and down the slope to the creek, already swollen past its banks.

"It's starting to lighten up," Beau shouted. He was right. The rain wasn't coming down as hard as it had been, and the sun was struggling to come out from behind some clouds to the west.

My teeth were chattering. "Why don't we head back to the house and get out of these wet clothes."

Dr. Brady nodded. "I'll be there in a moment—you boys go ahead," he said. "I'll get some clothes from my tent, try to secure the site a little more now that the rain's lessening. You go on ahead."

Beau and I walked back up the sloping road, slipping and falling as we went, trying to keep our feet from sinking into the mud as deep as the ground seemed to want, like it was trying to pull us down into—

Stop that, I told myself.

As we went up the steps to the mudroom, I looked at him and then at myself. We were soaked and covered in mud almost from head to toe. "We can't go in the house like this," I said.

Beau nodded. "Might as well hose off first." He grinned at me over the top of his water-spattered glasses. He gestured at himself. "What's a little more water?"

I went around to the side of the house where the hose was attached to a spigot. I turned the spigot on. The sun had come back out and felt good on my arms and legs as I carried the hose over to where Beau was standing at the bottom of the steps. I washed the mud off my legs, arms, and clothes. As I sprayed him down, Beau said with a laugh, "I hope my other clothes are dry now."

I laughed and went up to the mudroom. I opened the door and grinned back at him. "Yeah, the dryer's stopped."

He climbed the steps and hesitated. "Um, you won't track as much water into the house if you, um, leave your clothes in the dryer." His face flushed bright red.

I grabbed a towel from the laundry basket on top of the dryer. I tied it around my waist and stripped off my shorts and underwear, tossing them on the floor. I took a deep breath and added my shirt to the soggy pile. I grabbed another towel and tossed it to him.

"You dry off and change, then put our clothes in the washer while I go put some clothes on."

I stepped into the frigid air of the kitchen.

Geneva was coming out of my grandmother's room when I reached the staircase. She hurried soundlessly down the hallway toward me. "Where are your clothes? What's going on?"

"Beau and I heard Dr. Brady shouting, down at the ruins." I looked down the hall to Miss Sarah's closed door. "We went down there to see."

"And?"

"He found a skeleton at the ruins," I whispered, even though there was no way Miss Sarah could hear me. "Don't tell her, okay? At least until I check with Dewey, see what he thinks and what he wants to do."

A skeleton at the ruins was above my pay grade.

"A skeleton?" Her eyes widened as she shook her head. "Lord have mercy. Hasn't there been enough trouble at the house already?"

Trouble at the house already?

Before I could ask what she meant, she said, "Best be calling the sheriff, don't you think?"

"I don't know." I started up the steps, saying over the railing, "Beau's changing in the mudroom, and Dr. Brady's going to be coming up soon. I'll try to keep them quiet, try not to disturb her."

I didn't need to say her name.

"What are you—what are they—going to do about the skeleton?"

"I don't know."

I left her standing there and took the stairs two at a time, clutching the towel around my waist as I went up. When I reached the top, I heard a sound from the other end of the hallway. I glanced over and saw Kelly's bedroom door closing.

I didn't know he was home but had been in a such a rush to get out of the rain I hadn't noticed if his truck was parked outside. Weird he didn't even say hello. Whatever.

I dried off in my bedroom and put on dry clothes. When I got back downstairs, there was no sign of Geneva, and Miss Sarah's door was still closed. Beau was sitting at the kitchen table, hair still damp. He looked kind of adorable sitting there. Shivering, I started a pot of coffee. Once there was enough, I filled two mugs and handed one to Beau.

He clasped his hands around the cup. "Oh, this feels good."

I sat down at the table, cupping my hands around the mug. I heard footsteps on the back steps. I let Dr. Brady in. I handed him a towel and pointed out the dryer. "Just put your wet clothes in there with ours," I said. "There's coffee in the kitchen when you get dressed."

He was carrying clothes in a plastic bag. He beamed at me. "Thank you, son."

I went back inside and poured him a cup.

"Sorry to take so long," Dr. Brady said with a frown when he joined us in the kitchen. "I think the site's secure now as I can make it by myself, and I called the county sheriff. They'll be sending someone to take a look—and probably call the SBI."

"SBI?"

"State Bureau of Investigation." He sat down at the table with us. "Corinth County can't handle this kind of—well, whatever this is. They'll need the state's help."

"I should probably call my uncle," I said. What if it was one of the Lost Boys? This could turn into a media circus. I remembered the closed door to Miss Sarah's room. It'd be hard to keep the news from her, but she had to know something was going on out in the woods. The stroke didn't leave her deaf, after all…she's not oblivious.

I supposed it didn't really matter in the long run whether she knew or not.

She was dying, and there was nothing she could do to stop the dig, anyway.

I shivered.

You don't know what she's capable of.

"Yes, you're going to need to let him know," Dr. Brady agreed. He was a short man, maybe five feet five on a good day, and older, maybe in his late fifties. What's left of his graying hair was plastered to his egg-shaped head, which tapered down to the sharp point of his chin. He cleaned his glasses with a napkin and sipped his coffee. "This is good coffee, thank you."

"Did you have to call the sheriff?" I asked.

I gulped down more coffee.

He nodded. "We don't know how old the skeleton is, or how long it's been there," he said gravely. "And we have to report human remains whenever we turn them up." He held up his hands. "Believe me, son, the last thing in the world I want is my dig site turned into a crime scene."

"You think it's that recent?" I raised my eyebrows and looked at Beau, who gave me a little shrug and rueful smile. I remembered what he'd said about the Tuckers and their moonshine-slash-meth businesses.

"I can't be certain without a thorough examination, but no, I don't think it's one of the Lost Boys, if that's what you're wondering," Dr. Brady said. He wiped his glasses with a napkin.

Another flash of lightning made us jump. A few moments later the thunder roared. It started raining again. I walked over to the window and looked out. Kelly's truck was sitting out there next to mine and Geneva's.

"Why do you think that?" I asked, remembering the truck from last night. I wondered, for the first time, just how safe and secure we were inside the house at night. "I mean, it's possible, isn't it?"

Don't be silly. The Tuckers didn't care about getting in here.

"It is strange," Dr. Brady went on, rubbing his temples. "But the bones…the bones don't seem like they've been in the ground for over a hundred and fifty years. And I think there was some dental work done, fillings. They wouldn't have filled cavities in the 1860s."

"And it had to be a more recent burial, right?" Beau chimed in. "To be so close to the surface so that the rain would expose it…"

"Don't make assumptions or theories that aren't borne out by the facts." Dr. Brady frowned. "All we know is it's a male skeleton of indeterminate age, buried by the back corner of the original house exposed by flash flooding from the rain. We don't know when it was buried, or who it is, or what happened to whoever he was, although there's also a…" He swallowed. "There's a hole in the right temple where the skull was damaged. Maybe it was postmortem, we don't know. But it looks like he didn't die a natural death."

I shivered as Beau said, "Maybe it was from the family cemetery?"

Dr. Brady looked at us over the top of his glasses. "Boys, the cemetery wouldn't be that close to the house." He cleared his throat. "Do you know, Jake, where the old cemetery is? Your uncle doesn't seem to."

Caught off guard, I mumbled, "Everyone's buried up at Cross Roads." I didn't know where that came from, to be honest, but once I'd said it, I could see my grandfather's tombstone clearly in my head, the big gray marble stone with DONELSON carved into it in large letters, my grandfather's name with the birth and death dates on the lower left side, the plastic flowers stuck into the ground, dusty and dirty and waving in a breeze, my little hand clutched in my mother's. And there were three shadows, mine, Mom's, and another—it had to be Miss Sarah—and in my mind's eye I could see the little brick church on the other side of the orange dirt road.

How old had I been?

Dr. Brady smiled. "No, Jake, that's not where the prewar Blackwoods would be buried. I doubt that little church was around back during the war period. And there are records showing there was a family cemetery on the plantation, which was pretty common during those times."

I shrugged. "I don't know any of the family history," I replied. I didn't even know I had two other uncles. "If Dewey doesn't know, I can ask my mom the next time I talk to her."

Or I could ask Miss Sarah.

"There's a family cemetery somewhere on the grounds of the plantation, and probably another one for the enslaved people. I'll be looking for both, of course, it's part of the project. I just hoped that you might know." He took off his glasses and wiped his eyes again. "Make my life a little easier."

"I've always been under the impression that…" I tried to remember things Mom had said to me over the years. "That sometime around the Depression was when the Blackwoods went broke again and couldn't farm all the land anymore, so the forest came back." I swallowed. "So, if there were two cemeteries, they'd be in the woods somewhere, right?"

No wonder the woods always seemed haunted to me.

"Yes, it was too much to hope you'd know, to make it easier." He laughed. "But nothing about this dig has been easy, so why should it start getting easy now?"

"Aren't there records?" I asked as a vehicle pulled up alongside the house. I got up and walked over to the window. The sun was out, and it seemed steamy out there. I could clearly make out the markings on a sheriff's deputy vehicle, along with the bubble light on the top.

"Remarkably little," Beau said. "Is that the deputy?"

"Looks like it." I headed out the back door and almost slipped on the slick steps. "Hey, Deputy," I called as I came around the side of the house as he was getting out of his vehicle.

He unfolded into a very tall man, well over six feet, long and lanky and lean. His long arms were thin, tanned, road-mapped with blue veins. His brown uniform pants were borderline too short for his long legs, so I could see his navy-blue socks over his black patent-leather shoes. His face was gaunt, tanned skin pulled tightly over bone, deep hollows under the cheekbones, the nose long and thin with round nostrils over colorless thin lips. "And you are…?" he drawled. His eyes were hidden behind mirrored sunglasses with silver metal frames. As I got closer, I could see angry acne scars on his cheeks and chin and forehead.

"Jake Chapman. My grandmother is—"

"Pleased to meet ya. Deputy Seth Rowland. Someone found a corpse?" He shook my hand. His was long and bony, calloused, but strong.

"Dr. Brady, out by the ruins." I gestured back toward the woods. "Come on in, he can show you where it is."

But Dr. Brady was already coming down the back stairs, talking a mile a minute. Beau wasn't with him. Dr. Brady and Deputy Rowland start walking toward the woods, Rowland carrying a blue and orange umbrella he'd retrieved from his car, with AU written in orange on the blue sections.

I climbed back up to the porch, checked the dryer—still about half an hour to go—and went back into the kitchen. Beau was at the coffee maker, filling up his mug again.

I noticed his hands were shaking. "Beau, are you all right?"

"That's Seth Rowland." His eyes were panicked. "I just wish they'd sent someone besides him."

"Someone else?" I stared at him. "What's wrong with him?"

"He's trying," Kelly drawled from the kitchen door behind me, "to think of a polite way of telling you Seth's last name might be Rowland, but he's also a Tucker." I turned to look at Kelly, who wasn't smiling as he went on, "His mother's one."

Chapter Eleven

Everything was dripping, glistening with wet, and sparkling in the sunshine. The ruts between the gravel on the dirt road were darkened blood-orange mud.

Down at the foot of the hill in the little hollow, the creek was swollen with water, overflowing its banks, making the road a shallow orange bayou. The mud and water hadn't slowed down traffic at all—vehicles had been going up and coming back from Tucker Holler with a surprising regularity since I'd come out to the front porch. Sunday after church was clearly a busy time for the Tuckers. Another filthy truck, its windows down, turned onto Blackwood Road but didn't start picking up speed right away the way the others had, slowing and idling where our gravel parking area met the sporadic grass of the front lawn. I started to get up, wondering what they might want, but Deputy Rowland strode out there, gravel crunching beneath his boots. The passenger window came down, and Rowland stuck his head inside. After a few moments Rowland stepped back, the window went back up, and the truck began descending the hill, picking up speed and throwing up orange-brown water as he sped through the flooded hollow, the back shimmying a bit as the tires struggled to get a grip on the soupy mud. The tires finally grabbed hold and the truck shot forward, flying up the other side before disappearing over the ridge.

Rowland grinned at me from behind his mirrored sunglasses as he walked back around the house.

I shivered. How safe were we when the county sheriff's

department was clearly in cahoots with the criminals in the next hollow?

The blooms of the four o'clocks were opening, bees and wasps and hummingbirds weaving in and out of the pink and white blossoms. A cloud of gnats swarmed around the outside of the lilac bush.

Beau had gone back down to the ruins. A team from the university medical center was on its way, and another from the State Bureau of Investigation's Birmingham office. Dr. Brady insisted on supervising the removal of the skeleton. The skeleton had been there awhile, and the rain had washed away whatever other evidence might have remained. I'd pointed that out to Deputy Rowland after he went down and took a look.

"It's still human remains, and there's rules," was all he said.

I was going to have to clean the kitchen floor at some point, with so many people tracking in mud and water and forest debris. Wiping their feet in the mudroom hadn't helped at all.

And there was Miss Sarah to be dealt with.

I'd come out onto the porch to wait for Dewey.

He wasn't happy—he'd sworn a lot, then I heard him tell Tracy he wasn't going to make it to church tonight after all. I could almost sense her rage radiating from her room. I didn't envy him having to stick his head into the lion's mouth. And Deputy Rowland wanted to talk to her. I'd convinced him to wait for Dewey.

He didn't take much convincing.

Mom didn't pick up when I called her, so I left her a voice message.

The screen door opened, and Geneva stepped out onto the porch, wiping sweat out of her eyes. She opened her mouth to speak, then closed it again.

"Yes, Geneva?"

She cleared her throat, clearly uncomfortable. "Mr. Jake, someone has to tell Mrs. Donelson about what's going on out at the ruins, and it isn't going to be me." She folded her strong arms in front of her chest. "That's family business, and I don't get involved in that—it's not my job."

"No, Geneva, it's not," I replied. She visibly relaxed. "It's Dewey's job, and he's on his way here."

"Well, that's good." She opened the screen door, but before going inside, she added, "She should have been told before she was brought home. She's not going to be happy."

No, she wasn't—that was why Dewey never told her.

"Thanks, Geneva. You don't think…You don't think it will…"

She shrugged. "Who knows, Mr. Jake? She's a strong woman. She might get up out of that bed someday, or she might die in it. It's in God's hands at this point."

The screen door shut behind her.

No sooner had her steps faded away than I heard Kelly's heavy tread coming down the stairs. I closed my eyes and pressed the perspiring bottle of Coke to my forehead. He stepped out onto the porch in his Sonic uniform. It was tight in the shoulders and across the chest. "I'm going to work now," he said, letting the screen door slam shut with a loud bang. "Not sure when I'll be back. Probably do something with Bonnie after work."

Yeah, I knew exactly what. And right down the hall from me, too, Mr. Perfect.

"You didn't tell Miss Sarah about…" I l just gestured toward the woods.

His face reddened. His fists clenched. "No. Dewey can tell her, since he couldn't be bothered to tell her before what he was letting happen on her own property. Just because she got sick." He shook his head as he went down the steps to the flagstones, swatting at a horsefly. "None of this would have happened if he'd done what she wanted and not let them back there. But she's going to blame me for not telling her."

"You don't think she knows anything about the skeleton?"

He stopped and turned, scowling at me. "You think she killed someone and buried them back there? You're an even bigger fool than Dewey." He took a deep breath. "It probably—" He stopped, swallowed, darted a quick glance at Deputy Rowland's car before looking back at the ridge.

The Tuckers and their moonshine-slash-meth operation. They wouldn't bury someone they'd killed so close to their own hollow, would they?

"Are we safe here?"

"You think them Tuckers are going to come up here and kill

us in our sleep?" He laughed. "If that was someone that crossed them, they're not stupid enough to leave evidence behind that'd send them to prison." He gave me a sour smile. "They wouldn't still be in business if they were idiots."

He had a point.

When he reached the gravel, he looked back at me. "Where's that Hackworth kid?"

"Oh, he went back down to the ruins to help Dr. Brady."

He opened his truck door and said, "You need to be careful around that one. He's a fag, if you hadn't figured it out already."

I froze.

Did he just say that?

I stared at him, unable to move or speak. He slammed the door and started the truck, revving the engine and throwing up gravel as he backed out onto the dirt road and spun out, heading for the county road, spraying mud and gravel.

He didn't just call Beau a fag.

I felt sick.

I guess that answered my question about whether or not he knew I was gay.

But I kind of felt like he wouldn't care if he *did* know.

I was stuck in a house for the summer with a homophobe.

A big, strong, athletic homophobe who had about seventy pounds of solid muscle on me.

I'd heard the word before, of course, had it directed at me. The Archdiocese of Chicago wasn't exactly a shining example of tolerance, and their school system—while a good one—was riddled with homophobia.

It wasn't pleasant walking into a classroom and reading *Jake Chapman sucks dick* written on a desk in Magic Marker or heading to your hall locker to get a textbook for your next class and seeing someone wrote *Fags go to hell* in Sharpie on it.

But much as it hurt, much as it made me wish I was dead, I sucked it up.

I'd defiantly raised my chin into the air and looked around at the crowd of boys in navy blue corduroy slacks and white button-down shirts with *St. Sebastian's* sewn in script over the breast pocket and the gold and navy-blue striped ties, all waiting to see what I was going to do, how I'd react, if I'd cry or get mad, but I did neither, just letting out a contemptuous laugh and walking away, some of them clapping me on the back and making sympathetic noises that only made me feel even more alone.

I ran to the end of the porch, throwing up over the side as a horsefly buzzed around my head. My stomach kept heaving even after there was nothing left to come out but ropy strings of spit. I wiped my mouth and went back inside the house, which felt somehow different. I'd never felt home here, but I'd been getting used to it. But now…as I went up the stairs, the moaning and groaning and slight give of the soft wood seemed malevolent, like the house was alive and out to get me, the unwanted and unwelcome fag.

It was palpable, real, and terrifying.

Somehow, I made it into the bathroom, brushing my teeth thoroughly, rinsing my face, brushing my teeth again to try to get that raw feeling off them.

The house can't hate you.

"Don't let him get you down," I whispered to my reflection and headed back downstairs. Geneva was waiting for me at the bottom, a worried look on her face, her cell phone in her hands.

"There you are," she said, her voice shaky. "I was worried you'd gone off back down to the ruins." She glanced at the watch on her wrist. "I need you to sit with Miss Sarah."

I recoiled. "Why?"

"I wouldn't ask if it wasn't important."

I felt my face flush. "Of course, I'm sorry," I mumbled.

"There's been an accident, and I have to go meet my husband at the hospital," she said, and I realized she was barely holding it together. "My son—"

"Go," I said, cutting her off. "Geoffrey will be here soon enough, and I suppose I can sit with her awhile. Do I need to do anything?"

"She's sleeping right now." Geneva's entire body relaxed. "Thank you, Jake, thank you. She's had her medications and is resting now. You just need to sit with her. I called Geoffrey, and he's coming early." She shook her head. "Of all days."

"I'll just get my book," I replied, going back upstairs and grabbing my copy of *The Case of the Buried Clock* from the nightstand.

I heard Geneva's car leaving as I headed down the hallway to my grandmother's room.

The door was open. Her room smelled like…well, it smelled a little sour. The heavy green brocade curtains were closed, blocking out exterior light. The little reading lamp next to Geneva's chair was the only light on. It was gloomy in there, the corners dark, and I closed the door softly behind me, not wanting to wake her up.

I wanted her to sleep until Geoffrey or Dewey arrived.

I sat in Geneva's chair without making a sound and opened my book. Her breathing was shallow, but regular, an occasional slight snoring sound. The room felt…claustrophobic, like it was much smaller than it was. One entire wall was hidden behind an enormous wooden cabinet, several rows of four drawers at the bottom, with cabinets above the rows reaching almost all the way to the ceiling. I couldn't remember coming in here as a child, but I recognized the lily of the valley smell above the mustiness. There were water stains on the wallpaper and the ceiling. On one wall was a large framed photograph of a man in uniform I'd seen before. It was my grandfather in his military dress uniform, in some exotic location with palm trees and a beach behind him. Hawaii? I did the math in my head. He must have been in Vietnam, maybe? The Navy whites looked good on him, and there was a resemblance to both me and my mom, but he was a dead ringer for Dewey.

I closed my eyes and leaned back into the wingback chair. The whole room was stuffy, despite the chugging of the window unit beneath the thick, heavy drapes. Her hands were folded on top of the ragged quilt draped across her body, and she was wearing a long-sleeved crimson cotton nightgown which probably had *Roll Tide* written on it somewhere, given the shade. But other than the picture of my grandfather, there was nothing personal about the room, nothing that marked it as Sarah Donelson's space.

There were no pictures of her children or grandchildren.

Mom's bedroom at home was put together by one of the top interior decorators in Chicago and looked like something out of *House Beautiful* or the Sunday *Sun-Times* supplement—but it was clearly her room. There were pictures of me at all the various stages of my life framed on her walls and scattered across the top of her dresser. There were pictures of her with mayors and governors and congresspeople, other politicians, and important people in both city and state. Her room radiated Glynis Donelson Chapman.

I turned my eyes back to my grandmother.

She was looking at me.

"Hello," I said, trying to keep my voice from shaking.

Her eyes were watery, red-rimmed, cracked with red lines. Her grayish lips started trembling, like she was trying to speak. I could hear her labored breathing as her jaw moved and her lips sank farther into her mouth, over the gums, and I wondered where her teeth were. She struggled with the syllables. "Jay-jay-jay-cob," she said, closing her eyes as if the struggle to say my name had worn her out.

"Yes, Miss Sarah, that's right, it's me, Jacob," I said softly, hoping she'd fallen asleep again, but her eyes snapped open again, and that horrible gaze fell on me again. The watery eyes narrowed, the graying black brows knit together above the bridge of her nose, and she tried again. "Why yah here?" She hissed out the words.

"Well, you're sick, and Geneva had an emergency," I replied.

"Yah don't care."

Well, she had me there. Perceptive, even after a near-fatal series of strokes. Good for you, Miss Sarah! I smiled back at her and made a goofy face. "Of course I care—you're my grandmother."

She looked startled. "Guh-grandmother?"

Of course, she thought I was her son. "Yes, Miss Sarah. Glynis is my mother."

Her eyes narrowed.

"Yah never cared." Her hand flopped on the bed. "Sh-sh-she never cared."

"Yes, we do," I lied calmly. "You're my grandmother, and I came up here to keep an eye on you over the summer, help out as much as I can until school starts next semester."

Her mouth twisted.

"I'm sorry if I scared you the other day," I went on, my nerves starting to get to me. That cold stare! Mom was tough but fair, sure, but I was glad she was my mother instead of Miss Sarah. Her kids probably never got away with anything. That stare was making me want to tell her everything, about Tradd and the overdose and everything else, and so I kept talking to keep from blurting that out. "I didn't know I looked so much like my uncle. I didn't even know I had two more uncles, let alone was a dead ringer for one of them, kind of like how Dewey is a dead ringer for his dad—"

She waved a veined hand at me dismissively. I noticed her nails were trimmed, painted red.

Makeup is vanity. I heard Mom's voice, slightly slurred from the wine, in my head again. *Skirts above the knee are only worn by whores and sluts trying to tempt men into lust. No bare arms in public. Everything was sin, Jake.*

"You're just like him," she said clearly, her eyes hardening. "Like I told your mother. You won't amount to anything." She took a breath between each word, but those pauses didn't lessen the venom, the contempt, the dismissal. "I wasn't sorry when he was gone."

I closed my eyes. I'd heard those words before.

And remembered.

I was in the porch swing, a slice of watermelon in my hands, juice running between my fingers and down my chin as I took big healthy bites of the yellowish-orange meat—that couldn't be right, watermelon is red—and Mom and Miss Sarah were sitting in metal chairs, slightly rusty, not too far from me. She wouldn't let me swing because it was dangerous, so it was barely moving, my dirty bare feet not quite reaching the porch itself, and I heard my mother saying, "Don't talk like that, Mama."

"It's the truth." That deep, husky, gravelly voice. "He's like his uncle, and if you don't do something about it now, you'll live to regret it. Like I did. You'll know nothing but grief from that one, mark my words."

"What was the problem with Uncle Jacob?" I asked.

But my words were drowned out by the roaring of an engine of some sort outside that grew progressively louder, almost shaking the house. I smiled as I stood up and said, "Let me see what that is," before fleeing her room, glancing at the grandfather clock in the hallway, wondering how much longer before Geoffrey arrived and how much longer I'd be stuck with her.

And where the hell was Dewey?

I hurried through the kitchen and out the mudroom door to the back steps. As I clattered down the four concrete steps, I saw again a white flash in the woods out of the corner of my eye—only there for a moment, then gone, like every other time—and headed around the corner of the house.

There was an enormous tow truck there, with a huge construction machine on its bed. The noise was from a motor, tilting the bed so the machine could be backed off.

The county seal was on the driver's side door of the tow truck.

A man somewhere between thirty and fifty climbed down out from the cab, wearing dirty, paint-spattered jeans and a filthy white T-shirt. His arms, face, and neck were blackened by the sun, and he looked like he hadn't shaved in a couple of days. "Hey," he said, his big smile showing crooked yellow teeth with gaps here and there. "Somebody called for a backhoe? Would that be you?"

"Not me," I replied. "I'm Jacob Chapman. This is my grandmother's house. You say someone called you?"

He held out an enormous hand for me to shake. It was rough, calloused from years of hard work, and big—mine was enveloped almost entirely by his. He was taller and broader than me, but his legs were too thin for his big upper body. I could see steel gray hairs sticking out of the collar of his filthy T-shirt, and he smelled like stale sweat, old beer, and tobacco—which explained the teeth.

"Jimmy Wheeler's my name. Seth Rowland called me, said y'all needed my backhoe up here," he went on, reaching into his jeans pocket and pulling out a crumpled pack of unfiltered Camels. He shook one out and lit it before sticking it into the corner of his mouth, where it settled like it belonged there.

Rowland's county car was still parked in front of the little pump house, but there was no sign of him anywhere. "He must be down at the ruins," I said, pointing vaguely at the rough-hewn road into the woods. "We found a skeleton down there this afternoon."

He gave me a puzzled look. "Y'all don't need a backhoe for that," he said, scratching his head and puffing deeply on the cigarette, which smelled foul.

"I can't help you," I said, again pointing into the woods. "I imagine that's where you'll find them all." I could hear voices coming from the woods, voices getting louder as they got closer. And sure enough, Dr. Brady and Deputy Rowland showed up, walking out from the woods. "I'll leave this in your hands," I said, turning to go back into the house.

I poured myself a glass of ice water before braving the old woman's room again.

But once I'd settled myself back in the wingback chair, she was staring at me, her eyes and face clearly expecting an explanation. "It's Jimmy Wheeler with his backhoe," I said finally.

She kept staring at me, then said, slowly, taking her time with each word and pausing for breath after each, "Why…a…backhoe?"

The tone of her voice sent a chill down the back of my spine, so much so that I didn't notice at first that she was speaking easier.

Sorry, Mom. Sorry, Dewey.

I took a deep breath and said, "Now, don't get mad at me, I'm just the messenger. But Dewey's allowing a team from the university to dig at the ruins, and this afternoon they found a human skeleton out there and—"

Her eyes opened so wide and her breath started coming so fast that for a moment I worried she was having another stroke, which would be the perfect touch, right? Left alone with the care of his grandmother very briefly, Jacob managed to spill the beans about a big secret being kept from her by her family, and she had another stroke and died!

Yeah, not optimal.

But she wasn't having a stroke.

She was furious.

Spitting nails, as Mom said sometimes when she'd had some wine and her accent came back out.

"Dewey," she said clear as a bell. "I want Dewey."

"He's on his way, but yeah, I'll go call him right now," I said and ran back out into the hallway, shutting the door behind me.

Those eyes! They would haunt my nightmares for the rest of my life.

I called Dewey from the kitchen, just as Geoffrey came in through the mudroom. "I got here as soon as I could," he said as he walked through the kitchen. I just nodded and held up a finger. He winked and went into Miss Sarah's room, closing the door behind him.

I got Dewey's voice mail.

"Hey, Dewey, it's Jacob, your nephew, and we have a bit of a situation here...You really need to get here sooner rather than later."

CHAPTER TWELVE

"She's waiting for you." I didn't get up from the porch swing as Dewey walked up the flagstones to the steps. His face was red, and he was still wearing his church clothes. There were sweat marks at his armpits, beads of sweat on his face, and his thin blond hair was wetly plastered to his scalp. He'd loosened his tie and undone the top button of his shirt, but the tie was still around his neck. "And she's not happy. I'm sorry, but once Jimmy Wheeler got here with his backhoe, I had to tell her something." The backhoe was gone now, sent away by Deputy Rowland and Dr. Brady, who'd almost had an apoplectic stroke at the idea of a backhoe turned loose on his dig site. "And I couldn't think of anything plausible on the spur of the moment."

"It's not your fault—you weren't the one who lied to her in the first place," he replied, wiping his forehead with his bare hand. He exhaled and sat down in one of the rusty old iron rocking chairs on the porch. "I should have waited until she was dead before I gave them permission, or made them leave once she came home. A skeleton, you said? They found a skeleton down at the ruins?" I didn't think I'd ever seen anyone sweat that much. "And what the hell did they need a backhoe for?"

I waved my hand. "Deputy Rowland called for one. Geneva had a family emergency and had to leave early, and Geoffrey wasn't here yet…" I swallowed. "You know, she's doing much better than you said she was."

His eyes narrowed. "How do you mean?"

"Well, for one thing, she spoke to me," I replied. "Clearly. She struggled at first, but she's able to talk. I don't think—"

"Great." He got up without letting me finish, and the screen door slammed behind him.

"You also didn't tell me Kelly's a homophobe," I muttered as I followed him into the house. I watched as he opened her door and went inside. A few seconds later Geoffrey came out and crossed the hall into the kitchen.

Geoffrey was making a pot of coffee, pouring the water into the reservoir as I walked through the doorway. He glanced over his shoulder at me. "Not going to make it tonight without coffee," he said, getting a mug from the cabinet next to the refrigerator and adding Sweet'N Low to it.

"Can I ask you something?" I got another Coke from the fridge and straddled a chair at the battered table.

"Shoot." He sat down at the other side as the coffee started brewing.

"Are you originally from Corinth County?"

He gave me an odd look, then nodded. "Born and raised, went to Corinth County High. Why?"

"You're…you're…" I struggled with the words. I knew it wasn't polite to ask, but I had to know. "You're not straight, are you?"

He raised an eyebrow. "Are you?"

I laughed awkwardly. "No, I'm not."

"Me either." He widened his eyes comically and wiggled his ears. "I mean, thanks for asking, but I'm not exactly a macho man, you know?" He laughed. "Sure, I know how to skin a deer, and I can shoot a rifle pretty well, but I'd rather stay home." He pondered for a moment. "Why are you asking me this? Has something happened?"

I hesitated.

"Did Kelly or someone say *fag* or something worse in front of you? Did he call you that?" Geoffrey's eyes were kind, his voice soft and comforting. "Don't let it bother you." I must have made a face because he laughed again. "I couldn't get out of this county fast enough after high school, Jake. But you know, after being away for a while, I started to miss the place." He gestured with his hands. "And when the job came open here, I thought, sure, why not? My family and I…well, we don't exactly get on, you know, but we're getting there."

"Am I supposed to pretend he didn't say it?" I felt my face getting hot. "He was talking about Beau Hackworth, actually. He didn't say it about me. But he said it *to* me, like I wouldn't care."

"And if he knew you were gay, too, he wouldn't have, and he's going to be mortified." Geoffrey shook his head. "It's difficult, I know, to understand. But people down here, they'd give you the shirt off their back. They'd never harm you, and most of them would never even say anything ugly to your face. But they'll disapprove of your *lifestyle* and vote against your rights without even having to think twice because they think that's what God wants."

"But…" My voice died off as Dewey came out of my grandmother's bedroom and into the kitchen. His face was redder than before, his eyes bulging out of their sockets, and he was breathing hard. He looked awful. He turned on the cold-water spigot in the sink and splashed water onto his face. "Are you okay?"

He gave me a look and, without another word, went out the back door.

Geoffrey got up and poured himself a cup of coffee. "Look, if you want to tell Kelly your truth, go ahead. That's your call."

Easy for you to say, I thought as I watched him close my grandmother's door behind him.

As I stood over the sink, looking out at the woods, two men in dirty EMT uniforms came out carrying a stretcher between them, with a blanket over it—the skeleton from the ruins, of course. Shortly thereafter Deputy Rowland and Dewey came along, talking amongst themselves. The EMTs loaded the stretcher into the ambulance and pulled out. Dewey talked to Rowland for a moment or two, and then Rowland got into his deputy's car and followed the ambulance.

Dewey looked over at me in the kitchen window and shook his head. He came back into the kitchen with heavy strides. "I'm shutting down the dig and ordered them off the property," he said tersely.

"Why?"

He glanced over at Miss Sarah's closed bedroom door. "She doesn't want them here, and it's still her land, so she decides.

Rowland seems to think the skeleton isn't that old, and they need to figure out who it is and how he ended up back there at the ruins." He was sweating profusely. "So it's kind of a crime scene anyway. I told them to pack up everything and to get out as soon as possible." He wiped his face again. "All right, I'm heading back home. You need anything?"

I shook my head.

I watched as he drove off, sighing. She must have read him the riot act.

I was reading my Perry Mason novel in the porch swing when Beau came back to the porch. The sun was starting to set in the west, the golden light filtering through the towering pines. "Hey," he said, sitting down in the same iron chair he'd sat in before. "Um, I need a favor from you. Do you mind?"

"Depends." I dog-eared a page and looked into his big green eyes.

"I don't think I can get my car out of there tonight, or until the ground dries more," he said. "I don't want to spend the night here, but I was wondering, maybe you could drive me back to Tuscaloosa, stay overnight, and we could come back in the morning and see if I can get the car out then? We can have dinner, see a movie—and you can sleep on the couch. Or I can sleep on the couch, either or, I guess." He was talking very fast. "Or not."

I laughed. "I would love that. It'll be nice to get away from here for a bit," I replied. "Let me take a shower and get cleaned up, though, first."

Twenty minutes later we were driving through the countryside. "What was it like growing up here?" I asked when we turn left at Four Corners.

"Not easy," he replied. He rubbed his face. "I mean, I knew I was gay when I was little, even if I didn't know what it was. I mean, I always liked guys better than girls." He frowned. "I used to get bullied a lot, sure, fairy and homo and fag and all that stuff, but I also got picked on a lot because I'm a Hackworth, and Hackworths are good-for-nothings, you know? Trash. What about you?"

"I always knew." I accelerated and passed a slow-moving truck with a bed filled with watermelons. "I went to Catholic school, so I got some flak now and then, but nothing much I couldn't handle." *Given your history,* I heard Mom's voice in my head, and self-consciously rubbed the almost invisible scar on my right wrist. A suicide attempt at fifteen wasn't first-date conversation material. "Besides, Mom's a powerful lawyer, and the school was scared to death of her, so…It could have been a lot worse, I guess." I smiled. "Mom always says no matter how bad things are, they could have been worse."

Was I going to tell him about Tradd? The real reason I was spending the summer here?

"My dad—he thinks I'm a disgrace, and Mama goes along with whatever he says, and my brothers and sisters…" He sighed. "I guess I've always known I was, and that meant I wouldn't have much of a relationship with my family when I got older. I studied and worked hard, and I got a scholarship to Bama. I work and have student loans to help pay for things. My roommate is gone for the summer—she went back to Chattanooga to spend it with her family—but we're keeping the apartment, so I don't have to go back to Corinth and stay with my family."

"Would you have, if you'd had to?"

"Well, it's better than sleeping in my car," he replied. "Can we not talk about this anymore?"

"I don't really know much about dating," I replied. Tradd didn't count, did he? He was never really my boyfriend anyway. "I kind of thought I was involved with someone…" I took a deep breath and told him my sad, sordid history with Tradd.

He touched my arm. "He sounds like a first-class jerk to me."

"He was," I admitted. "I don't know why I lost my mind the way I did, I really don't. But—" He was the first gay guy who showed me any real attention other than just hooking up. He made me feel special, made me feel not so lonely anymore. I bit my lower lip. That was really it, wasn't it? He made me feel like I wasn't alone anymore. "What about you? Have you dated anyone serious?"

"I've dated a couple of guys but, yeah, nothing deep." He looked out the window. "They always just kind of fizzled out, and when they did, it didn't really bother me. Do you still have feelings for Tradd?"

"I don't…I don't think so," I replied. "I mean, whenever I think about him, I just get embarrassed." It was hard to believe it had been about two weeks since I woke up in the hospital.

It had only been two weeks, but it felt like I'd been here forever.

"Let's change the subject. How do you like going to school in New Orleans? I've only been once, but I loved it."

So, we talked as we drove through the darkening evening, about colleges and my mother and the ruins, his dreams about what he wanted to do with his life and my dreams about what I wanted to do with my life, and before I knew it, we'd made it to Tuscaloosa. He directed me to an apartment building near the campus. His place was a nice, clean two-bedroom apartment, sparsely decorated, with a small kitchen and a bathroom. The bedrooms were at the end of the short hallway, which ended at the bathroom door. I sat down on the couch. Beau rifled through the paper, but there wasn't anything playing that either one of us wanted to see, so we settled in to watch one of the Avengers movies on Netflix.

Beau was a big Marvel Universe fan, so he could explain what I didn't understand. We ordered a pizza and drank beers he had stashed in the refrigerator.

After the movie, we sat on the little balcony just off his living room. There was a little Weber grill out there, and two lawn chairs. We sat and watched the stars, listening to the sounds of the night.

"Tell me about Kelly Donovan," I said carefully. I wasn't going to tell him what Kelly said but wanted to know more about the guy I was sharing a house with.

"Kelly's nice enough. You know he's a Tucker—his mom was a Tucker before she married Jerry Donovan. He died a couple of years ago—drunk driving, no one else was involved—but she had Kelly long before she married Jerry Donovan. No one is sure who Kelly's father is...She would never say, and she died last year. You could have knocked everyone down with a feather when he went to live with your grandmother."

"The story I was told is that his mother was a distant relative of Miss Sarah," I said slowly. "But if his mother was a Tucker—"

"Everyone in Corinth County is connected in one way or another," Beau cut me off. "I think maybe one of Miss Sarah's first cousins might have married a Tucker. I swear I'd heard that before someplace, but even so, it was a real surprise. No one had the slightest idea that Sarah Donelson even knew Kelly existed, but once Barbara Sue was in the ground, he packed up and went to live out there."

"But what's he like?"

"You sound like you have a crush on him."

I couldn't see his face clearly in the darkness—he'd turned off the balcony light to not attract bugs—but he sounded a little jealous. Tradd was never jealous about anyone. He hoped I'd find someone, so I'd leave him alone.

"I don't have a crush on him," I said, taking his hand. "Sure, that body is ridiculous, and he's good looking, but not my type." Which was a lie, of course—Kelly was everybody's type.

"He's one of the good ones, I suppose," Beau said. He hadn't pulled away from my hand, which was nice.

It was the kind of thing I'd been dreaming of since seventh grade.

I wished I had a friend I could text *I'm on a date and holding hands with a cute boy!*

"He was never mean," Beau was saying, "and you know, he could easily have been an asshole. But he's like me, you know? He was pretty much white trash until he got so big and so good at sports, and everyone started kissing his ass, especially when we started winning games, you know?" He smiled at me. "We do love our football in Alabama."

"And this girl he's dating? I've not met her." But she's spent the night more than once in my grandmother's house.

"Bonnie Burleson?" Beau rolled his eyes. "Her daddy is chief of staff at the hospital, you know. No one in Corinth County is good enough for his daughter, and he doesn't care if Kelly's a jock or not. He's not good enough for the Burlesons. I know they wouldn't let her date him for a while but gave in eventually because they were sneaking around anyway. Maybe Dr. Burleson thinks Mrs. Donelson is going to leave everything to Kelly."

"Why would she do that?" I always assumed when Miss Sarah died everything would go to Mom and Dewey.

But would they want it?

The house was a wreck. It needed some serious work done.

The county probably would have condemned it by now if it wasn't the Blackwood house.

"But it's not worth anything, is it? I mean, the house—"

"The land has a lot of wood," Beau replied. "Mrs. Donelson has been selling the timber for years, tree farming. And of course, if the excavations around the ruins yield anything, Blackwood Hall could easily become a tourist attraction."

"No one in their right minds would drive all the way out there just to look at ruins," I said.

"You'd be surprised," Beau replied. "I know Dr. Brady hopes that Mrs. Donelson will leave the ruins, at least, to the university, or to the state, to manage. And if we find anything important—"

"Besides a skeleton? Do you think Dr. Brady was right, about it being more recent than the Civil War?"

"Well, I don't think they used silver fillings back then," Beau replied. "I wonder…" He stopped and looked up at the sky.

"What?"

"I just wonder who it could be, is all. But it's not one of the Lost Boys," he said after a few moments. He swallowed. "Did you notice the skull?"

"I didn't really pay a whole lot of attention," I replied, thinking back and shivering.

"Whoever it was, well, he didn't die of natural causes." Beau squeezed my hand. "Like Dr. Brady said, the skull looked damaged."

"But it was a long time ago, right?" I exhaled. "Probably someone who crossed the Tuckers, don't you think? And they hid the body up there, thinking no one would ever find it."

"Maybe."

I opened my mouth to tell him about…about the weird things that had been going on since I arrived, the weird feelings, the white flash I kept seeing in the woods.

But how to do that without sounding crazy?

I was so emotionally unbalanced two weeks ago that I went on a drug and alcohol binge that almost killed me. Who knew? Maybe the drugs rewired my brain or fucked it up somehow. Doesn't it make more sense that my mind is delusional now, rather than the house and woods are haunted?

There're no such things as ghosts.

I closed my mouth. I'd already told him about the whole Tradd thing and hadn't scared him off. I liked him. He was cute and sweet and smart, and I enjoyed being around him.

No, I wasn't going to say anything. At least not yet.

"Your uncle was really upset." Beau yawned and stretched.

"Well, he had to face down Miss Sarah," I replied. "I wouldn't wish that on someone I hated."

His face looked puzzled. "You know, you keep saying you haven't been down here since you were a kid, and you really don't know her all that well, but you sure are afraid of her. Why is that?"

"Everyone in my family is afraid of her," I replied. "I mean, I remember some things from when I was a kid, and the way my mom and Dewey talk about her...I guess maybe it's something I've picked up on."

It was strange.

But everything down here was strange.

He yawned again. "I think I'm going to go lie down. It's been a long day. I can make up the couch—"

"No," I said, standing up and looking him right in the eyes. "I'll share the bed, but we're just going to sleep. Nothing's going to happen, okay?"

"Not even a little cuddling?" he teased, leaning over and brushing my lips with his.

I smiled back. "Well, maybe a little."

CHAPTER THIRTEEN

I opened my eyes and didn't know where I was.

I sat up, rubbing my eyes. I could smell bacon frying. My stomach growled. I remembered I was in Tuscaloosa, in Beau's apartment and his bed. I glanced around the room. It was a standard college student apartment bedroom. The walls were beige and covered with thumbtacked posters. The carpet was brownish beige. There was a store-bought particleboard desk against one wall, a closed silver MacBook Pro on top of it. A stack of textbooks teetered dangerously on the edge, next to a stack of mail, a printer, a stack of opened copy paper, and his phone—plugged into the outlet under the desk.

The posters were of hot men—Dwayne Johnson doing some exercise involving cables, every muscle straining and veins bulging, the skin sparkling with sweat; Chris Hemsworth in the famous photo from *Thor*; in jeans and no shirt, enormous muscles pumped; and Shawn Mendes pouting at the camera, his lips glistening.

Self-consciously I looked down at my own body. If that's what he likes, what was I doing here?

"Stop that," I whispered. "There's nothing wrong with you."

I yawned and stretched, debated whether to get back under the covers and sleep a little longer. The bed was very warm and comfortable and smelled slightly like Beau. I started to lie back down but...if he was frying bacon, he was making me breakfast. A guy had never done that for me before.

Tradd would never spend the night and never let me stay at his place. Whenever Tradd and I had sex, it had to be at my place—I guess so no one would see me leaving. If I fell asleep after we'd had sex, I'd wake up in the morning and find him gone.

That was all Tradd's problem, not mine. I wouldn't let his issues define who I was.

I got out of the bed and pulled my shorts back on over my underwear.

I got my toothbrush out of my duffel bag. I wished I had a friend I could call, dish over the details, talk to and giggle about having a boyfriend, the way Tradd's friends did with him whenever they started seeing someone.

That's really what it was all about, wasn't it? I thought with a flash of clarity. I'd never had any real friends before, and I was attracted to Tradd. I got confused about my feelings.

I wandered into the bathroom. I flipped on the lights and turned on the water spigots, splashing hot water up into my face. I used some of Beau's toothpaste. The bathroom was nondescript and utilitarian, small, painted pale blue with yellow trim. The hand towels were red. The sink, the toilet, and the bathtub were white. The shower door needed to be scoured.

If I ever moved into a place like this, Mom would hire a deep cleaning service before moving in. *Can you imagine what's in that* carpet? I could hear her voice in my head, complete with the physical shudder.

I did like my cozy apartment in New Orleans, even if it was expensive for how small it was. It was a one bedroom carved out of a massive old Victorian. It had high ceilings, ceiling fans, and amazing hardwood floors. I liked it much better than the house Tradd shared with three other college students.

I was scrubbing away at my teeth when Beau popped his head through the bathroom doorway. He was wearing a Roll Tide baseball cap pulled down low on his forehead, a black tank top, and gray shorts.

I was grateful I'd remembered to pull on my shorts.

"I'm making breakfast. I hope bacon and eggs and toast are okay," he said, awkwardly leaning over and kissing my cheek. "You want to take a shower first, or…?"

My heart was racing from the touch of his lips against my skin.

I hadn't expected the kiss and wasn't sure how to respond. Kiss him back? Pull him in close to my body? Or just take it for what it probably was, a casual show of affection?

There really needed to be a manual. How were we supposed to figure this stuff out on our own?

I spat toothpaste suds into the sink and rinsed out my mouth. "Eat first," I replied, smiling at him. "Then shower, and I suppose we need to drive back out and see if the ground is dry enough for you to get your car out. If not…" I shrugged. "Maybe you should pack a bag just in case."

He smiled back at me, delighted. "Yeah. I can't keep expecting you to drive me back and forth every day. Better make sure nothing's burning." He hesitated, pecked me on the cheek again, and disappeared back down the hallway, his face burning red.

It was cute. He was cute. And sweet.

And I liked him.

This was different from Tradd in every way.

But that was a good thing, right?

I brushed my messy hair into some semblance of order before heading into the kitchen. I poured myself a cup of coffee. Bacon was drying on a paper towel, crispy, just the way I liked it, and he was scrambling eggs. Buttered toast was stacked on a plate. "You didn't have to do this," I said, picking up a piece of bacon and popping it into my mouth.

"I like to cook," he replied. "I'm good at breakfast."

"I can't cook at all." I sat down at the table and sipped the coffee. It was good, hot and strong, and I could feel the caffeine starting to ping through my body.

He set a plate in front of me—scrambled eggs, toast, more bacon—and went back to the stove to make his own plate. I sprinkled salt and pepper on the eggs.

"Can I ask you something?" He put down his knife and fork. "Why does your uncle not want us on the property anymore?"

"Dewey doesn't care. Miss Sarah is the one who cares," I replied, getting up for more coffee. "She never wanted you guys there in the first place. As long as she didn't know—"

"That stupid backhoe." Beau shook his head. "I don't understand why Seth called for one. He knew Dr. Brady wouldn't let him use it down there, and the ground was too soggy and wet for it to go into the woods even if he would have. Why did he do that?"

"Well, he's a Tucker," I reminded him. "Maybe the Tuckers don't want y'all there any more than Miss Sarah does."

A ghost of a smile played across his lips. "Did you just say *y'all?* We're turning you into a Southerner."

"It slips out every now and then," I admitted. "Mom says it. I try not to—people mocked me in Chicago." And the less ammunition I gave them, the better. "But I think we should consider the idea that the Tuckers don't want *your team*"—I emphasized the words—"back there in the woods." I scratched my chin. "I don't really know the geography. How far is the ridge where the hollow starts from the ruins?"

"You know, I don't actually know," Beau replied. "We really hadn't really explored much—we were busy getting things set up to get started on the dig, you know, staking out and surveying the ruins themselves. But we intended to go looking for the original family cemetery at some point."

"Well, we could do that today," I said. I liked him a lot. I liked his dimples and the way he smiled, the way his green eyes sparkled. He wasn't as sexy or handsome as Tradd, but I could see myself dating him.

And Tradd was garbage, wasn't he?

And I was sick of doing the inventory, of breathing in dust and cobwebs and avoiding spiders and digging through musty boxes. Sure, there were snakes in the woods, but maybe…maybe a day in the outdoors *was* exactly what I needed.

"You sure you won't mind the heat?" Beau grinned. "It's cooler in the woods, because there's shade, but there's humidity. Maybe we could stop at the Pig in Corinth on the way, barbecue burgers or something at the ruins site."

"It would be like camping." I'd never been camping in my life. But it sounded like a good idea, and to be fair, anything that meant spending more time with Beau would sound good.

We drove out of Tuscaloosa and headed back to Corinth County. All the way we listened to Kylie Minogue—Beau was a big fan—and stopped at the Piggly Wiggly in Corinth. Kelly's truck wasn't there when we got back, but Geneva's Toyota was. I checked on her—her husband was fine, just a little shaken up after a fender-bender—and we stored everything in the refrigerator, leaving the charcoal bag in the mudroom before heading into the woods.

As we walked, I said, "Can I tell you something? Promise you won't think I'm crazy."

"Any crazier than I already do?" he teased. "Of course."

I bit my lip as we descended a slight slope. It was incredibly still back in the woods, no wind, just the heavy wet air hanging, but he was right—in the shade of the towering pines, it was a lot cooler. The woods smelled wet, green, fresh. There were flies buzzing around everywhere. I paused, looking into the woods on the left side of the path. I saw underbrush, vines, trees, dead pine needles, and pine cones, but nothing white, nothing that would account for what I'd seen—more than once. Haltingly, as I stared into the green darkness, I told him about the times I'd seen the white flash from the kitchen windows, and how it always unsettled me, made me feel a little sick momentarily.

"Something happened the first time you came down to the ruins." He squinted at me, tilting his head to one side. "Do you remember? I asked you if you were okay."

"I do." I tried to remember. As I thought, I put my hand against a mossy pine trunk and leaned on it. "It was weird, I felt…I don't know, sick and scared? And then you said something, and the feeling went away."

"But you've been back down to the ruins a couple of times since then. Did you feel anything the other times?"

"The second time, yes." I started walking again. The ground was still wet, but it felt more solid than yesterday. "But I didn't…" I stopped speaking.

Something was rustling through the underbrush near me. My eyes widened, and I stepped back away from the side of the road, moving closer to the center. Probably just an opossum or a rabbit or a raccoon…

Or maybe a snake.

A memory flashed through my mind.

I'm walking behind someone, an adult, a woman who is a lot bigger than I am, and I am just a child, and I realize when I look it's my grandmother. She's wearing a loose blue and white checked cotton housedress and brown shoes that look worse for wear—the sole of the right one is loose under her heel and starting to flap a little as she walks. A bird sings overhead, and the sun goes behind a cloud, making it even darker in the woods than it already is. I don't like the woods, I don't like them at all, and never come in here unless she makes me. She doesn't have any patience, and she'll hit me with a hairbrush if I don't help take the garbage down to the dump. It's just ahead, and she's carrying a brown paper grocery bag with a big grease spot in the lower right corner, and it's full, almost too full, and I can hear the horseflies buzzing around the garbage dump, and then I hear the same sound—something rustling through the underbrush— and I freeze. So does she. She stops walking and cocks her head, listening, and the sound is coming closer to me, and I can feel the scream welling up inside me, but I choke it down because I know she'll hit me and yell at me, and I don't want to be punished. I don't want to make her mad—she gets so angry and her eyes go black and her face gets red and that's when the bad things happen and then she pinches my arm so hard it hurts, my skin bruising between her fingers, and she hisses at me, "Go on back to the house, ya hear? Go on!" and I don't understand, and that's when the snake, oh my God, it's enormous, slithers out onto the path and starts coiling, and I know that means it's going to strike, and it moves so fast I don't even see anything besides a blur of browns and a sharp pain in my leg, my right leg, and she kicks it, the garbage bag falling onto the path and the empty cans and greasy paper towels, and she kicks the snake, and it's flying into the trees, hits one with a smack, and then I don't know anything else because my leg is burning, it feels like it's on fire, and I start screaming and she picks me up and starts running back up the path—

"Jake?"

My ears were ringing, and spots danced in front of my eyes. I returned to the present, the memory fading. I bent over and pushed my right sock down and checked the back of my leg. There were no scars there, no fang marks left behind from the snake attacking me when I was so little, but now I knew why I hated and feared snakes so much. I could still feel the terror, the burning in my leg. "Wow."

I shook my head. "I just had a really intense memory of being bitten by a snake when I was a kid." I told him what I remembered.

When I finished, he said, "Yikes. Mrs. Donelson must have been terrified. You know she's never driven or owned a car."

"What?" He was right. I remembered she'd never had a car. The only cars that were ever around the place were either my uncle's or the one my mom rented at the airport in Birmingham. I vaguely remembered hearing she'd never learned how to drive.

"I wonder how she got you to the hospital?"

"I don't remember going to the hospital." I checked my leg again. Nope, nothing there—but I could remember the feeling, the sharp sudden pain of the fangs going into my leg, the burning sensation as the poison moved through my bloodstream. "I never remembered being bitten by a snake before now, either."

We started walking again. "How much time did you spend down here?"

"I don't know." I wiped sweat out of my eyes. "Mom says she used to bring me down here every summer until I was about eight, but to be honest, I don't remember much of those trips, you know?"

"You haven't been here in eleven years?" Beau looked at me. "That's—"

"I know, I know. It's weird. We're not a close family." I frowned as we started up the low rise to the plain where the ruins sat. I wiped sweat off my face with the tail of my shirt. "But Miss Sarah...I can't imagine what it would be like to grow up with her as your mother, you know? I mean, Mom and Dewey turned out okay, but..." I could now see the blackened columns standing upright, reaching for the sky.

I tensed up but didn't feel anything.

Maybe those other times it was just exhaustion from the heat? From traveling? I didn't know.

I didn't *think* I was losing my mind.

But I could be wrong.

"Who do you think the skeleton is?" I asked.

Beau stopped walking. "I don't know," he replied. "I guess it would depend on how old it is. Dr. Brady felt, because of the dental work, that it's more recent, and he'd know, I suppose."

"I guess we could do an online search for people who went missing in this area," I replied.

"The *Weekly* has a website, but I don't know if they have back issues archived and accessible," he said. "I suppose they have an archive at their office. Maybe we could just do a general search online for people missing from this area and then go look at the papers from around that time. If they don't have them at the newspaper office, I bet the library would."

We walked to where his car was parked. The ground was still soft around it. "I don't know if I should risk it," he said, clicking the door unlocked. "I should have left my car up at the main house. I won't make that mistake again."

"Give it a try," I said. "If it gets stuck, it gets stuck. Kelly can help push when he gets home."

He laughed and got into the car. He started the engine and slowly backed up. The car sank a bit, but eventually the tires grabbed hold, and it began moving. He turned the car around, and I watched him go, waved, and started walking back through the woods to the house.

I heard the rustling in the bushes again as I walked and tried not to look over where the noise was coming from.

But out of the corner of my eye I saw something white flash in the woods, near the area where I usually saw it. I could hear Beau's car making it out of the woods, and the sound of his tires on pavement. I turned my attention to the woods. I walked over to the side and looked at the underbrush.

Poison ivy, if I wasn't mistaken, and what did poison oak look like? I wondered as I watched for movement in the underbrush, listening for the sounds of movement. I started pushing my way through the bushes, my feet crunching on dead pine needles. I was vaguely aware of his car engine shutting off. It was deathly silent in the woods now, just the rustling of branches and leaves moving in the slight breeze, the song of cicadas, the occasional croak of a tree frog, and the annoying buzzing of gnats trying to land in my ears. I kept walking forward, watching the ground for dangerous things. The ground was still a bit squishy under the crunching pine needles, and the ground itself sloped, so keeping my balance wasn't easy. I had to grab a tree for balance every now and then as I kept walking.

"Jacob?" I heard Beau's voice calling me. "Jake?"

"Here!" I called back, still making my way forward. I looked up the hill and realized I couldn't see over the ridge lip. I could see the upper floors of the house, but not the kitchen windows, so whatever I kept seeing must be up higher. I stopped walking and looked up.

And saw a white sheet tangled in the lower branches of a towering pine.

Beau came crashing through the underbrush.

"How good are you at climbing trees?" I asked, pointing up.

He raised an eyebrow. "You think that's what you see?" His voice was skeptical, and I knew what he was thinking.

"What I see is more like a light," I said. "Like a flashlight being turned on and off quickly?"

"So…"

"I've never climbed a tree," I said, holding up my hands. "City boy."

He started climbing the tree like a squirrel. I couldn't believe how fast he got up there. He dislodged the sheet, and it came sailing down, floating through the air like a dust mote.

"Oh," he said, his voice disgusted. He grabbed something else from the branch and started back down.

I caught the falling sheet when it came within reach. It was wet, cold, and old, smelled dirty and musty.

"What's that?" I asked Beau as he jumped down the last four feet, holding the other piece of cloth.

He held it up, and I felt nauseous.

It was a Klan hood.

CHAPTER FOURTEEN

I t was vile, nauseating and almost…almost seemed *alive.*
I felt hot, feverish, sick to my stomach.

My head began to ache, and my eyes began to blur, like everything around me was fading out of focus. I could feel the fear, the terror, rising inside of me…

And it was dark, it was night, and they were after me.

They wanted to kill me.

I could barely catch my breath, and there was a stitch in my side, but I couldn't stop for breath. I couldn't stop for anything because they would catch me and kill me. There was no question about it in my mind—I had to get away. If I stayed if I stopped if I didn't keep moving, I would die.

It was so hot, and the sky was clear above my head. Above the tops of the trees, I could see stars in a dark blue-black sky. How long had they known? When did they decide? It didn't have to be like this, but I knew now they were beyond listening, beyond caring, I wasn't a person but a thing that had to be destroyed. And I choked back a sob, wondering if I dared to stop, to find a place to hide, to let them run past me and then double back, somehow, get somewhere safe—

But that was the point. There wasn't any place safe.

So, so much hatred.

I kept running, stumbling over roots and bushes, avoiding the trunks of the trees. If I stuck to the woods, they might not ever catch me or find me. I could stay in the woods and head for Four Corners, maybe flag a car down, but who would care, who would believe me? They'd just bring me back, turn me over to those who wish—no, not wish, but want—those who want me dead, and I just wanted to rest, stop, maybe drink some water, but no, I can hear them crashing through the brush behind me. They're too close, and I have to keep going—

Someone slapped me hard across the face.

And it was gone.

And I was back to a summer afternoon in the woods behind my grandmother's house again.

"Are you okay?" Beau's eyes were wide open, his face pale beneath the tan. "Do we need to get you to a doctor?"

"I—" And I gagged, turning my head and leaning to one side.

I threw up my breakfast, a witch's brew of eggs and bacon and toast and bile and spittle, long strands of spit dangling from my mouth as I gagged again, my stomach convulsing and clenching, another load coming up, and it was sour and acidic in my mouth, and my eyes were watering, and my nose was running, and it was humiliating. I wished I was anywhere but here, throwing up in front of the first guy to ever ask me out on a date, the guy whose arms I slept in last night, feeling his skin against mine, the rhythmic regularity of his chest rising and falling as he breathed, and somehow even more food came up, my stomach clenching and cramping, and I could feel it splashing off the damp soggy pine needles and onto my lower legs, and I didn't care—it just came and came and came, so much puke, more puke than I could have imagined.

I continued gagging even after my stomach was empty, and I put my head down, taking deep breaths and spitting to try to clear out my mouth. I felt Beau's hand, hot on my shaking shoulder. He didn't say anything, but I couldn't...I couldn't calm down enough to think clearly.

A Klan mask.

A *fucking* Ku Klux Klan mask, complete with the pointy end and the eye slits, here in the woods behind my grandmother's house.

It's a bad place, I heard my mother muttering into the phone, her slightly slurred voice coming through the speakers in the car.

No wonder she left and seldom returned.

It felt like a punch in the gut, a slap in the face.

I felt stupid.

Did I really think it was just history?

We'd studied the Klan in Twentieth Century History my sophomore year in high school.

In my mind's eye I could see the black-and-white films of thousands of people marching, wearing the robes and the hoods, marching down whatever avenue that was in New York in the 1920s, the screaming mobs of white people, faces twisted with hate, crowding around the soldiers walking the dignified Black children into the schools they were desegregating. The fire hoses and dogs turned loose on peaceful protestors who just wanted to be treated like human beings. The film of burning crosses and smiling white faces next to the strange fruit hanging from the Southern trees, Black bodies broken and limp as they slowly spun from the nooses around their necks.

Was this why Mom kept her distance? Why she's kept me away?

I could hear her saying again, *Don't ever let anyone tell you it's heritage—the heritage is hate, Jake. White supremacy. And there's nothing uglier than bigotry.*

I reached out with my right hand and pressed it against the rough bark of a pine tree, still coughing and spitting and trying to clear my mouth. My stomach was burning, my throat aflame, and my tongue and teeth felt scraped and raw.

I wiped my eyes and mouth with my T-shirt and took some deep breaths.

"Are you okay?" I heard Beau's voice. It sounded like it was a thousand yards away, hollow, empty, not real.

And I felt again that fear, all-encompassing, that need to run and get away, hide, something, anything, because they were after me and wanted to hurt me, maybe even kill me, and everything shifted, even the air, and it's cooler, so much cooler, and the humidity is gone, and I turn my head, but everything is hazy, like one of those old movies where they smeared Vaseline on the lens to soften the harsh lights on the face of an aging screen queen, and I can hear the footsteps, the dogs barking, and I know they are going to kill me, they are going to slip that noose around my neck and hang me until I'm dead, and they're going to pose with me and—

"Jake?"

And I snapped back into the present again. Everything cleared. It was hot and humid again. A mosquito was buzzing around my head, and enormous black horseflies and gnats were swarming around the puddle that used to be my breakfast, and my stomach clenched yet again…but there was nothing left to come up.

I felt hollow.

He was still holding the hood. He looked concerned.

"I'm okay." I spat again and slowly started to get back to my feet.

A Klan hood.

Even during all the hubbub about taking down Confederate statues, renaming army bases and high schools and buildings on college campuses, I'd somehow thought, believed, the Klan was something from way back in the past, something historical, and sure, there were still white supremacists and Confederate apologists, a group of people holding on to a myth about their past but were nothing more than a very loud and vocal minority, that things had changed and gotten better.

Kelly called Beau a fag to my face yesterday. Did I think he liked Black people any better than he liked gay ones?

Enlightened, my ass.

I was in Alabama. I could never forget that. I needed to watch my back, to let Kelly keep thinking I was straight.

I shook my head. I wasn't making sense.

I didn't have to be afraid of Kelly.

Did I?

My hand still resting against the tree trunk, I straightened up, still spitting, the back of my teeth and tongue both feeling raw still from the acid I'd just puked up. "I need to brush my teeth," I mumbled. I felt dizzy.

"Are you sure you're all right?" Beau's voice was low, shaking slightly. "You scared the crap out of me there."

"I'll be okay—just give me a minute."

"Your eyes rolled up in your head, and you just went down," Beau went on. "You were trembling, shaking, and mumbling. I could barely make out what you were saying." He shivered.

"Let's get back to the house." I took a step. I was a little wobbly still, but starting to feel better. "What was I saying?"

He was still holding the hood. I looked at it, and whatever it had triggered in me—whatever that was—was over. It was just a piece of cloth, cut to make a hood symbolizing evil, but it couldn't hurt me.

"You kept saying you couldn't let them catch you, they wanted to kill you." He took a deep breath. "I mean, what happened, Jake? Have you had fits before?"

Fits.

"No," I replied. My mouth tasted disgusting. I made a decision: I didn't care if he thought I was crazy. "Nothing like that has ever happened to me before. Until I came here."

"That day you came out to the ruins"—he nodded—"it wasn't quite as bad as this time, but it was sort of the same kind of thing."

"And it happened to me in the attic." I rubbed my eyes. "And then I keep seeing that white flash out here in the woods."

"This can't be what you were seeing," he said, turning the hood over and over in his hands. "For one thing, it's been up in that tree forever. Look, it's rotten in places, and it hasn't been white in years." He held the repulsive thing up for me to see better, and he was right. It had been exposed to the elements for a long time. It was dirty and yellowed and rotted in places, but not so weather damaged that you couldn't tell its original purpose.

Whatever it was I'd seen—been seeing—through the windows was bright white, so bright it almost seemed like a light bulb—there one minute, gone the next.

Whatever I'd been seeing was not yellowed and faded and rotting with age and exposure.

"I need to brush my teeth," I said again, louder this time. My head still felt dizzy, and my stomach was aching and empty. My throat felt like I've been drinking battery acid. "Let's get back up to the house, get out of the heat." My voice sounded as raw as my throat. Beau started to throw the hood on the ground beside the sheet, but I stopped him. "No, bring that," I rasped.

He nodded and we started walking back up the slope to the house, soggy pine needles crunching beneath our shoes.

"Is there still a Klan around here?" I asked. "Tell me the truth."

He opened his mouth to reply but shut it again, turning a little pink in his cheeks. "I don't know," he said as we walked. "I've not heard anything about it, but it wouldn't surprise me." He shook his head. "It's the way everyone is down here, you know? I grew up hearing the N-word—nobody says Black, unless they're in a public place and they feel they have to hide it."

"That's horrible."

"Yeah." He blew out his breath in a sigh. "We're not supposed to be, you know, segregated anymore, but all the white people who can afford it send their kids to the private school, Corinth Christian Academy." He shot a glance at me. "I went to the public school."

"Wow."

His face twisted for a moment. "How many Black kids were there in your Catholic private school? You're not even Catholic, are you?"

"No." I stopped walking for a moment. Mom always said she sent me to Catholic schools so I could get a better education.

Was that the real reason?

But there were Black kids at St. Sebastian's.

Athletes on scholarship. How many Black kids were actually enrolled there that weren't?

I didn't know the answer.

Or…was Mom a racist, deep down?

All white people are racist, I heard her voice in my head. *We benefit from a system designed to benefit white people at a cost to others. That makes us all racists by default. Never forget that, and never think you're better than someone else because you're white and they aren't. People are people, Jacob, always remember that.*

People are people.

I glanced over at the hood in his hands. "But is there a history of the Klan in Corinth County?"

He hesitated. "Yes. But I've not heard anything about there being a Klan, or the Klan being active, around here in years." He sighed, and his body sagged a little bit. "Back in the 1950s a Black boy was lynched in Corinth. He was visiting from up north, and a"—he swallowed—"a Hackworth woman—I think she might be a cousin of my grandfather's? I don't know, but she was my kin— anyway, she worked at the curbside farmers' market on the edge of town and claimed the boy said something to her. She would never tell anyone what he said, claimed it was too ugly." He swallowed. "They strung that kid up. There was even a picture on the front page of the paper."

"Wow. How old was the kid?"

Beau shifted uncomfortably. "Thirteen."

"*Thirteen?*" My voice rose.

Beau kicked at the ground miserably. "I know how it sounds."

"So this kid got lynched. What happened to her?"

"She moved away. No one's heard from her in years." Beau swallowed as we stepped up over the lip onto the plateau. "It caused some trouble, and after that there really wasn't much Klan stuff around here." He coughed. "I wrote a paper for a class I took on social justice—that's how I know about the lynching. No one talks about it."

And if they did, I bet they weren't sorry some Klan thugs murdered a thirteen-year-old.

"Really? No Klan activity here after 1950? Not even in the sixties, with the march on Selma and everything else that was going on in Alabama? Nothing in Corinth?"

"We didn't have riots or problems here," he replied. "I told you, I wrote a paper on Klan activity in Corinth County last year. There was no unrest here. And that was really the only time the Klan was involved in violence here—at least since the 1800s. There was a lot of it then. But reading the papers"—he swallowed—"what they said about it all was pretty ugly."

I stopped next to the pump house. My head ached, and I still felt sick to my stomach. "Am I safe here, Beau?"

"Why don't you go get cleaned up, and we'll talk some more?"

"There's a meth lab and a still in the hollow." I managed to keep my voice calm, even though every instinct in my mind was telling me to start screaming, to run upstairs and pack everything into my suitcases and drive back to New Orleans—the inventory and my grandmother be damned. "It's bad enough I have to worry about *that* shit. But the Klan, too? How homophobic is it down here?"

"My parents don't know I'm gay," Beau said finally in a half whisper. "I've not come out to anyone in my family. They'll disown me."

"You don't know that," I replied, but I suspected he was right.

"We belong to the Church of Christ the Lord." Beau smiled crookedly, but it didn't reach his eyes. "Do you know how many Sundays I've sat in that church and listened to the preacher rail against sodomites?"

Jacob, I'm worried about your immortal soul. The Lord teaches us to love the sinner and hate the sin. Father Ambrose said that to me in the eighth grade.

I've never figured out how he knew. I barely knew myself when I was thirteen. Puberty and hormones were making me crazy, and in the locker room and showers after gym class, I could see I wasn't the only one. Others were getting hair in places they'd never had hair before, and I tried to only look when no one else would notice.

Somehow, I already knew that who and what I was put me in danger, and I needed to be careful, and the way all the other boys talked about boys like me—*fags, faggots, fairies, cocksuckers, homos*—made it clear it was something to be ashamed of, to hide, to never, ever tell anyone.

I tried to imagine what it was like to have parents who thought like Father Ambrose and felt sick all over again.

"I can't imagine." I followed Beau up the steps to the house. I heard Kelly's voice sneering *He's a fag* at me again and was glad there was nothing left to throw up.

"I don't want you to feel sorry for me," he said, putting his hand on my shoulder. "I don't know what it was like for you in Chicago—"

Not as easy as you'd think.

"But it's…" He swallowed, eyes filling with tears, and his voice caught in his throat. He took a deep breath. "Corinth County has very definite ideas about what's manly and what's not." He shook his head. "As you can see, I'm not the football type." He smiled weakly. "I don't have the body for it, and I'm not very athletic, really. As my dad says all the time, I run like a girl."

"Sexist, too," I replied. "Do you not have girl athletes here?"

He nodded. "It doesn't matter, though. Gender roles are pretty rigid here. I've never been into sports, so I've always been a little suspect. My dad is ashamed of me." He stepped into the mudroom and grinned at me. "Trust me, I can't wait to finish my degree and get as far away from here as possible."

"I'll be right back," I said, stepping into the kitchen and gesturing at the refrigerator, "Help yourself to anything you want."

The stairs to the second floor seemed to go on forever as I started up. I put my hand on the railing, but it wobbled, and I stepped away from it, putting my left hand on the wall. The wall felt moist, damp. The air was heavy, and I could see dust floating in the sunbeams coming in through the windows. The stairs groaned and moaned and complained about my weight as I walked, my head still racing.

Poor Beau. What a shitty existence, what a terrible childhood, what an awful church.

I was lucky. Mom was terrific. I couldn't imagine having to hide who I am from her.

I scrubbed my teeth and rinsed out my mouth and washed my face until my teeth and tongue didn't feel quite so raw anymore. I changed into a fresh shirt and looked out the window again at the woods. I didn't see the white flash.

Maybe the hood was what I'd been seeing.

Maybe I was losing my mind.

Maybe the overdose had fucked up my brain somehow.

What was that I felt in the woods when I was getting sick, when Beau showed me the hood?

Fear, terror, a gut feeling from the diaphragm, but why?

What was going on around here?

As I came down the stairs, I saw Beau going out the front door. I joined him on the front porch and sat in the swing. Beau started to sit down with me, but the swing shuddered and sank a few inches with a jolt. He hopped back up. "Wow, are you sure you want to sit in that swing?" he asked, sitting instead in one of the rusty iron chairs.

"The whole house is going to come down around our ears," I said as I heard a car slowing down to turn onto the gravel road. The driver—a man, which was about all I could see—waved as the car moved past the house down the road.

"Does anyone else live down that road besides Tuckers?" I asked.

Beau smiled. "Well, the Tuckers are all in the holler. That road keeps going for a good while, and then it comes out on another county road a good twenty miles down. There are other farms and houses past the holler, but it's mostly woods. The people live closer to the other road, and that's how they'd get in and out. You're just going to see Tuckers and their customers. That truck was Royce Hackworth's, another cousin of mine." He frowned. "He's a moonshine drinker, not a meth head."

"Who do you think that hood belonged to?" I asked. "And how did it get back there?"

Beau hesitated before speaking. "I don't know, but I know someone who might." He stood up. "You up for a drive?"

CHAPTER FIFTEEN

"Maybe we should take my car," I said, looking at Beau's car dubiously.

It was an old luxury car, long past its prime. It looked like it was held together with rust, baling wire, and some Band-Aids. Its dark blue paint was scabby looking—like the car had psoriasis or something. The windshield was spider-webbed with cracks, and the driver's side rearview mirror was dangling from some metallic wires. It was filthy, crusted with dried red mud beneath the fresh new coat of mud from extracting it out of the woods.

It also looked like it would break down at any moment.

"It runs fine," he replied defensively. "The mechanic who changed the oil last time said the engine looked good enough to last for another fifty thousand miles."

"I didn't mean that the way it sounded," I said. It wasn't *his* fault his mom wasn't a lawyer who could buy him a new car—I didn't want him to think I was a snob. "I mean, what I meant was…I need to get gas anyway." I had about a half tank left, which would last for a while, but he didn't need to know that.

He scratched his head. "It's probably better if we don't take mine anyway. I don't want to deal with my relatives, and they'd know my car if they saw it." He hopped down from the porch and walked around my car to the passenger side.

The sun was slowly setting in the west, throwing shadows of the pines across the blacktop. "So where are we going?" I asked as a passing 18-wheeler rocked us with its backdraft. I glanced warily over to the right side of the road. I would *never* get used to those sharp drop-offs just beyond the side of the road.

"My high school history teacher, Mr. Marren—he's an expert on Alabama history, and he does a lot of research on county history. I think he might be writing a book," Beau replied. "If anyone would know about the Klan in Corinth County, it would be him."

"Are you sure it's okay for us to just drop in on him without notice?"

Beau laughed. "It's Monday night. Mr. Marren goes to church at Gethsemane Baptist on the Tuscaloosa road, and he's got choir practice every Monday night," he said. "And after the six o'clock practice on Mondays, he hits the Hardee's drive-through on his way home, then eats on his porch and watches the cars go by until it's dark, and then he goes inside and streams a movie. Same thing every Monday—you can set your clock by it." He laughed again. "You're sure not from around here. Nobody calls first. You always just drop in. And if you don't lock your doors, people will just knock on the door and walk right into your house."

I shook my head. Mom hates when someone drops by without warning, and I wondered if this county custom is why.

She seemed to hate everything about Alabama.

"Mr. Marren is a good guy," Beau went on. "He's been teaching at the high school since he graduated from UAB. He's originally from the county, too. He grew up in the country, though, not in town. His family…" He hesitated, took a deep breath before continuing, "His daddy worked in the coal mines, and his mama had a small plot of land out here somewhere. They're long gone. His brothers and sisters all took off for Atlanta once they were old enough to get out of here." He tapped his knuckles against the window. "Mr. Marren came back here and took care of his mama. She died a few years back." He squinted. "I think she died when I was a freshman."

I couldn't help but think about Miss Sarah, dying in her crumbling house. Neither Mom nor Dewey would give up their careers and lives to move here to take care of her.

I glanced over at Beau and wondered if he—and other county people—judged my mom for not dropping everything to take care of her mother.

She never talked about why she left Alabama, but whenever the subject came up, her distaste for where she grew up was obvious. She didn't have a good childhood, and her refusal to talk much about it—or her mother—made it clear she still had issues from back then.

She raised me to be independent, to want my own life, to not tie myself to family expectations. Anytime my dad tried to push me, one way or another, about my future, she came down on him like a Fury.

But now I wondered what her childhood had been like. She'd dropped random little bits here and there. I'd always gotten the impression Miss Sarah hadn't been supportive. There hadn't been money for her or Dewey for college—when I was accepted at Tulane, and she wrote the check for my first semester's tuition, she said, *I sure hope you appreciate this. My mother wouldn't give me lunch money when I went to college.*

She'd kept me away from her relatives, from her family, from Alabama, as much as she could. I hadn't been down here in over ten years. I barely knew my cousins, my uncle, his wife, or my grandmother, for that matter.

My dad's family? I knew them all quite well. I'd spent holidays with my dad's parents, cousins on that side, but they all lived in the Chicagoland area. I'd taken the commuter train to visit my dad's parents when a ride couldn't be arranged. She never had any problem with me spending time with that side of my family whenever I wanted.

But her family was a different story.

But if there was Klan activity down here—yeah, couldn't blame her about that one bit.

I wanted to burn that disgusting mask.

But how did the mask and robe get up in that tree in the first place?

I wanted to think it was just a joke, a trick someone had been playing on someone that had been forgotten, but…

There was always a *but* when it came to Alabama, wasn't there?

We passed over the Sipsey River bridge. The river was high on its banks—with all the rain we'd been having lately, it was surprising it hadn't flooded, to be honest. A quick flash of memory: *The water, still, like it wasn't moving, not quite as high, as I came out from the trees and stood on its banks. I was carrying a fishing pole—*

"Are you even listening to me?" Beau interrupted the daydream, and I snapped back to attention.

I shouldn't daydream when I'm driving. Just because these backcountry roads never had much traffic didn't mean I couldn't wreck the damned car and kill us both.

Duncan was killed in a car accident.

"What were you saying? I'm sorry, I was…I was thinking about that Klan mask," I lied. I didn't want to tell him about the weird memories—or whatever they were—I'd been having since I got here, at least, not yet.

I liked him. I didn't want him to think I'm crazy.

Nobody wanted to go out with the crazy guy, right, Tradd?

He was so cute. I glanced over at him, and he smiled back. I liked the way his face lit up when he smiled, the little dimples in his cheeks, the way his eyes flashed. He wasn't as handsome or as built or as sexy as Tradd, but not being like Tradd was a good thing. He was smart and funny.

I also liked that he wasn't a horndog like every other guy our age seemed to be.

"I said, I'm getting a bit hungry. Do you want to get something to eat before we go over to Mr. Marren's?"

My stomach growled loud enough for him to hear, and he laughed. "I guess that's my answer."

We reached the intersection where the county road dead-ended. I flipped my turn signal on as I coasted to a stop, waiting for a beat-up old pickup truck to go past on its way into Corinth. Beau waved, and the driver waved back.

"You know everyone down here, don't you?"

"It's not that big of a place," he replied. "Less than five thousand in town, and probably not much more than seven thousand in the whole county." He made a face as I started turning. "And I'm related to at least half of them."

I passed the truck on the right, and Beau waved again. The driver was an old man, his face leathered from the sun, wearing an Auburn baseball cap. "Roll Tide," Beau shouted as we went past, and the old man shook his fist but kept smiling, yelling, "War Eagle," back at him.

Ah, Southern football tribalism.

We passed the *Now Entering Corinth Population 4760* sign, and I slowed as I approached the forty-five mile per hour speed limit sign. Just beyond was another sign: *Slower Speed Zones Ahead*. Both signs were pocked with rusty bullet holes.

"Do people just go out with guns when they're bored and shoot things around here?" I asked, half joking. I wasn't a big fan of guns. Mom had a couple of pistols in the house and took me to the shooting range to learn how to use them—but I didn't like shooting, didn't like having them in the house.

Mom might have moved up north and become a Yankee liberal, but she still had enough Alabama in her to want guns in the house.

"Liquor's usually involved," Beau replied as the fields and trees started giving way to houses and stores and gas stations. I slowed down again when I saw the speed limit sign for twenty-five. There weren't many cars or signs of life in Corinth as we headed into town. "Just keep going, past the square," Beau instructed me. "Do you want to go to Hardee's?"

"Not if Kelly's working."

"He won't be working the drive-through window," Beau replied. "But we can go to the Sonic instead if you'd rather."

He didn't ask me why I was avoiding Kelly, which was a relief. I could still hear Kelly's voice in my head. *Beau's a fag.*

I didn't want to tell Beau that.

We pulled into a slot at the Sonic—there were only two other cars, both pickup trucks, parked there.

I pressed the button to place our order.

I put my window back up and turned the air-conditioning up a notch.

"Was it hard growing up here?"

"I think it's hard growing up anywhere," he replied. "I mean, I don't know what it's like to grow up somewhere else, you know? This is all I know." He slumped down in the seat and pulled the brim of his cap down a little bit, putting his knees up against the glove box. "I wasn't an athlete, so I was a disappointment to my family, but I made good grades, so that made up for it. My older brother was a football player." His eyes drifted over to look out the window. "He works in the condom plant now."

"Condom plant?"

Beau laughed. "The main industry in Corinth is the condom factory. Isn't that great? This stupid backward county with all its religious hang-ups and everything, and the main source of employment is a factory that makes rubbers. My brother works the graveyard shift—the plant runs twenty-four hours. It's fun watching the religious wingnuts who put food on the table making condoms wrap themselves in knots justifying it. Cause you shouldn't ever use a condom, oh no. Sex is for procreation only, so if you're having sex, you should be doing it to have a baby." He shook his head. "They hate abortion, think it's murder, that babies are sacred, but how is forcing someone to have a child they don't want, a sacred baby…a punishment?"

"They don't make sense," I replied. "None of it makes sense."

A teenage girl in a uniform carrying a tray came out to the car, hanging it off my window. I handed her a twenty, and she made change while I took the bags off the tray and handed them to Beau.

Her nametag said *Kayla*. "Beau Hackworth, is that you?" she said in a drawl so thick it could've been cut with a knife. She bent down to look in the window.

"Hey, Kayla, how are you?"

She rolled her eyes. "Working." She gave me an appraising look. "Who's your friend?"

"Kayla, this is Jake Chapman—ole Miz Donelson's grandson. He's down here with her being so sick and all. Jake, this is Kayla Collinsworth. She's a cousin of mine somehow."

"Oh, Beau, you know our granddaddies are first cousins. Nice to meet you, Jake." She batted her eyelashes. She was flirting with me. "You gonna be around all summer?"

I stopped myself from saying *I sure as hell hope not* and smiled instead. "I don't know."

"Well, don't be a stranger. Beau, there's a party over at Brent Bullard's parents' lake house later tonight. Why don't you come and bring your cute friend?"

I felt color creeping into my face.

"We'll keep that in mind, Kayla."

I tipped her a couple of bucks, and she winked at me with a smile before taking the tray back inside.

"You don't want to go to that party, do you?" I asked.

He laughed. "The only reason she invited me is because she thinks you're cute." He took a bite from his cheeseburger. "Trash like the Hackworths generally don't get invited to parties Kayla Collinsworth and her friends go to."

"Trash? Isn't she your cousin?" I was confused. "Twice removed or something? Anyway, don't call yourself trash." I watched Kayla go back inside the little building where steam was rising from the grill. "And she works at a fast-food joint."

"She does it for spending money," Beau replied. "Her daddy owns the funeral parlor in town." He rolled his eyes. "Her mom—my mom's cousin—made her get a job when she got suspended for smoking on the school grounds last semester. She got a job as *punishment*. Most kids who work have to."

We finished eating in silence. Beau gathered the trash and got out of the car to throw it in the garbage can halfway to the building. As he was walking back, a filthy pickup truck pulled into the parking area and revved its engine. I watched it pass behind my car in the rearview mirror, and I heard them shout something at Beau as he walked back. He didn't even look over at them, just lowered his head and walked faster. When he got into the car he said, "Start the car and let's get out of here."

"What's going on?"

"Just do what I say, okay?"

I backed out of the spot but had to drive all the way around to get to the exit on the other side. The big truck had pulled into one of the spots on the other side, and I could hear the thumping bass of some hip-hop music over the sound of my own engine.

"Turn right," Beau instructed me.

Main Street was still relatively deserted. No cars were parked in front of any of the businesses, the parking lots empty. The sun was setting in a violent explosion of reds and oranges and purples and blues in the western sky. Beau was rattled, tense.

"Are you okay?" I asked when I reached the red light at the town square.

He took a deep breath and turned down the stereo. "I don't

want to bore you with the sad drama of my life." He wiped at his eyes. "That was my cousin Frankie in that trunk. Frankie's a jerk and a bully and borderline criminal. He's going to wind up in jail someday, and that someday can't come soon enough."

"What did he yell at you?"

"It wasn't Frankie, it was his girlfriend Liza." He hesitated before the words came tumbling out in a rush. "Liza's trash—I know I'm not supposed to say that, and I know people think that about me and my family, but she is trash, absolutely trash. Her mother is a prostitute, and Liza doesn't even know who her father is—he could be anyone, you know? And her mother lives in a trailer, and people pay her for sex, and I can't imagine who ever would, how she would even be worth five dollars—she's so dirty and nasty. And I know she smokes crack and probably meth—she's always out at Tucker Holler when she gets her check, buying more meth—and Liza is just mean, the kind of person who'd kick an injured dog or smother a baby, and they've made me miserable for so many years, and I just hate them so much, and I didn't want them to…"

He took a deep breath.

"Never mind, okay, forget I said anything. Just keep driving. After we cross the railroad tracks, take the second right."

The wrong side of the tracks was such a cliché I'd never imagined I would ever experience it for real. But once we crossed the forlorn railroad tracks, Corinth became a different town.

The houses needed paint, or some other kind of repair. The yards weren't neat and orderly, but filled with junk and garbage and bare spots where the grass and weeds had worn away. The streetlights were broken, looked like they'd been shot out or something, and I felt myself recoiling inside.

"It's this house up here, the one with the weeping willow."

I pulled over to the side of the road in front of the sad little house. This yard was neat and tidy. There was an old car parked on the lawn next to the side of the house. The porch light was on, and there was a light in one of the windows. It looked small, tiny, not big enough for a family.

The front door opened, and a man stepped out. "Beau Hackworth?" he called out into the darkness. "Who is that out there?"

"Mr. Marren, it's me and a friend."

We crossed the lawn and stepped into the light cast from the porch.

Mr. Marren turned gray when he saw us and reached out to one of the iron columns supporting the porch roof.

"Jacob?" he asked hoarsely. "How…how is this possible?"

And then he slumped down to the porch.

Chapter Sixteen

"M r. Marren!" Beau ran up the cracked walk to the front porch, skipping the steps by hopping up. Beau took him by the arm, and Mr. Marren smiled, putting his hand over Beau's.

"Thank you, son." He looked back at me. "Just caught me by surprise, is all. It's not every day you see a ghost."

Goose bumps came up on my arms, and I felt weird, hollow headed, and a little scared.

He knew my name because he knew my uncle. He thought I was my missing uncle, somehow returned from wherever he ran away to. But he also said *ghost*. Did he know something about my uncle we didn't?

"Come on, boys, let's get out of this heat and inside," Mr. Marren said, gently removing Beau's hand from his arm. He beckoned me forward. "I'm fine, young man. I'm not going to bite you or anything." He laughed. "You sure gave me a shock, though. You must be Glynnie's boy. I'd heard you looked just like him."

I walked up to the porch. A black cat ran out of the shadows with a screech and disappeared into the lengthening shadows across the lawn. I climbed the steps.

"God, just look at you." Mr. Marren smiled at me, shaking his head. He was maybe in his early fifties, his hairline receded. What little brownish-gray hair he had left was loosely scattered over his brown scalp. His face was tanned, his teeth stained yellow from nicotine. He also smelled like sweat and stale smoke, and the skin under his jawline sagged a bit. He was wearing a brown and yellow plaid shirt, open at the neck to reveal a white undershirt. His casual brown slacks were pressed crisply, and he was wearing dark brown and yellow Oxford shoes. He held the battered screen door open, and Beau and I stepped into the cool darkness inside the house.

The only light came from a fake hurricane lamp on an end table next to the couch. The light seemed to get sucked into the darkness, because the walls were covered with dark, faux-wood paneling. There was dark carpet covering the floor. Magazines and paperback books and hardcovers in their plastic library covers were piled high on the coffee table—several of the piles leaned dangerously. The big-screen television mounted on the front wall was tuned in to Wolf Blitzer on CNN, the sound muted.

"Would you mind getting me a glass of water?" Mr. Marren asked, sinking into a reclining chair with a wheeze. "I'm feeling a bit light-headed. There's a pitcher in the refrigerator."

The kitchen was also small, painted yellow, with old particleboard cabinets mounted on the back wall over a counter. Dishes were drying in a rack next to the single porcelain sink. There was a light on over the small table for two pushed against the opposite wall, newspapers piled on one side, and I found glasses in a cabinet. I opened the ancient refrigerator door. A plastic Brita pitcher filled with water sat next to a half-full plastic milk carton. There was a plastic bin in the freezer filled with ice cubes. I grabbed a couple and filled the glass from the pitcher.

I handed it to Mr. Marren, who was mopping sweat from his forehead with a handkerchief. He still looked a little washed-out and pale. There were deep lines on his face, laugh lines and crow's feet radiating out from his dark brown eyes. "Boy, you gave me quite a fright," he said with a slight laugh as he took the water glass from me. "I seriously thought Jacob Donelson was getting out of that car, after all these years." He laughed again. "Like he wouldn't have aged or something. It don't make sense, I know." He took a long drink from the glass, his Adam's apple in his long thin neck bobbing with each gulp. He set the glass down on the little table next to his chair.

"I guess he looks a lot like his uncle," Beau said.

He closed his eyes and nodded. "So, you're Glynnie's boy," he said. "Jacob."

"Jake," I said, sticking out my hand for him to shake. "I prefer Jake."

He shook my hand. "I'm sorry, but the resemblance"—he stared at me—"is uncanny. It's like you're him, back again, but it can't be. You would have aged surely in all this time." He shook his head. "Listen to me, talking like an old fool. It's nice to meet you Jacob—Jake." He peered at me a little closer. "No, it's not exact. Your chin isn't as sharp, and his dimples were deeper than yours. His face was a little rounder. But it's close enough for horseshoes and hand grenades. His hair was lighter, too." He held out the glass to me again. "Do you mind getting more?"

I could hear Beau and him talking while I filled up the glass again, and when I walked back into the living room, the overhead light was on, the front door closed. I glanced around as I walked the glass to him. Bookshelves lined one entire wall, and each shelf was crammed full of books, so tightly the bindings looked like they hurt. Books were stacked on top of the ones lined up on the shelves, paperbacks with cracked and worn spines, and I saw names I recognizes and others I didn't: Janet Evanovich, Stephen King, Laura Lippman, Michael Connelly, James Baldwin, Kellye Garrett.

Beau sat down on the couch, and I sat at the opposite end. "I'm not much of a host, am I?" Mr. Marren pushed himself up to his feet. "You boys want a Coke?" When we both said okay, he walked into the kitchen and returned with three glasses of ice and three sweating red cans of Coke. He stared at me again as I poured mine over the ice and looked away, embarrassed, when I caught him.

"I'm sorry," he said, his voice sounding emotional. "I just never thought I'd see Jacob again, and the resemblance…the resemblance is uncanny. It's like him, all over again." He got up and walked out of the living room through the door opening into the next room in the front. He came back with a yearbook, black with gold lettering on the front: *Kenilworth High 1974*. He sat down in the easy chair and started flipping through the pages. "There he is." He passed the book over to me, a gnarled finger pointing at the page.

I glanced down the names and saw it: *Donelson, Jacob*. I looked at the small black-and-white head shots. Like when I'd found the picture in the attic, it was disorienting to see my own face staring back up at me from a picture I'd never taken. But there were subtler differences.

We didn't look exactly alike—but it was pretty damned close.

A memory flashed through my mind. I was picking the green seeds out of the four o'clocks and slitting them open with my thumbnail, childishly delighted to see the milky inside. My mother and Miss Sarah were sitting on the porch—Miss Sarah in a faded old wooden rocking chair, Mom in a rusted metal chair that rocked on its rods—talking.

He looks just like your brother when he was that age, Miss Sarah said disdainfully. *And you need to make a man out of him. You don't want him to turn out like your brother.*

He's fine the way he is, Mother. Mom sounded tired. *All I care about is if he's happy.*

God doesn't care about happiness! Miss Sarah snapped back. *You need to take him to church and get him right with God!*

I shivered.

I looked down at my uncle's smiling face. What was so wrong with you?

"Are you okay, Jake?" Beau asked.

"Yeah." I showed him the picture. "It's just weird to see my face in a yearbook from before I was born."

"You don't look exactly like him." Beau peered at the picture and then back at my face. "There are differences, but you could be twins."

I looked at the top of the page. *Juniors,* it said. I turned back a page to *Seniors,* and there was Mr. Marren—*Marren, Linus*—Linus, just like in *Peanuts.* I looked at the face and then at Mr. Marren. I could still see the teenager in the old man's face—the sparkle in the eyes and the smile were the same, even though the boy in the picture had a big gap between his front two teeth.

"Kenilworth High?" Kelly's face was on the facing page, only the name read *Donelson, Duncan.* The resemblance to Kelly was also striking, but if you looked closer, just like with Jacob, there were differences. Kelly's face was fuller, his shoulders thicker, his blond hair curlier. Duncan's hair was cut shorter than his brother's—the hair not even covering his ears—but he had the same rosy cheeks Kelly had, the same lips, the same dimples in his cheeks. But there was a cruel set to Duncan's eyes Kelly's didn't have.

I handed the book back to Mr. Marren.

"That was the year before they desegregated Kenilworth High

School." Mr. Marren leaned back in his chair, the yearbook resting in his lap. "They'd closed the schools for Black kids a few years before, but the county sent its Black kids to Corinth County High for a few years."

"I thought that happened in the 1960s?"

"The court orders happened then," Mr. Marren explained. "It took a while for it to, you know, take effect everywhere. Corinth County was a late adopter."

"They had to finish building Corinth Christian Academy," Beau said bitterly. "So the parents who could afford to have their kids go to an all-white school had one to send them to instead."

"It was a hard time in the county," Mr. Marren said, agreeing. "There weren't any protests, and there wasn't any violence, but not for lack of trying. The Klan was still around then—not as organized as it had been, and not near enough members to do anything." He placed the book on the table carefully. "Your uncle was one of my best friends, Jake. I still can't believe he ran away the way he did."

"What happened?" I asked. "No one can tell me. Mom and Uncle Dewey were too young. Miss Sarah had a stroke, so I can't ask her."

"After Dunk was killed in the car accident, he ran away." Mr. Marren closed his eyes. "He talked about it all the time, but I never thought he would actually do it, you know? All kids talk about running away at times, but to go when his mother was still grieving…" He shook his head. "People said some pretty harsh things about Jacob. Miss Sarah wouldn't talk about him—just said he'd gone, she didn't know where, and she didn't care if he ever came back."

Beau looked sick. "She didn't care?"

"She was grieving—you should make allowances," Mr. Marren said quietly. "The resemblance is so uncanny," Mr. Marren said. "That's the other funny thing, too, you know? Jacob looked just like one of the Lost Boys."

All the hair on my arms stood up, and I felt the skin on the back of my neck moving. "The Lost Boys? I didn't think there were any pictures of them."

"You know about the Lost Boys?" Mr. Marren grinned at me, gesturing at Beau with his hand. "He and his fancy professor from

Tuscaloosa think they can find the boys if they dig in the right place. Nobody's ever going to find those boys." He shook his head again. "It's just like the Lost Cause, a whole lot of romantic nonsense about something that was bad to begin with."

"You don't believe in the Lost Boys story?"

Mr. Marren waved his hand. "The boys disappeared during the war, and their mother was dead and buried. There's no telling whatever happened to those boys, but if their mother died of typhus, then the boys probably did as well. All the rest is just romantic nonsense." He pushed himself to his feet and walked into the next room. When he came back, he had a photograph in his hands. It was of an oil painting, with what looked like Blackwood Hall before the fire in the background. A man stood next to his seated wife, and there were four boys gathered around them. The two kneeling in front of their mother resembled me and Kelly. "This is at the state museum in Montgomery," he said as I passed it to Beau. "It's the only known image of the Blackwood family before the war. You see the resemblance?"

"To Kelly, too," Beau said, frowning. "But he's a distant relative, right?"

"Sort of," I replied. "No one really seems to know how he's related."

"Your grandmother is a hard woman." Mr. Marren got a faraway look on his face. "Always was. She married late, you know, and everyone figured your granddaddy married her for her land. There used to be a lot more of it back then, you know. She's gradually sold it off when the money from tree farming wasn't there anymore."

"Tree farming?"

"Most of her land was covered with forest back then, not as much now as it was then, but she used to let the loggers come in, sold the wood to them. Made some nice money from that. Your grandpa, her husband, farmed, of course. But they had that big house, and he was a lot younger than she was. She was a handsome woman—not what you'd call pretty, but she was handsome, a big woman, too. Most everybody thought she'd die an old maid, the last of the Blackwoods like she was. The Blackwoods used to be a big deal in this part of the country, you know, but it was her daddy who drove them down into the ground. He drank, you know." Mr.

Marren took a sip from his water. "Or so my mama told me." He got that faraway look in his eyes again.

"You said the Klan was still around then, when the schools desegregated?" Beau asked.

"Yes, they were still around. Nowhere near what they were in the past, of course, but yeah," Mr. Marren said, narrowing his eyes. "And you can be sure there are still sympathizers around here. There was some serious trouble during the marches and the civil rights fight, some crosses burned and windows got broken, but not near as bad here as some other places. We never made the national news here." He shook his head. "The people in this county were always too damned poor to organize, but there used to be lynchings. They strung up that Black Yankee boy in the early 1950s, but after that, it was more underground than out in the public."

"We found an old Klan mask in the woods behind the Donelson house," Beau went on. "And I thought you'd be the person to ask. It's in the car."

"You run on and get it then," Mr. Marren replied.

After the screen door slammed shut, Mr. Marren looked at me. "You want to know about your uncle, don't you?"

I nodded.

"Jacob was my friend." His eyes watered a little bit. "Such a great guy." He wiped at his eyes angrily. "Duncan was older than Jacob," he went on. "He was a big deal, best athlete to come to Kenilworth High in decades. Winning teams, you know, matter more than anything else to the people around here, so having the *coloreds*"—his tone was bitter—"on the Kenilworth team, playing alongside Duncan, helped them start winning for the first time since before Pearl Harbor. Duncan, though, he was a racist and an asshole." His face screwed up into a scowl. "Off the field he didn't want anything to do with the Black kids, you know, and he picked on some of them. He was the ringleader. And the school wouldn't do anything about it, of course. The principal didn't want us there in the first place, and neither did the teachers. But Jacob, he stood up for us. He sat with us in the lunchroom and wouldn't let anyone say anything to us. He was brave. They called him terrible names, of course, and he'd just say *No, I'm just a decent human being, you should try it sometime*." He smiled at the memory. "He was such a great guy, your uncle. Even though he'd talked about getting out of here, it was just strange he'd run away *then*, you know? I was so glad to get out of here and go to UAB. It felt like escaping."

"Why did you come back here?"

"To take care of my mother." He made a face. "And just stayed after she went. She left me this house, and well, it's home."

I opened my mouth but had nothing to say.

"After Duncan died…" He exhaled. "You know about that?"

"All I know is he died in a car accident," I replied. "My uncle Dewey and Mom don't really know much more than that."

"Duncan and his buddies liked to drink and party and whoop it up. Corinth was a dry county back then, and so the only way to get liquor was to drive over to Tuscaloosa or Carbon Hill, or buy moonshine from the Tuckers." He raised an eyebrow. "You know your grandmother owns Tucker Holler, don't you? That's Donelson land—they pay her rent. And no Tucker was going to say no when Miz Donelson's son said he wanted shine." His eyes got a faraway look. "There was a party that night, up in the woods on McCallum Mountain. The story I was told was Duncan rode along with Caleb McCallum in a drag race on those mountain roads—I don't recall who the other driver was—and they came over the top of a rise, and Caleb and Duncan were in the wrong lane, and another car was coming, and Caleb slammed on the brakes, but the car went off the road and flipped a few times before blowing up." He shook his head. "No one knows if they were killed in the crash or they died in the fire."

My stomach felt queasy.

"Ole Miz Donelson took it hard, you know. The sun rose and set on that boy in her eyes, and she never did give much of a shit about Jacob or the babies. She leaned a lot on Dunk after Mr. Donelson died." He shook his head. "She even stopped going to church for a while after the funeral. And it wasn't long after that Jacob ran away. I know he wasn't happy at home—him and Duncan never got along too well. Him and Miz Donelson weren't getting along too well at the time either. It never made sense to me, you know." He rubbed his eyes again. "He never said anything to me. That was what I never understood. We'd been like brothers since we were in diapers. I still can't believe he didn't tell me."

The screen door opened, and Beau walked in, holding out the mask by the pointed top, so it hung from his hand the way it would drape if someone was wearing it. The eye holes stared at me, and I felt a chill go down my spine, the hairs on my arms standing up.

A memory flashed through my head, of someone wearing it, brown eyes staring at me as I pressed back against a tree.

I shivered. Where the hell did that come from?

"It's not very old," Mr. Marren said, taking it from Beau and examining it. "This is a cheap cotton blend. I'd say it's no more than two or three years old, tops, and even that's pushing it a bit." He laughed. "Fabric left out to the elements rots pretty fast around here. But I haven't heard about any Klan activity or organizing or anything. I'll ask around, though." He pointed a finger at me. "But if I were you, I'd make sure that house is locked up tight every night before I'd be able to sleep."

"Is there anyone else we could talk to, Mr. Marren?"

He laughed. "About the Klan? I don't know any white people who'd admit to being in the Klan, at least, not recently. Lately, though…"

"But you said you'd ask around?" I replied.

He grinned at me. "Black people. They won't talk to you, but they might talk to me."

"Thank you." I stood up, and he offered the mask back to me. I didn't want to take it from him, but Beau grabbed it.

"Tomorrow we can head down to the library and maybe the newspaper office, to check on the times," Beau said.

"What part of town are you from?" I asked.

"This side of the tracks," he replied. He grabbed my arm and gasped.

Written on the windshield of the car, in what looked like shaving cream, was the word *faggots*.

CHAPTER SEVENTEEN

Beau's face turned white in the glow of the streetlight. "Oh my God," he half moaned and clamped his hand over his mouth.

I walked up to the car and touched it. Yes, it was shaving cream. I reached into the back floorboards for the towel I always keep there. The humidity in New Orleans often fogged up the windows and created condensation, so I'd taken to keeping a ratty towel in the car to wipe the windows down. It was dirty, sure, but would work.

My hands were shaking slightly as I wiped the shaving cream off. Deep breaths there, Jacob, I told myself as I balled up the towel and tossed it into the back seat. My heart was beating so fast it felt like it might jump out of my ribcage, and I could also hear my own ragged breathing. Deep breaths, stay focused, it didn't mean anything, just some kids being dicks and playing pranks, was all. Nobody in this town really knew you, so it couldn't be personal.

I hated the word *faggot*.

I was maybe eleven or twelve when I first heard someone use it. I was in the seventh grade, at St. Sebastian's middle school.

I was in the locker room, after gym class. I hated gym class in the seventh grade. We didn't have gym in grade school, but that changed in junior high school. We had to buy gym suits at the school bookstore, along with a lock for the tiny locker we were assigned— moving the lock from the small locker to the bigger ones for storing our school uniforms. Changing—and being naked—in front of my classmates took a while for me to get used to, and I never liked it. We were required to shower after gym class—with Father Ambrose situated outside the walk-through showers and the tiled room where we were given towels to dry off, checking us off by name as our naked bodies trooped past him to get dressed and ready for our next class. The junior high showers were strange, old, from when the school was built back in the late 1960s, showers mounted on a kind of tiled maze you walked through after getting undressed. You had to get your hair wet—something else Father Ambrose was checking for—and if your hair wasn't wet, he'd send you back through. I tried not to look at other boys, standing under showerheads and letting the hot water run down their bodies, transitioning from childhood to manhood, but couldn't help it sometimes.

I already knew I was different, thinking about boys the way everyone else thought about girls, and seeing other naked boys was both scary and exciting.

Everything we did in gym was some macho-hetero bullshit, sports I wasn't interested in. We never did badminton or volleyball or anything I was good at, no, it was always things I didn't know how to play, didn't know anything about. I wasn't the most graceful of kids and my body had started changing that summer between sixth and seventh grades—black hairs growing out of my calves, under my arms, in my groin. My voice was also changing, getting deeper, sometimes cracking embarrassingly what I talked, and I started having dreams. Dreams about movie stars, TV stars, the boys on *Teen Wolf* on MTV, and I knew what that meant, and it scared me.

I tried not to attract attention, either from Father Ambrose or any of the other kids. I changed as fast as I could, got through the showers quickly, getting dressed and out of there. I couldn't help stealing glances at the other naked bodies, comparing my own with theirs, seeing who was getting through puberty faster and who hadn't gotten there yet.

I was always terrified someone would catch me looking.

I'd heard them talking about fags before, fairies and homos and faggots. I didn't know what any of those things were, but I knew it wasn't anything good.

I never dreamed one of them, any of them, would figure it out about me as I was just figuring it out myself.

"Are you a faggot, Chapman?"

I was drying my hair when I heard the words, and I knew who spoke them.

Troy Alexander, the tough guy, already had hairy legs and hair on his chest, powerful muscles developed from sports and exercise, the bluish-black shadow on his face meaning he was also already shaving. He was taller than me, already about five ten, and I had a crush on him of sorts, the man-boy that he was, and I furtively checked him out from time to time, snapping pictures with the camera in my head so I could remember his body in vivid detail later, alone in my room. My crush was so strong it sometimes hurt, wanting him to notice me, be his friend, and in my wildest fantasies, my boyfriend. I imagined his thick pouty lips kissing me, wrapping me up in his big strong arms, the warmth of his velvety skin against mine as we pressed our bodies close against each other.

No one could know.

My number one goal was to make it through high school with nobody finding out. I knew I wasn't the only gay person in the world. But I was sure I was the only one at St. Sebastian's.

I imagined college would be different, an entirely different world of people interested in learning and talking about smart things, reading books and discussing them under trees on beautiful sunny afternoons. I'd get away from these boys with their nasty locker room talk and disrespectful comments about women and what they'd do to them, what they did with their girlfriends, the way they referred to girls, and spend my time with people who wanted to learn, to think, to expand their minds and their horizons.

And now I'd somehow caught Troy Alexander's attention, but not in the way I had dreamed.

"No," I said, my heart pounding.

"I think you are." Troy laughed, rubbing his towel over his crotch suggestively. "I don't think you like girls at all."

Some of the boys in his circle, idiotic thugs who breathed through their mouths, smelled the blood in the water, and I started to worry, to get afraid of what was going to happen in the drying area. I glanced around furtively. No one was going to stand up for me.

I could tell. Everyone else had their eyes down, not watching, pretending this encounter wasn't happening, drying themselves off faster than usual so they could get out of there and away from whatever was about to happen.

There was no worse insult in junior high than *faggot*. The toughest guy in the class was calling me one, and this wasn't going to end well for me. And it didn't. Kids didn't want to hang out with me anymore, sit with me in the cafeteria, be seen with me in the hallways. Troy and his friends would mock me, call me names, knock my books out of my hands, threaten me with violence, bump into me hard enough to almost knock me down.

Eventually my mother found out—I never told her, I was too ashamed—and I don't know what she said to Father Dominic, the principal, but in the eighth grade the harassment died away to almost nothing. Most kids still acted like I had two heads, but the outright bullying stopped.

But every now and then I'd see *Jake Chapman sucks dick* written on a desk or a bathroom wall.

Every time it was like being punched in the face.

Once the shaving cream was nothing more than just a greenish-white smear across the window, I started the car. I pressed the button to send a spray of blue fluid up onto the glass and shifted the lever to get the wipers going as quickly as they'd go. I kept spraying fluid, the wipers kept moving, back and forth, back and forth, smearing the residue at first before clearing it off, but I could see the letters still there, burned indelibly on my brain.

"It's just kids," Beau was saying, bringing me out of the terrible memory. "Not anything to worry about. It's the kind of thing kids think is funny. They don't know you, and they don't know your car."

"So we're not in any danger here?"

He chewed on his lip for a moment before answering. "I don't think so."

"But you don't know," I replied, resting my forehead on the steering wheel. "Have you always felt safe here?"

"I'm alive, aren't I?"

It wasn't an answer.

"Are you okay to drive? Do you want me to?"

"No, I'm fine." I turned on the headlights and put the car in drive, making a U-turn in the middle of the road to head back the way we'd originally come. "I'm good. It was just a shock, is all."

"Yeah, well, if anything it was directed at me and not you," he said. "I get hassled sometimes—it's why I'm not really out here. But some kids were just out fucking around and tagging cars. At least it wasn't spray paint."

Good point.

"It must have been rough growing up here," I said, signaling and making a right turn back onto Main Street.

"It could've been worse," Beau replied, looking out his window as we rolled through downtown Corinth, which was a ghost town. The only thing really missing were tumbleweeds rolling down the road.

"That's not comforting." I stopped at the main intersection when the light turned red. There were no cars coming from either direction, but tempting as it was to just run the damned light, I was afraid to. It was a small town in Alabama, and weren't the cops just itching to write a ticket to someone with out of state license plates?

I felt sick to my stomach.

Or was I just buying into stereotypes from movies and TV shows?

Stereotypes exist for a reason, I heard my mother's voice inside my head.

Calm down, drama queen. Some kids wrote a slur on my windshield. It's not like they tied me to a fence and beat me to death.

"I got picked on a lot," Beau admitted in a low voice. "And my older brothers were the worst. It was like they were afraid if they didn't join in, you know, if they actually stood up for their brother, everyone would think they were fags, too." His jaw set. "No, all they told me to do was toughen up, like my dad did, basically blaming me for being picked on."

"That's terrible. I'm so sorry."

The light turned green after an eternity. I stayed below the posted speed limit, but it was so eerie that there were no other cars around. The sidewalks were all nice and rolled up, no sign of life anywhere, other than lights in the windows of some of the houses.

"Yeah. I'll never forgive my brothers," Beau went on. "Or my dad either."

"What about your mom?"

"She took off when I was twelve." Beau shrugged. "No big loss." He mimed sticking a needle in his arm. "She's a junkie, has been for as long as I can remember. It's a wonder my brothers and

I were born without, you know, birth defects from her drinking and shooting up." He looked out the window. "She's probably dead somewhere now."

I didn't know what to say to that so didn't say anything. Soon we left the city limits and were out in the darkness of the country again. I started speeding up. It felt good to leave Corinth behind. Beau and I rode in silence. But once again at Four Corners, a big black truck turned and started following our car.

Just like the night I came back from Dewey's.

But unlike that time, the truck hung back a little bit, didn't crowd my rear bumper, didn't seem menacing. Just another vehicle going the same way we were, but my palms were sweating, and I couldn't stop checking my rearview mirror every few seconds.

I just…I just had a feeling.

The history of this county is written in blood.

But as we went up and down slopes and around curves in the darkness, it stayed back. The insects smashing themselves to death on the windshield didn't bother me as much as they did before.

I guess you *can* get used to anything.

And finally, at long last, I could see the mailbox on the side of the road up ahead, flipping on my turn signal and slowing down. I glanced into the rearview mirror and saw that the truck was also slowing, also had its signal on.

Why were they turning? Were they coming after us, or were they customers of the Tuckers?

I knew I was panicking because of the shaving cream, but that didn't help.

I was just rattled. It's not the same people who shaving-creamed my windshield. They would have followed me from Corinth if it was. Just more meth customers of the Tuckers, is all.

Not that *that* was any better. Didn't people go crazy when they were on meth?

I made the turn and pulled into the parking area next to the house. Kelly's truck wasn't there, but Geoffrey's car was parked right next to the pump house. I turned off the lights and the ignition.

The headlights of the truck lit up the inside of the car.

"What the hell?" Beau turned and looked behind, shielding his eyes from the glare.

"Go get in the house," I said, gesturing. "Go in the back door"—I handed him the keys, separating out the back door key—"and watch from the window. I'm going to go see what they want."

I hoped the *Have your phone out and ready to call the sheriff* was implied.

Before he could stop me, before I understood what an incredibly stupid idea this was, I got out, giving a friendly wave as I started walking back to where the truck was idling, less than three feet behind the back of my car. *This is stupid are you crazy what are you doing this is crazy you're going to get killed are you crazy run for the house run for the house run for the house…*

The driver's window rolled down as I got closer. The driver was a man in his early twenties with that thick dark hair so common down here, cut so it looked like a Q-tip. He was starting to lose his looks a bit though—his teeth were yellowed and crooked, and there were pockmarks on his cheeks. He jerked a thumb, directing me to walk around to the other side of the truck. I could see someone sitting there but couldn't tell if it was a man or a woman or a rottweiler. I went back around the front of the truck, feeling the heat of the engine, the heavy, wet hot night air making me sweat.

"You're a Blackwood, all right," a woman's voice said in a heavy drawl as I got closer to the passenger window.

"Technically, a Chapman," I replied, stepping close to the window. "And you are?"

She laughed, a pleasant sound, from deep inside. "Alberta Tucker, pleased to meet you." She was an older woman, wearing a plaid cotton housedress, her flabby arms bare. Her teeth were dark yellow, her right incisor gold. Her limp, wavy black hair was latticed with gray and silver and white, and her face had been ravaged by time. Deep wrinkles, eyes deepset in their sockets, the lips bloodless and thin, a fold of skin hanging just below her chin. The eyes were arresting, suspicious, and brown. "You can call me Ma, like everyone does." She laughed again. "I heard Miz Sarah's grandson had come down to look after her, but I didn't recognize that car from around here, so I told Rafe over here to follow you when I saw you pass through Four Corners, and you pulled in here, and I knew who you were then, and I wanted to come get a look at you." She looked me over like I was a piece of meat. "You know, we Tuckers live down in the holler." She gestured in the vague direction. "I knew your mama when she was a little girl. And I'll be goddamned if you aren't the spitting image of your uncle Jacob."

"I was named after him."

"Your mama sure knew what she was doing when she named you." She laughed again. "Glynis was always the smartest Donelson, not that it's saying much." She held her liver-spotted tanned hand out the window for me to shake, and I did. "Pleased to meet you. Call me Ma, like I said, Jacob."

"I prefer Jake, actually."

"I'll call you Jake if you call me Ma."

"Okay, Ma."

"How's your mama doing? We don't see her much around here anymore. She went up to Chicago and now she's too good for us back here at home?"

"I don't think she thinks that. She's just busy, is all. She's in California now, working on a case."

"Well, isn't that special? I guess I always knew she was destined to be a big thing." She seemed to think that was funny, and when she stopped laughing, she asked, "So, how's the old lady doing?"

"Not as bad as everyone seemed to think before I came down here."

"She's a tough old broad, she is! Too ornery and mean to die, like me." She looked at me. The smile faded. "We're all a little concerned about what's going to happen around here if she dies." She coughed and spat out a nasty wad of phlegm that hit the dirt near my right foot. "We're not about to get turned off land we've been living on for a good long time—you tell your mama and Dewey that for old Ma, will you?"

I nodded. "Sure."

"You're a good one." She smiled at me, then looked past me, to my car. "Is that Beau Hackworth I see? Beau! You git over here and say hello! Where's your manners?"

Reluctantly, he walked through the gravel, shuffling his feet and kicking stones aside. He stood next to me. "Hey, Ma."

"Git over here and let me hug your neck," she commanded. He held back for a moment, then stepped over to the truck. The door swung open, and she leaned down to hug him, her fleshy arms going around his neck. "I haven't seen you since—well, since I don't know when. What are you doing out here so late? Ain't you living in Tuscaloosa now?"

"I, uh, well, I'm working with Dr. Brady at the ruins." He gestured vaguely toward the woods. "And Jake and I have become friends…"

Her eyes darted back and forth between the two of us. "Not getting up to anything, are you boys?"

"No."

"Make sure that you don't. Jake, you feel free to come down to the holler if you need anything, you hear? Anything at all, just come on down the road." She waved as the truck backed out, turned around, and spun gravel. Soon the taillights were just a red glow in the dirt cloud stirred up by its tires as it headed up the other side of the rise.

"Well," I said.

"I think I'd better head on home." Beau shivered.

"You sure you want to make that drive?" I felt strange, a bit woozy and dizzy. I walked over to the back of my car and placed my hand against the trunk to steady myself.

"No offense, but I'd rather not have Ma Tucker—any Tucker— see my car here in the morning. They aren't the tolerant type."

Great. It wasn't bad enough that they were running both a meth lab and a still, but they were homophobes, too?

He opened his car door. "I'll be okay driving home. Are you sure you're okay? You look a little green."

I just nodded and stood on the porch, holding on to one of the porch posts, until he turned onto the county road. My head was feeling even stranger, and things were getting blurry…

I managed to make it inside before it came over me completely.

Chapter Eighteen

I closed the front door behind me and turned the dead bolt before putting the chain on. I flipped the light switch on, and the dusty chandelier blazed to light.

I staggered into the front room, heading for the kitchen. I was dehydrated and sweating and overheated. My head was swimming. I flipped on the kitchen light and staggered to the refrigerator, grabbed a bottle of water, and held it up against my hot face.

My grandmother knowingly rented land to people who were drug dealers. Did Dewey and Mom know?

I opened the bottle and took a long pull on it. Of course they knew, how could they not? The Tuckers have been renting that land for almost a hundred years, Ma Tucker said. How could they not know?

Just something else no one thought was important enough to tell me.

Seriously, what the fuck, Mom? Why did you send me here?

Clearly, I should have chosen the rehab option.

But that didn't explain this weird hollow feeling I had in my head.

I sat down at the kitchen table and drank some more water.

This had been going on ever since I got here.

I thought back to that first day, when I had that weird, exhilarated feeling when I got into my bedroom. The way I reacted when I first saw the house when I pulled up to it off the county road. Whatever that white flash was that I kept seeing in the woods right around where we found the Klan costume. The feeling of terror I experienced in the attic.

And he couldn't forget the nightmares. Or the skeleton at the ruins. And the meth lab and the still in Tucker Holler.

"I should go upstairs and pack and drive back to New Orleans tomorrow morning," I whispered.

But it didn't seem right.

I had to stay for some reason I didn't understand.

As I took another sip of water, I realized I hadn't felt homesick for New Orleans at all since I'd arrived and hadn't stalked Tradd and his friends on social media in days. Coming here had helped me get over that dysfunctional mess that wasn't a relationship.

I hadn't, in fact, had any desire to have a drink or do any drugs or go dancing or partying or anything since I'd arrived here. My weed stash was still in my laptop case, up in my bedroom.

I hadn't even *thought* about getting high.

Something was definitely…well, off about this place.

I finished the water and tossed the bottle into the trash can by the sink. That weird feeling was still there, just not as strong as it had been before I'd come inside.

I could be in danger here. That Klan robe wasn't that old. So someone around here was either in the Klan or knew something about Klan activity.

When I got to my room, I grabbed my laptop and googled *Corinth County Alabama Klan*. I wasn't expecting them to have a website or anything—certainly not under that name, even the biggest racists like David Duke never used those words anymore—but there had to be something, right?

Only one thing came up that fit all the search parameters: an article published in something called *The Crimson White*, which didn't sound all that promising. I clicked on the link and was a little surprised to discover *The Crimson White* was the student newspaper at the University of Alabama. The article itself was several years old and wasn't about Corinth County specifically. It was a feature article about an archival project the university was funding to keep track of the history of the Klan and racism in the state. There was an old black-and-white photograph, not well reproduced, of a burning cross with a young Black man hanging from a large oak tree. There was a crowd around the tree, some wearing complete robes, others with the hoods off. They were all smiling at the camera while a cross burned in the background. Some were holding cans of beer, others bottles of Coke. Some of the completely robed had to be children, given how short they appeared next to the grown men. The unhooded man closest to the camera looked familiar, and I realized he looked like a Tucker. The resemblance to the guy driving Ma Tucker's truck was uncanny.

Almost as uncanny as the resemblance between me and my uncle.

Beyond the burning cross I could see a sloping lawn in the darkness, and at the top of the slope was a house with columns.

I felt sick to my stomach and the ringing in my ears started again.

I knew exactly where that picture was taken. Every time I drove into Corinth, I drove past that tree, and that house.

I didn't read the article. I closed my laptop and walked to the window. The air conditioner was chugging along, condensation dripping, and the towel I'd put down to catch the drops was soaked through.

The white light flashed out there in the darkness again—

And I was running, out of breath, a stitch in my side but I had to keep going, I had to get away, I didn't want to die and that's what would happen if they caught me, I didn't want to die, oh God please help me…

—and my stomach lurched, and I almost threw up.

Breathing heavy, my eyes burning and my throat raw, I picked up the wet towel and staggered down the hall to the bathroom. I thought for a moment I heard a voice from behind Kelly's door—I couldn't remember if his truck had been outside when Beau and I got back, I hadn't been paying attention—and made it into the bathroom. I tossed the towel into the hamper and grabbed one from the linen closet. I turned the cold-water spigot on and splashed some onto my hot face.

As I stepped out of the bathroom, I heard the voice again from down the hall, and yes, it was a girl's voice. Jesus, Kelly—nothing like pushing your luck.

I walked back down to my bedroom and opened my laptop again.

The caption on the picture of the lynching just read: *The only documented lynching in Corinth County was thirteen-year-old Abraham Baker, visiting his grandmother from Chicago and accused of propositioning a white woman. This picture ran in the* Corinth County Weekly, *in August 1952.*

I felt sick to my stomach.

Thirteen?

Who did that skeleton out there belong to?

Another thirteen-year-old Black kid who didn't deserve to be murdered like Abraham Baker?

I started reading the article. The project's mission was documenting, and giving names to, those who died from racial violence in Alabama since the Civil War. They combed through newspaper archives, documenting the lives and deaths of the victims. The Abraham Baker case, for example, wasn't as well known or notorious as those of Emmett Till, Thomas Shipp, or James Chaney. Corinth in the 1950s was a backwater, and so Abraham didn't get the same national attention the others had. The project wouldn't have known about Abraham had they not received a letter from his sister, begging them to remember her brother and what happened to him. And the woman who'd accused him—her name was Vernita Hackworth.

Hackworth.

Hands trembling, I typed the name into my search engine.

No hits. Lots of Hackworths on the internet, but no Vernita.

I closed the laptop and placed it on my nightstand. I took another drink of water and stripped out of my shirt and shorts. Beau said the Hackworths were a big family, and that lynching had happened almost three-quarters of a century ago. The article didn't say whether Hackworth was her married or birth name. She would have to be in her late seventies at least if she was still alive.

A great-aunt, maybe?

I stretched out on the bed and closed my eyes. Suddenly I was tired, exhausted, worn-out—it had been quite a day.

The last two weeks had been a lot to handle. It had only been two weeks or so since Tradd and I had our—well, it wasn't really a breakup, was it?

He'd never been my boyfriend, had he? I'd thought he was, but all I'd been was a friend with occasional benefits, benefits when he didn't think he could do better, or didn't want to bother trying.

All he had to do was text me and I'd reply *sure come on over*.

Had I really been that desperate for someone that I settled for being treated like a fucking sex doll?

He wasn't innocent, though. He'd encouraged me, making me feel like maybe someday when he was ready to settle down it would be with *someone like you*—words he'd never meant. That was his way to keep me waiting, hooked, and available whenever he needed me. I could only imagine what he said to his friends about me—no wonder none of them tried to get closer to me or warned me about what a self-absorbed narcissistic sociopath he was.

He never loved me—and he never would, either.

But I didn't feel angry or sad or depressed or upset.

Tradd was Tradd. That's just who he was, and it wasn't personal.

I was the one who made it personal.

I exhaled. Maybe coming here was a good idea after all, giving me the distance I needed to see my life in New Orleans with greater clarity, the reality instead of the fantasy I'd created in my mind.

It was embarrassing to remember how desperate I'd been to have Tradd love me, and what I'd put up with, hoping one day he'd realize I was the right guy for him.

I was never going to be the right guy for him, ever. He'd seen that from the very beginning, and he'd kept me around for his ego.

I deserved better than that.

I didn't even take the time to turn out the lamp on my nightstand before I fell asleep.

❖

I woke up, sitting up in the bed.

The house was silent, other than the ticking and humming of my window unit.

What woke me up?

Thirsty and nervous, I slid out of the bed and walked as quietly as I could over to the door. I opened it and peered down the hallway.

There was no light under Kelly's door, and the house was still—almost like it, too, was waiting for something to happen, something inevitable.

Stop freaking yourself out, I scolded myself, gently closing the door without a sound. This place was creepy enough without my imagination running wild.

But I couldn't shake the feeling that the house was waiting for something.

It wasn't the first time I'd had the sense that the house was alive, sentient.

But that was crazy…wasn't it?

A lot of crazy things had happened since I came here. Almost like the house—or something—was just waiting for me to get here.

I didn't believe in ghosts. I didn't believe in the supernatural. I'd never had any experience of that kind in New Orleans, arguably the most haunted city in North America, but here?

Here? I could believe.

I walked carefully over to the window. The moon was high, stars scattered across the cloudless blue-black velvety sky. It was bright enough for me to see the lawn, the pump house, and even the shape of the ivy-covered rotting outhouse down the slope close to the creek. I turned my eyes to the forest itself.

The forest looked dark, impenetrable, imposing.

And then I saw it—a flash of white, out in the trees, just out of the corner of my eye.

I turned my head to look again, my eyes straining against the dark.

There it was again!

Someone—or something—was out there with a flashlight.

Near where we'd found the Klan robe.

I pulled a shirt over my head, slipped on my shorts, and slid my feet into my flip-flops. I crossed the room, worried about stepping on a board that might make a noise and wake Kelly. When I reached the door, I took a deep breath and eased it open.

Why are you so afraid to make a sound?

I didn't know, but the feeling that I needed to be quiet was intense. It was instinct, deep and primal, but felt right.

I made my way down the hallway to the stairs. There was still no light coming from underneath Kelly's door, and I listened. Hearing nothing, I headed down the stairs, tracing my hand along the wall. When I got to the bottom, I headed down the hallway to the back door. The door to Miss Sarah's room was open. She was sleeping, her mouth open. Geoffrey was also asleep, the book he was reading—*Sunburn* by Laura Lippman—open across his chest, and he was snoring a little bit. I reached in and closed the door almost all the way—I didn't want the sound of the latch catching to wake either of them—and moved to the back door. The moonlight made the tortured and bloody Christ on his cross seem creepier than in daylight. I eased the door open and stepped down onto the concrete stairs.

Are you crazy? I asked myself. The hum of insects was the only sound in the still of the night, the occasional hoot from an owl, the rustle of wings as a bird in the forest took flight as I walked along the cool grass, wet with condensation, toward the red dirt path into the forest, all the while watching to see if the white light flashed again. Was I nuts, walking out into the woods at night, with no idea who or what could be waiting for me out there in the green darkness of the forest, lurking in the shadows?

Maybe the idea was to lure me out there.

A shiver went through my body despite the heavy warm wet air. I was sweating already, the air thick, and I was thirsty—I should have grabbed a fresh bottle of water from the refrigerator.

And yet on I walked, my flip-flops sinking into the cool damp red dirt when I reached the path, my eyes still focused on the darkness inside the woods.

The sound of a car on the county road slowing down to turn onto the dirt road stopped me, and its headlights soon skittering across the empty parking area in front of the rotting old house on the other side of the road from Miss Sarah's. I froze, unable to move, a sense of terror rising up from deep inside me, and as the car began to head down the dirt road, its headlights beaming brightly out in front of it, I caught a glimpse of the red taillights as they vanished down the road, glowing through the cloud of red dirt the tires had stirred up.

I turned back to the woods, breathing hard. There was a cool, green-smelling breeze coming out of the woods, and I tentatively started down the path, keeping my eyes on the woods to my left.

Maybe—maybe I should go out there?

And then I heard it.

It was very faint, quiet, barely louder than a whisper, but it was the sound of someone—or something—moving in the woods.

In the woods to my left.

Where we found the hood.

Where I always saw the white flash.

I felt a scream forming in the base of my throat but swallowed hard, afraid to move, afraid to make any sound at all.

It wasn't my imagination, I told myself as I heard the distinct crack of a stick snapping under a footfall.

And it was—whoever it is—a lot closer than I'd thought.

Run! Every nerve ending in my body was on edge, begging me to get the hell out there, to go back to the house and into bed, shake a Xanax out of the bottle, and pull the covers up over my head, pretend this had never happened at all, it was all just a bad dream—

There was another cracking sound.

And then I heard it—a voice, so soft and quiet it almost sounded hollow—calling softly, *Are you there?*

My stomach clenched tightly.

Are you there?

The voice came again, hollow and empty, almost like an echo from another time, another place, from anywhere but here. I sensed that it was almost human, but not quite.

There were no such things as ghosts, I reminded myself.

My rational brain rejected the idea, but my instincts didn't care.

Because if ghosts weren't real, whatever I was hearing, whatever was out there, was human.

And that was even more terrifying.

I saw movement in the trees ahead of me. I strained to see through the darkness, wishing I'd thought to bring my phone with me, so I could shine it into that inky velvet black ahead of me, then was overwhelmed with emotion, a desire, a feeling of love so strong it almost knocked me down, almost made it impossible for me to breathe. I'd never felt anything, any emotion, this strongly, and I reached out to a pine tree for support, as tears filled my eyes and—

The feeling emptied out of me as quickly as it came, leaving me empty and hollow and weak.

There was another cracking sound in the trees, and all the bugs, the insects, the birds, everything in the woods, went completely silent.

And now the emptiness was being filled, filled with absolute terror, a fear for my life, because whatever was out here in the woods with me wanted to kill me, wanted me dead, and before I knew what I was doing, I started running, running away from the big old run-down house and toward the ruins, the flip-flops slapping against the soles of my feet as I ran down into the gully and across the little bridge over the creek and up the other side, the dirt giving way beneath me, and they're close, whoever it was, right behind me, and they wanted me to die, they hated me and I could almost feel the hate—it's palpable and alive, so alive I can almost feel its breath on my back, and I ran, still I ran on, down into the gully, and then I tripped, skinning my knees and going down hard, my breath knocked out of me, and I sobbed in terror and fear and frustration yet managed to get back up. On I ran, hearing whoever—whatever—it was behind me, I could sense their hate, how much they wanted me dead, and I gave in to the emotions. Sobs were coming out of me, broken sobs, tears running down my face. I kept running, my calves and thighs on fire as I went up the slope and finally got to the top and broke into the clearing where the ruins stood—

And it was gone.

Whatever it was I'd felt was gone.

I sat down, hard, in the dirt, gasping for air. The moon was so bright out there in the clearing…

And for just a moment, I saw Blackwood Hall as it looked before it burned.

Rising up from its foundations, majestic and beautiful, painted a white that glowed in the moonlight, the white marble columns rising up to the roof they supported.

And there was a light…There was a light in one of the windows on the second floor.

I got to my feet.

It was like I'd gone back in time.

The trees were gone. All I could see was grass, spreading out in inky-black darkness over the hills and slopes. I could see where the road was, and as I stood watching the house, the front door opened and a form slipped out, quietly, secretly, shutting the door carefully.

I must be losing my mind raced through my head as I watched the form, a young boy I thought but wasn't sure. His form was shadowy as it moved down the front steps of the house.

An owl hooted in the silence, hooted again. Everything shimmered and was gone, like it had all been a dream.

Chapter Nineteen

I was rudely dragged from the depths of sleep by someone shaking my shoulder roughly.

I opened my eyes and looked up at Kelly. I blinked a few times before it registered that he was in my room and didn't look happy. "What are you doing?" I finally managed to get out in a sticky mumble. I reached for the water bottle on my table and sat up farther in bed. "What do you want?"

"Your boyfriend's here," he sneered at me, stepping away from the bed. He was wearing a mutilated T-shirt—the kind guys like him wear, cutting off not just the sleeves but also the sides, so the front and back were only held together at the bottom by about an inch of cotton. His left nipple was peeking out the right side. He was also wearing blue board shorts. I glanced over at the clock on the nightstand as I took a nice drink of water. It was almost ten. I shouldn't still be in bed.

"For one thing, he isn't my boyfriend," I said, "and for another, don't just come into my room without knocking." *This has happened before* went through my head.

How was that even possible?

His hand clenched, and his face turned red. I thought he was going to hit me *—he has hit me before* went through my head, immediately followed by *no, he hasn't*—but he had the decency to flush. "Beau's in the kitchen waiting for you," was all he said and went out the door.

I got out of bed and felt that weird sense of déjà vu again. *It's all happened before* kept running through my head as I walked to the bathroom, and as I brushed my teeth, washed my face, and ran a brush through my mop of tangled hair. I knew what déjà vu was, of course, but had never experienced it before.

And it was happening a lot.

I heard Kelly's truck pulling out as I walked down the stairs. When I walked into the kitchen, Beau was sitting at the table, drinking coffee. He gave me an odd look. "How was *your* night?"

I poured myself a cup of coffee and sighed. "Are you hungry?" I asked, opening the refrigerator and getting the eggs and bacon.

"Sure."

"This is going to sound crazy, but I have to tell someone." I started talking as I put the skillet on for the bacon and started cracking eggs into a bowl. I started from the beginning, with the way I'd reacted to the house when I saw it the day I arrived, to the weird feelings I'd been experiencing all along that I couldn't explain. I told him about walking out into the woods last night. I told him about the weird feelings I'd been having as I melted some butter in the hot skillet and poured the eggs into it. Bacon was already cooking in the microwave.

"You're sure you weren't just dreaming?" Beau took another drink from his coffee cup.

I turned back to the eggs and start stirring them with a rubber spatula. "I wasn't dreaming, Beau."

"Maybe you were sleepwalking," he replied. "My sister used to do that. One time she wandered out of the house and into the road and almost got killed."

I hesitated, unsure. It sounded so much more reasonable in the light of day that I walked in my sleep than had—had been having—some paranormal experience. It was possible I could have walked in my sleep and dreamed it all. "No, I don't think so." I started spooning eggs onto plates, alongside the bacon and the buttered toast. I turned off the stove and placed the skillet in the sink, carrying both plates over to the table. I took another drink of my coffee. "It was so real," I said, remembering, a chill running down my back, and the hairs on my arms standing back up. "If it was just a dream—"

Beau's phone interrupted with a snippet of "Telephone" by

Lady Gaga and Beyoncé, over and over. He grabbed for his phone, placed his finger on the screen, and said, "Hello, Dr. Brady." He listened for a moment.

I kept eating. With the bright sunlight streaming through the windows, it did all seem unreal to me. But I hadn't been imagining those flashes, had I, and those *had* led us to find the Klan robe. And the skeleton out at the ruins was very real.

Something was going on around here—I just didn't know what. Was I in danger?

You're such a drama queen, Tradd's voice taunted inside my head. *You didn't worry when you found out a meth lab was over the ridge, did you?*

Beau put his phone down on the table and cleared his throat. "That was Dr. Brady," he said, his voice trembling slightly. "The medical examiner finished checking out the skeleton."

"Is it one of the Lost Boys?" I asked, even though I was certain it wasn't.

Beau shook his head. "Well, it's a boy—a young man at any rate—but it can't be one of the Lost Boys. Dr. Brady was right—the skeleton, whoever he was, apparently, he had some work done on his teeth, something that dates him to the second half of the twentieth century. And his neck was broken—that's what killed him." He cleared his throat. "They can't tell if the head wound happened before or after he died."

The second half of the twentieth century.

"Uncle Jacob," I said. "He didn't run away. Someone killed him and buried him out there by the ruins."

"Jacob was seventeen when he ran away." Beau shrugged. "Why would anyone kill him?"

"I don't know," I said, "Maybe the white trash crime family down the road? Maybe he saw something he wasn't supposed to?"

Other than the ticking of the window unit and the clicking of the ceiling fan, there was silence in the kitchen.

I got up, taking his dirty plate and stacking it on top of mine. "I wonder how Miss Sarah got the idea he'd run away," I mused, rinsing off the dishes before placing them in the dishwasher. "Mom hired a private eye to try to find him years ago, and they couldn't find any trace of him anywhere," I went on. "If he was dead and buried out at the ruins..." I shivered.

I glanced through the doorway to the closed door to Miss Sarah's room. I remembered the way she'd reacted when she'd first seen me. She'd been terrified.

Why would she react that way if he'd just run away?

She knew more than she'd ever told anyone.

I don't know how I knew, but I did.

"Kelly was acting weird this morning," Beau replied. "Did something happen between you two?"

"Other than him being a homophobe, not really." I put some detergent in the dishwasher and turned it on. "But he's going to behave himself, or I'm going to have Uncle Dewey kick him out." I leaned back against the counter. "Miss Sarah is *my* grandmother. This house belongs to my family. He is here as a guest, and if he's not going to treat me or my friends decent, he can pack his shit up and move to Troy now."

"Kelly's not a homophobe." Beau frowned. "Trust me. He's one of the good ones, believe me." His face flushed. "He was two years behind me in school, but he's always been big, you know? And he used to stop kids from picking on me, stuck up for me, when they were, you know, bullying me?" His brow furrowed. "I mean, he might be an asshole, but he's not a homophobe."

I hesitated. The last thing in the world I wanted to do was hurt Beau, but sticking up for Kelly? "He warned me about you," I said slowly. "He called you a fag and warned me to stay away from you."

"I find that hard to believe."

"I'm not making it up!"

"I guess," Beau replied. He sounded confused. "But I'm telling you, he used to stick up for me. Things would have been really rough for me in high school if not for him."

"You must be glad to be out of here," I said. "Maybe he just didn't like seeing you get picked on—but that doesn't mean he can't be a homophobe. Anyway, what do you feel like doing today?"

He swallowed. "Um, if you don't mind, I was thinking..." His face flushed a dark red that was almost purple. "If you don't mind, or you don't have anything else to do..."

There was the unfinished inventory, but the thought of going up to the attic and digging through boxes and trunks wasn't appealing. The window units had helped, but it was still stuffy and dusty up there, and the cooler air didn't get rid of the spiders. "What did you have in mind?"

"Your uncle closed down the dig," he went on. "But there's nothing stopping *us* from exploring, is there?" His eyes shone. "I want to look for the family cemetery."

We sprayed ourselves down with bug spray in the mudroom before heading into the woods.

When we reached where the path began at the tree line, Beau pointed down at the red dirt. "Look." The footprints from my flip-flops were clearly visible.

"I told you I didn't dream it," I replied.

"Doesn't mean you weren't sleepwalking," he said as he knelt down by the first footprint. He looked down the path.

A strange stillness dropped over us. Every so often I heard the rustle of wings as a bird took flight, and the cicadas were still making that annoying humming sound. Crickets were chirping, and gnats and fleas were flying around—every so often there was that horrible close buzzing sound as one flew into my ear before I smashed it with a well-placed index finger—but other than that, it was curiously quiet and still. No animal noises, no dogs barking in the distance, no cars going by on the county road. We continued down the steady decline. I looked back. Once the house was no longer in sight over the top of the ridge, it seemed like we were deep inside an untamed forest.

I wondered if this was how my ancestors felt when they first came to this place.

"Do you believe in ghosts?" I stopped and asked.

"Ghosts?" He paused too and looked at me, confused. "Restless spirits? Rattling chains and all that? Of course not. There's no such thing as ghosts." He put his hands on his hips again, his eyebrows drawing together over the bridge of his nose. "Are you thinking it's a ghost you've been seeing?"

"I don't know," I replied.

"And you think the skeleton is your uncle?"

I nodded. "I do. It makes sense. I mean, how many other teenage boys have disappeared from around here in the last fifty years?"

"I guess we could look it up at the library," Beau replied, starting to walk down the gradual slope.

I followed. "You've not heard any stories?"

"Not about boys disappearing," he said, picking up a long, mossy stick with a fork at the end. "And you'd hear about that, don't you think? It's the kind of thing my crazy mother would have tried to scare me with, you know, *If you stay out late or you don't do what I say, you'll disappear, too.*" He rolled his eyes. "I mean, I never even heard the story about your uncle. Of course, by the time I was in school, there weren't any Donelsons my age. I mean, everyone knows who your family is, and the old stories…but there aren't any recent ones."

"Not even about Miss Sarah?" I was panting a little as we crossed over the little bridge at the bottom of the slope and started up the gentle slope leading to the ruins. "There had to be stories about her."

"No, not really," he replied. He stopped for a minute and wiped his face with his T-shirt. He took a drink of his water. "It's amazing how the humidity just settles into these low-lying areas, isn't it? Miss Sarah was someone you didn't want to mess with," he went on. "Miss Sarah didn't give a fuck what anyone thought, and she didn't care about hurting anyone's feelings. She spoke her mind. If she thought you were a fool, she made sure you knew she thought you were a fool. What was it like having her for a grand-mother?"

"I don't know—our family isn't close. I haven't been down here in over ten years, at least. I only see Dewey and his family when they came up to visit us in Chicago. I've not seen Miss Sarah in—wow, I don't know, eleven years?"

"Wow. That's so not how kinfolk are down here." He stared at me. "I mean, I don't see my family that much but they're *there*, you know? I mean…wow."

"I don't…" I stopped walking. I took a deep breath. "I've always thought something must have happened," I finally said, giving voice to a suspicion I've never shared with anyone before. "Between Miss

Sarah and my mother. I don't know what it was, but my mother never talks about her—she refuses to talk about Miss Sarah, only brings her up when she has to, you know?"

My childhood memories weren't clear. I remembered the house, the woods, being afraid of Miss Sarah, but I couldn't remember why. I couldn't remember if I actually *was* afraid of her, or if my mother somehow made me afraid of her—why would I think that?—in some way.

I didn't remember ever being hugged or kissed by Miss Sarah. No birthday cards, no Christmas cards, no acknowledgments of milestones like graduating from high school or anything. It wasn't disappointing because there wasn't anything to miss. It was just how the Donelsons were.

But Dewey and his kids—the warm and happy way they were with each other and all the pictures of his kids in the house, family pictures framed and hung everywhere, every little thing commemorated, made much of, a big deal.

My mom...not so much.

She was not demonstrative, even with her husbands.

Dad never talked about their brief marriage—it was a no-win for him, really, and she could be a shark.

We reached the ruins in silence, other than our breathing and the sloshing of water in our bottles. The sky was shockingly blue, not even a wisp of a cloud daring to dance across its expanse, like a gorgeous baby-blue canopy being held up by the tops of the pine trees.

As soon as we stepped into the little clearing, I saw the crime scene tape fluttering in the light breeze. The area where we found the skeleton was a mess. The little wooden fence-like thing we'd built around the skeleton to keep it from being washed away by the storm runoff was still there, covered in dried red dirt. The crime scene tape was stapled to it. An entire area of the edge of the plateau had crumbled away, right where the runoff had been going over the edge.

"This area must look completely different than it did before the house burned," I said, turning to look at the ruins. I'd never noticed before how exposed the cellar walls were. An image fluttered through my mind—

—and the house is still there, the columns dirty but solid and not blackened from flame and smoke. There is glass in the windows, and where the cracks between the lumber boards are in the sides of the house there's red dirt and some greenish moss or mold or something. There are no trees, and I hear a horse neighing somewhere nearby. I can smell smoke—someone is cooking over an open flame. There are other houses, farther down the slope on the other side of the house, thatched roofs with chimneys jutting up into the sky, and I realize, with horror, that those must be where the enslaved people lived.

"Hello?" I call but there's no response, no sign of life anywhere, everything frozen in place there's no wind or no bugs or anything, just the smell of a cooking fire and the baby blue sky up overhead, free of clouds and free of—

"Jamie?" A boy's voice calls out, and I freeze, unable to move, unable to say anything.

I hear someone approaching, coming around from the back of the house.

And that frozen sensation is gone, now things are moving, there's wisps of clouds drifting across the blue expanse of sky, bees buzzing around the rosebushes in front of the house, the smell of roses and lilacs, mimosa and honeysuckle and jasmine all mixing together.

"Jamie, where are you?" the voice calls again, and just at that moment the boy comes around the back of the house, and he looks like Kelly.

"Jake? Jake, are you okay?"

I snapped back into the present. I had gone cold all over. I was so cold, it didn't make sense—it was a hot summer afternoon in rural Alabama, and I shouldn't be cold, but I was. "Yeah," I finally managed to say. I looked at the far slope and saw nothing but trees and underbrush and bushes.

No cabin roofs, no fire, no jasmine or roses or lilacs or honeysuckle in the air.

"What happened?" Beau's face was pale. "It was scary." He shook his head. "You scared me."

"I—I don't know, Beau." I didn't know how to explain it to him.

"You went away somewhere." He shivered, too, despite the heat.

"Come on," I said, and led him around to the front of the ruins, sat on the front porch steps, covered in moss and mildew and damp. "I don't know what happened, but let me try to explain it to you."

"You think you went back in time?" Beau said when I finished. His voice was skeptical, doubt written plainly on his tanned face.

"I don't know. Maybe it was a vision. I don't know." I took a few deep breaths. It was fading away, taking the fear and concern with it. "What did you see?"

"You just…stopped." Beau wiped his face with his hand. "One minute you were talking, and you just stopped, midsentence, like someone switched you off. You just stood there, staring, not saying anything, not doing anything, barely breathing. I didn't know what to do. I just kept calling your name. I shook you a few times. I was about to slap you when you came out of it. I've never seen anyone do that before."

I shivered, wrapping my arms around myself. "Did you—did you feel anything?"

"What do you mean?"

I didn't know how to explain it. How did I tell him that this place felt bad to me, wrong?

"The guy looked just like Kelly," I went on. "There's something about this place—this place in particular, but this whole place, including the main house." I pointed in that direction. "There's something wrong here. I don't know why or who or how or what, but it's just not right. There's something off here."

"Well, if you believe in ghosts, the ruins are supposed to be haunted, but you know that."

I stared at him. "No, I didn't. I've never been told anything about ghosts."

"I can't believe you know so little of your family history." He sighed. "I guess you weren't kidding about not being a close family. The ghosts of the ruins of Blackwood Hall? You never came across that, reading about the Lost Boys?"

"Let me guess—they haunt the place."

Beau laughed. "No, not them. The Yankee who killed them and burned the place to the ground."

"Why would he haunt this place?"

"There's a story that Louisa Blackwood killed him and buried him somewhere on the property."

Just like *Gone with the Wind*. Seriously, Confederate apologists needed to be more creative.

"I thought she died of typhus. Tell me the story while we look for the cemetery." I stood up. "I don't want to hang around here for much longer."

"Okay." Beau stood up. "Well, according to the records, the family plot was behind the house." He started around the corner of the house, and I caught up with him. We walked back to the plateau's edge. "What story did you read about the Lost Boys?"

"It was a chapter in *Civil War Legends of Alabama*," I replied. "Just that the house burned and the boys and their mother disappeared." I shrugged as we found a place where the edge wasn't so crumbly and started down. The slope was steep behind the house, and we grabbed hold of trees occasionally to help keep our balance. "It never made any sense to me—I just figured it was some romantic legend Confederates clung to after they lost the war."

"Not quite." Beau laughed. "According to this story, the boys did disappear, but Louisa didn't. The house burned, but when her second son, named Ezekiel like his father, came home from the war, Louisa was living in one of the slave cabins. The enslaved people were also long gone. But she was completely insane. Zeke tried taking care of her but eventually had to put her in an asylum over in Birmingham. The story he got from her, or what he pieced together, was simple." We reached the bottom of the slope.

"Wouldn't the cemetery be on level ground somewhere?" I asked. "I mean, given what the rain does around here, wouldn't the graves wash away?"

"Yeah." We started climbing the other side. "Anyway, Louisa was out picking berries apparently when the soldier came. She never saw what happened to the boys, or so she said." Beau tapped a finger to his temple. "The story was that he killed her sons in front of her, and that made her crazy. He set the house on fire and tried to rape her, but she killed him and buried him somewhere."

"So which story is true? Did she die of typhus or in a mental hospital?" I asked as we climbed up the slope. My legs and butt were burning by the time we reached the top, and Beau gasped. "What's the matter?"

Ahead of us, on another flat plain, was a rickety wooden

structure with a rusted tin roof, surrounded by trees and bushes. Kudzu was climbing up one side, the leafy vine beginning to crawl across the roof.

"Shhh," he whispered and started backing away, pointing to something off to one side of the structure.

I didn't recognize it at first, but then a memory of something— some movie or television show, something—popped into my mind, and I knew immediately what it was.

It was a still. For making moonshine whiskey.

The Tuckers.

CHAPTER TWENTY

I was afraid to breathe.

I glanced back over my shoulder. This shed was in an almost direct line to where we found the skeleton. Someone inside the shack was humming tunelessly, occasionally breaking the humming to sing—badly—lyrics to some song I didn't recognize, and the singer didn't know all the words—once he was finished with what I took to be the chorus, he went back to humming again. There were some other noises from inside the shed, clinking and clanking, and I caught a big whiff of a bleach smell, and my eyes started watering.

Beau grabbed me by the arm, and when I turned to look at him, he was holding an index finger up to his lips.

Like I needed to be told to be quiet? Please.

No, that wasn't bleach—it was ammonia. And you used ammonia to make meth.

This was getting better and better by the minute.

Of course, it was their meth lab. Why make meth somewhere else when you've got a perfect setup already in place for the moonshine?

Maybe the skeleton wasn't my uncle. Maybe—maybe it was someone the Tuckers had killed for some reason.

But no one had gone missing besides my uncle.

If we weren't careful, they'd be digging up *our* skeletons in the future.

I heard some twigs snapping behind us in the woods, and my blood ran cold.

The last place in the world I wanted to be caught was outside the Tucker combination meth lab and corn whiskey still.

I was terrified.

To our left, I could hear an electrical buzzing getting louder. It was a sound I recognized, and it took me a moment to realize what it was.

It had been a while.

When I was young, my father thought I might have an interest in sports, like he did. He'd been a star athlete in his high school, the big three: football, basketball, and baseball. When it soon became apparent that not only did none of those sports interest me, but I also had no aptitude for them, Dad was puzzled. He must have thought sports was a genetic thing. But he had started playing golf after college, and since I didn't have any interest in team sports, he thought maybe I was an individual sport kid. He paid for my lessons with a pro at his country club, but it never really took. I thought it was boring. My father was a great guy but never had a lot of patience, at least not with me. After three lessons, he took me out to a driving range because I needed to practice. I didn't want to do it and just teed up a ball and swung wildly at it. There was so much to remember—balance your weight, keep your left arm straight, don't move your head, swing the club with your head as the centerpoint of the swing—and I didn't care enough to focus. My mind wandered while I was teeing up and swinging, and the ball never went far or flew off into the air the way it was supposed to.

I never could understand why he bought me clubs, why he kept insisting every weekend I spent with his family with nice weather that we go hit a bucket of balls. I hated it, just wanted it to be over, so I could get back home and curl up with a book or play a video game or watch a movie. He even tried to enlist Mom in his campaign to turn me into a golfer.

That didn't go well for him.

Before Dad finally gave up on me as a golfer, he took me to play a round at his country club.

And that was where I'd first heard this sound.

It was an electric golf cart, coming up the dirt path leading to the raw earth surrounding the shack.

I pointed back the way we'd come, and Beau nodded. We moved carefully back down the slope, trying not to make noise, and once we were low enough to be concealed by a bush, I peered through the branches to see the golf cart pull up in front of the shack. Ma Tucker was behind the wheel, puffing on a cigarette and sweating through her cotton housedress. A lanky, rangy guy wearing filthy jeans, flip-flops, and a dirty ribbed white tank top climbed down from the passenger seat and picked up two enormous jugs of something from the back of the golf cart. Despite his leanness—I could see his bones through the reddish-brown leathery tanned skin—he swung the heavy looking jugs off the back without any difficulty or strain and carried them to the shack's front door. He kicked the door open and stepped inside, and Ma Tucker turned the cart around.

She paused for a moment, like she'd heard something, her lumpy form becoming alert. She looked up, around, and finally turned to look directly at the bush we were hiding behind.

I don't even think I breathed, I was so still. Beau was perfectly still beside me as we waited.

My legs wanted to take off running and get as far away from here as I could get—maybe even get in the damned car and head back to New Orleans.

Seriously, Mom, what the ever-loving *fuck* were you thinking, sending me here for the summer?

I was just about ready to take off running when she tossed the cigarette out into the dirt, resettled herself in the cart, and headed back down the path.

When she disappeared from view, we started inching our way back down the way we came. We didn't speak, didn't make any noise, just carefully picked our way back down the hill, waiting until we were so deep into the woods that no one could see or hear us before we spoke.

"What are we going to do?" I half whispered when we reached the ruins again.

"What do you mean? About what?" Beau looked at me like I'd lost my mind. "If you think the sheriff doesn't know about their business, think again. Everyone knows what the Tuckers get up to, how they make money. You saw that guy, right? That was Poochie

Tucker. He's mean as a snake and just looking for a reason to cut someone up. They call him Poochie because he killed a dog when he was about three years old." He kicked at a clod of dirt. "The Tuckers think that kind of shit is funny."

I felt sick to my stomach. "Nice." I looked back in the direction of Miss Sarah's house. "Miss Sarah—does she know?"

"I don't see how she can't." Beau slapped at a mosquito on his tan arm, leaving a bloody smear behind. "Everyone knows. And yes, it helps that the Tuckers are related to most of the people in the county sheriff's office."

"Moonshine." I shook my head. "I can't believe that's still a thing."

Beau laughed. "Corinth County used to be dry, so they did a good business for a real long time. The county's still dry, but Corinth—the town—is wet. There's a liquor store there, it's the only place you can legally buy booze in the whole county, and they have limited hours and aren't open on Sundays. So if you want booze in a pinch, you come to the Tuckers." He frowned. "I'm not sure when they branched out into meth, but…"

In New Orleans you could buy liquor at gas stations. Meth was harder to come by, but not by much. Meth was never my drug of choice, well, until the episode that landed me here—I preferred weed—but Tradd and his friends had introduced me to Molly and Ecstasy and cocaine and Special K and even GHB.

Meth scared me, always had. Tradd and his friends wouldn't touch it. *Highly addictive, and it makes you ugly*, Tradd told me once. *Your teeth rot, your skin gets nasty, you get sores, and your hair falls out.* He'd gestured at himself. *I've worked too hard to look this good to throw it all away on meth when there are better, more fun drugs out there.*

God, what an asshole he'd been! Why hadn't I seen it before?

"So, the sheriff's department is crooked?"

"I wouldn't say it in front of one of them, but"—he gestured back toward the shed—"how else have they operated so long without cooperation from the cops?"

I knew being a law enforcement officer of any kind wasn't a guarantee of noble purpose, and there were crooked cops, but this? This was insane. And my grandmother knew about it?

Hell, she probably got a cut from them.

No wonder Mom never wanted to come down here.

"And that's our land?" I said as we started walking along the side of the slope.

"Tuckers have been renting that land for generations," Beau said. It was getting darker—at first, I thought it was the tree cover, but glancing up I saw dark clouds coming in. The air was getting cooler and wetter, which meant it was going to rain again.

And I'd thought it rained a lot in New Orleans.

"Shall we head back to the house?"

Beau started to protest, but when I pointed up to the sky, he nodded. We didn't speak as we walked back through the woods to the house. "I think I'm going to head home," Beau said when we came out of the woods. "I need to do some stuff around my place. Tell you what, I'll come back out tomorrow, and we can look for the graveyard some more. At least we know now where not to look."

If the cemetery was near that shed, it could stay lost forever as far as I was concerned.

He drove off, just as the big heavy drops of rain started falling and lightning forked through the sky. The wind was also picking up.

I headed inside through the mudroom, and as I entered the kitchen, I looked off to the right, through the hall door. Miss Sarah's door was closed. I resisted the urge to go in there and ask her about the Tucker operation, but at the same time, yeah, I didn't really want to know.

It's not like she would answer my questions, anyway.

I'd just gotten a bottle of water from the refrigerator when I heard a vehicle pulling in outside. I glanced out the side window and saw Kelly getting out of his truck in the pouring rain. He was already drenched in sweat, his hair plastered to the side of his head, and he was carrying a gym bag. He dashed for the front porch, and just as lightning lit up the house, I heard the front door open and shut. I didn't want to talk to him and hoped he didn't come into the kitchen. I heard the stairs moaning and sighed with relief as I realized he was going upstairs.

I listened to his footsteps head down the upstairs hallway and into his bedroom. The coast finally clear, I was about to head upstairs when Miss Sarah's door opened. I could hear Geneva's voice, reading out loud to her, and Geneva smiled at me, book in hand and still reading, as she walked back to her chair. What the hell, I thought and stood in the doorway looking in. Geneva was seated in a chair on the other side of Miss Sarah's bed, and Miss Sarah's head was turned to look at her as she read. It was a library book—I could tell by the shiny cellophane wrap around the cover. Geneva looked up. "Jake! I was just fixin' to come look for you."

Miss Sarah's head rolled on the pillow to glare at me.

"Why?"

"Child, I need to eat." She laughed and put the book down on the nightstand. It was *Dare Me*, by Megan Abbott. "You mind reading to Miss Sarah while I have my lunch?"

I didn't see how I could say no. It was part of my job and why Mom was paying me to be here, after all, and Geneva didn't take advantage of me the way she could have.

"Sure." I crossed the room and picked up the book, sitting down in the chair as Geneva left the room. I started reading out loud, stumbling over words at first, but eventually picking up a rhythm. The rain drummed a steady pattern on the roof, but at least it wasn't one of those horrible gully washer storms.

"*Ja-cob.*"

Her voice was low, so low I wasn't sure whether I'd heard or imagined it, but when I looked at her over the top of the book, her eyes were focused on me, her lips moving as she tried to form more words. That stare of hers, though—it sent chills down my spine.

I wondered again what it must have been like growing up in the house.

And was grateful I hadn't.

I marked the place in the book and set it in my lap. "Yes?"

"Stay...away...from...the...ruins," she whispered, sweat beading up on her forehead from the effort to talk. "Danger... dangerous."

"Dangerous?" What did she mean? "Why is it dangerous out there?"

She shook her head weakly and closed her eyes. Within moments I could tell by her breathing that she'd fallen asleep, or she wanted me to think she had.

I walked over to the warped, leaning bookcase resting in the far corner of the room, next to the enormous armoire. No sense in reading to her while she was sleeping, and maybe there was something else for me to read in here. The top shelves were filled with well-thumbed paperbacks, everything from Agatha Christie to Stephen King. The bottom shelf was filled with yearbooks from Kenilworth High School. The years on the spines meant they must have been her children's, running from 1961–1989, eighteen years. I pulled out the oldest one, and the spine creaked as I opened it to the index at the back. I found the *D*s and saw, sure enough, Duncan Donelson was the only Donelson in the book. I flipped to the indicated page, and it was the first grade.

And there he was. He had a gap in his front teeth, grinning wide for the camera, and his hair was cut short, with a cowlick standing up at the back of his head. I calculated my mother's age and grabbed the book that must have been her senior yearbook. I flipped to the page for the seniors, and there she was, smiling at the camera, so young I almost caught my breath. Her hair was parted in the center and feathered back away from her face, and that smile! I don't think I'd ever seen her smile like that, so joyful and happy. Beneath her picture read: *Glynis Donelson, cheerleader 1, 2, 3, 4, Homecoming Queen, Pep Club 1, 2, 3, 4, class secretary 1, 4, National Honor Society 2, 3, 4.*

Somehow, I never pictured my mother as either a cheerleader or a Homecoming Queen.

I flipped through the pages, seeing her cheerleading at football and basketball games, candid shots with friends, and she was voted Most Popular in the senior class, as well as Most Likely to Succeed.

Her classmates had no idea how right they were.

I started working my way back through the yearbooks, looking for pictures of my namesake uncle, the one who ran away.

I knew he didn't run away.

The resemblance was there, I noticed, as I paged through yearbook after yearbook, flipping pages, but there were some images where the pictures could have been me, and others where there was only a slight resemblance.

"All right, I'm back." I jumped when Geneva came back into the room. "Studying your family history?" She smiled.

"Yeah." I started putting the books back on the shelf in date order. She was about my mother's age, I realized, and I asked, "You're from Corinth County originally, right, Geneva?"

She nodded. "Born and raised, Jake."

I stood up, gesturing at the older yearbooks. "It strikes me as weird there weren't any Black kids at Kenilworth."

"We used to have our own schools," Geneva replied. "They didn't close down the colored schools—that's what they called them—until, I don't know, I was about ready to start high school. They decided to bus us to town to go to County High rather than have us at Kenilworth." She sniffed. "Wondering why it took so long to desegregate? They had to have time to build and start the private school, Corinth Christian Academy, so the richer kids didn't have to mix with the lesser folk." She made a face. "Eventually the county kids got to go to Kenilworth instead of taking a bus into town. It was a rough time."

"I'm sorry." It seemed inadequate.

"It is what it is," Geneva replied. "Your mom was the smartest girl in the county. We all knew she'd wind up going someplace."

"It's hard for me to picture her growing up here."

Geneva laughed. "Lord, Jake, it's hard for anyone to imagine their parents were ever young!"

"You knew my uncles, too? The ones who—"

"Shh." She glanced over at the bed. Miss Sarah hadn't moved. "She never got over that, you know. Her whole world revolved around those boys."

Miss Sarah murmured something, shifted in her sleep.

"Go on, get out of here, go do something fun," Geneva whispered. "If you want, I can talk to you after Geoffrey gets here."

She closed the door gently behind me.

I walked back into the kitchen. It was still raining.

"Is your boyfriend going to be spending the night?"

Kelly could move soundlessly when he wanted to. I hadn't even heard him walk into the kitchen, let alone get so close behind me. He had a protein shake in one hand and a smirk on his face.

He was also standing way too close to me.

I tried to move to my right, but he moved with me. "What are you doing?" I said. "Stop it—you're making me uncomfortable."

"Having your boyfriend in the house makes me uncomfortable." Still that dangerous look in his eye, that nasty smirk on his face. He flexed his arm as he drank the rest of the shake. His arm looked gigantic, menacing, dangerous. He tossed the plastic cup into the sink and leaned closer toward me.

I had to tilt my head back to look up at him. "He's not my boyfriend, for one thing, and for another, too bad if you don't like it." I was quaking inside but would die before I let him see it.

Always stand up to bullies. I heard my mother's voice inside my head.

Yeah, easy for her to say. She didn't have a two-hundred-thirty-pound muscular redneck homophobe standing right in front of her, either.

"You expect me to believe you spent the night at his place and nothing happened?"

"I don't care what you believe." I raised my chin defiantly. "And it's none of your business. I'm her only family in this house, so I'm in charge whether you like it or not. If I want to have Cirque du Soleil over for an orgy in the living room, I can do it."

I regretted the words as soon as I said them. Sure, kick the orphan in the nuts while you're at it.

Kelly took a step back and bit his lower lip.

"I'm sorry," I stammered. "I shouldn't have said that, Kelly. This is your home, of course. But don't tell me what I can and can't do, okay? I'm sorry you have a problem with gay people, but I'm one, and Beau is my friend, and as long as I'm staying here, he's welcome here. If it bothers you that much, just stay away from us."

I was terrified—and again, had that weird feeling that this had happened before.

He stepped back again. "Just don't get any ideas."

"Don't fucking flatter yourself." I walked past him and headed for the doorway, but when I got there, he said my name.

"For the record, I'm family, too."

I rolled my eyes. "I know you're a distant cousin—"

"No, it's more than that." He stepped closer to where I was

standing. "It didn't strike you as weird, that picture of your uncles? That looked so much like you and me? You never wondered about that?"

"No. Should I have?"

He crossed his arms across his chest and smirked again. "Dewey is my father."

CHAPTER TWENTY-ONE

Of course.

His resemblance to my dead uncle had never made sense. I wasn't an expert on genetics, but I'd never understood how a distant relative could look so much like a close relative. My uncles had been brothers. The Lost Boys, who'd also born a striking resemblance to us, were also brothers.

Kelly and I were first cousins. I wondered if my mother knew and hadn't told me.

He stood there, his big arms folded in front of his chest, smirking.

"Does Miss Sarah—" I stopped. Of course she knew. It was why she let him come live here, why she'd taken in the child of a relative so distant no one was able to explain the connection. She wasn't a Good Samaritan—she was housing her grandson.

Who just happened to look like the favorite child she'd lost years ago.

Kelly's Tucker mother wasn't a relative. That was just a cover story Miss Sarah made up to hide that Dewey had a bastard son. Couldn't have any scandal attached to the Donelson name, no sir.

No wonder seeing me had such an effect on her. Kelly and I looked just like her dead sons.

"I have just as much a right to be here as you do," Kelly went on. "I'm family, too."

"You know," I said slowly, "I don't know what your problem with me is, or why you've been such a dick to me, but Beau told me he thought you were one of the good ones. He didn't believe me when I told him you called him a fag." His smirk faltered. "You used to stick up for him when kids were bullying him, giving him a hard time. He still thinks you're one of the good guys. But you aren't, are you."

It was a good exit line, and I took it, hoping he wouldn't come after me. I was shaking. I've never liked conflict—one of the reasons, I supposed, it was so easy for me to let Tradd walk all over me.

No more, I told myself as I went up the stairs, ignoring the moaning and groaning of the wood beneath my feet. I wasn't going to put up with anyone's crap anymore. That Jake was gone forever.

There were so many secrets hidden inside this house. What other secrets was this haunted house of horrors keeping?

I grabbed my laptop and headed down the hall to the attic staircase. I'd been neglecting the inventory, and maybe focusing on doing the job Mom was paying me to do would help calm me down, make me forget all the crazy shit going on around here.

A wave of cold air washed over me as I opened the door to the staircase. I flipped on the light switch and started climbing the steps. My nostrils filled with the musty, moldy smell of the attic when I reached the doorway at the top of the stairs. I closed my eye and hesitated, waiting to see if I reacted in some way to the attic. The only sounds I could hear were the air conditioners humming and the rain on the roof. I didn't feel anything. It was just an old attic, filled with cobwebs and dust and old furniture and boxes. I flipped on those lights and walked into the attic.

I pulled my phone out of my pocket and texted Mom: *Why didn't you tell me Kelly is Dewey's son? Why the big secret?*

That should get her attention. If she didn't already know, well, surprise!

If she did, she had some explaining to do.

I set up my laptop on top of a box and opened the spreadsheet I'd been using.

I walked to the other end of the attic, where I'd left off working the last time. It felt like it had been weeks since I'd last been up here. The boxes I'd already gone through were marked with an *X* written with a black Sharpie, still sitting on top of the last box I opened. I stepped over to the unmarked box next to it and noticed out the grimy window that I could see the shed on top of the hill, where the

Tuckers manufactured their illegal shit. It seemed like we'd climbed up forever to get up there, but from here it didn't look that high. I could also see the ridge on the other side of the hollow from the shack, which was a lot higher. In fact, the ridges seemed to go up in size the farther they were from this house.

I put my hand on the dirty window, leaving a handprint in the dust.

Why would the Tuckers put their workshop up so high on the ridge? If I could see it from here, it stood to reason that you could see Miss Sarah's house from the shack. Maybe they didn't realize the shed was visible from the attic windows. Given how filthy it was up here, it had been years since anyone had been up here. It seemed a little bold to me if Miss Sarah didn't know what they were doing on the land she rented them.

She had to know. Beau knew, and he grew up in town. Everyone in the county knew what kind of business the Tuckers ran on Donelson land.

Did Mom and Dewey know was the real question. What would happen when Miss Sarah died, and they inherited this place? Mom was an officer of the court—she could be disbarred for knowing of a criminal enterprise and not reporting it. I couldn't see Dewey moving his family out here, nor could I see Mom selling our place in Chicago, giving up her partnership in the firm, and moving down here.

And the house wasn't livable, not really. It would cost a fortune renovating and repairing this place after all these years of neglect.

I couldn't see them selling the place, though.

The Tuckers would have to go. I couldn't see them being evicted. Ma Tucker had been pretty clear they wouldn't go without a fight.

I wondered why Miss Sarah had never just sold them their land.

I used the box cutter to slice through the yellowed, brittle tape and opened the flaps. Dust flew up from inside the box. I wiped the dust off my face and coughed again. The box was filled with more clothes from another time period, musty and dirty and smelly.

Terrific.

I started working and got lost in the mindless chore. The clothes were decades older than me, and I tried to remember old television shows and movies from the 1950s. Yes, I thought with a slight smile as I put all the clothes back into the box and marked it with an *X* and added the corresponding number on the spreadsheet, these were from the Eisenhower administration. I typed quickly, *Box of women's clothes from the 1950s, probably worthless. Musty, dirty, and smelly.* I folded the flaps of the box back down and retaped it shut. I moved it from the top of its stack and reached for the next one.

I opened it and found myself staring down at my own face.

I lifted the framed photograph and wiped the dust off the glass. Christ, the resemblance was eerie. I opened the camera function on my laptop and held the picture next to my face. Most people would think it was a picture of me, wearing the hairstyle and clothes from a different era. Hair parted in the center and a little long, feathered back from the forehead, the big smile, the enormous brown eyes. The slight differences were there, too, of course—the slightly sharper chin, the wider set eyes. But it would fool most people.

It was close enough to make his own mother think she was seeing a ghost.

But if that was his skeleton out by the ruins, he didn't run away, did he?

Everyone thought Jacob had run away, and after Duncan died in the car accident, no one would push the grieving mother about her other son's disappearance.

She had to know that he was out there, buried by the ruins. Of course she knew—that was why she wouldn't let Dr. Brady's team excavate the ruins. But who killed him, and why?

I sat down on a dusty chair and stared at the picture. There was a pimple on his chin, right in the same spot where I always got one if I didn't wash my face enough. I smiled. I couldn't imagine ever wearing my hair like that, and the wide lapels on his blue suit jacket...ugh, how could anyone have ever thought that looked good on anyone? I traced my index finger along his jawline. He looked so happy in the picture. This was clearly his senior picture. I touched the pimple on his chin, wondering why it hadn't been airbrushed out. I smiled. I'd had a zit in the same place when I had my senior picture taken—but they'd Photoshopped it out.

I put the picture aside and pulled out a letterman jacket, maroon with white leather sleeves. There was a maroon *K* in chenille sewn on to the front, outlined in white. There was a little gold football on the stem of the *K*, with three gold bars beneath it. Beneath the bars was a little gold baseball, above bats crossed into an X, but there were only two gold bars beneath the baseball symbols. He'd lettered three years in football and two in baseball. On the left arm, chenille numbers—75, again, maroon outlined in white—were sewn on the upper sleeve. So we might be look-alikes, but he'd been a jock. I slid my arms through the sleeves and shrugged it up to my shoulders. It smelled musty—it had probably been up here in the attic since he ran away—and it needed to be cleaned, but it fit me perfectly.

We were the same size.

The light in the attic dimmed, and I could hear a marching band playing faintly in the distance. I closed my eyes and was looking through a thick plastic faceguard out onto a football field lit up by stadium lights. Two teams were facing off against each other near an end zone. There were people shouting behind me, girlish voices chanting *Touch! Down! Touch! Down!* The ball snapped and the teams converged in grunts, bodies and pads colliding against each other. The quarterback gave the ball to someone who burst through the crowd of players struggling against each other, and people started shouting louder, sounding more frenzied and excited as he sprinted for the end zone, and a whistle blew, and everyone around me was cheering and shouting and jumping up and down—

And I opened my eyes, back in the dusty attic, wearing a dead man's letter jacket.

I took it off quickly, my heart pounding in my ears, my breathing quick.

It was fucking creepy as hell.

I thought about the weird dreams I'd been having, barely remembered on waking, of running through the woods, terrified.

I remembered running for my life through this house, coming up to the attic, heading for the balcony in the rounded tower, thinking *He'll kill me if he catches me.*

And I knew, I *knew*, that skeleton belonged to my uncle Jacob.

He didn't run away. He'd been murdered and buried by the ruins.

A wave of sadness washed over me, so strong and deep and

heartfelt that I had to sit back down on the arm of the filthy chair next to the box. That's when I saw it, written in faded black in very small letters, near the bottom of the box by the floor.

Jacob's things.

I knew that neat, precise handwriting. It was Miss Sarah's. I'd seen it before, on letters and cards sent to my mother with the Corinth cancellation mark on the stamps, the rural route return address.

What did she know about Jacob? And what happened to him?

She had to know what happened to him.

She was the one who told everyone he'd run away.

She would only lie if she was covering for someone.

The runaway story meant no one looked for him, no one wondered about him, no one questioned her.

I carefully folded the jacket and placed it in the chair. I decided to keep it, have it dry-cleaned, take it back to New Orleans with me. We looked alike, of course, that was part of it, but since coming here, I'd felt some weird kinship with my namesake uncle. I couldn't help but wonder how different everything would be had he lived and was a part of our lives.

I started removing the top layer of clothes from the box. They were all my size, and I tried to imagine what it must have been like for Miss Sarah to pack up her son's things, to store away in the attic, neatly folded and boxed up, taped shut, stored in the attic, his life nothing but a closed chapter.

The clothes were years out of style, velour short-sleeved shirts and faded, bell-bottomed blue jeans, rotting T-shirts with iron-on pictures on the front, with names like Grand Funk and The Eagles and Led Zeppelin. I refolded the clothes, which smelled of age and mildew. But when I reached the bottom of the box, there was an old brown scrapbook, with the word *Memories* written across the front in gold script, not bound but rather held together by gold laces tied into an extravagant bow in front.

As I put my hands on it, I felt an almost electrical charge, a weird rush of excitement, similar to the one I felt when I went inside my bedroom that first time when I'd arrived, that exultant feeling, almost like joy, like every nerve ending in my body was waking up with a sense of *at last!*

Like I was meant to find this scrapbook.

I sat down and opened the cover. Inside, in faded blue ink and curling script, were the words *Jake Donelson, RFD Kenilworth, Alabama, Class of '75, KHS, GO LIONS!!!*

The first page had yellowed Polaroid photographs taped to it. The page itself was brittle, like it had gotten wet. The tape was yellowed and no longer adhered to the stiff pages, so the photos moved and slid around as I shifted the scrapbook in my lap. The faded sepia-toned pictures were of teenagers, the boys shirtless and wearing jeans cut off so short that you could see the bottoms of their pockets hanging down below the fringed strings. Daisy Dukes, I remembered with a smile, long out of style for guys, coming back into style for girls. The girls' shorts in the pictures were cut just as short, and they were also wearing bikini tops. They were on the bank of a river whose dirty orange water was visible off to the side. They smiled for the camera, crooked white teeth exposed. They all had long hair, both boys and girls, and their hair wasn't wet, either—so they hadn't gone into the water yet. Some of the boys had hair on their chests, their stomachs flat, muscles showing in their arms and shoulders. I picked up one of the pictures that had fallen to the floor. My own face stared back from the faded photo, yellowed with age, his right arm draped around the shoulder of a young Black boy about the same age as my uncle. Both grinned at the camera.

There was something about the way they were posed…

Across the bottom of the picture, on the wide white border at the bottom, was written *Jake and Cash.*

Cash.

Memories crowded through my mind.

A hot summer day, the air laying thick and heavy and damp, not a breeze anywhere to be found.

A sky so blue and bright it almost hurts to look at.

Splashing, water rushing, voices laughing and calling to each other, joking tones, happy young men.

So in love with each other.

I felt dizzy.

Cash.

I put the picture aside and started looking through the others. Cash, whoever he was, wasn't in any of the pictures with the other white kids. I turned the page and handwritten report cards were taped to the following pages: freshman, sophomore, and junior years' worth, spread out over the next few pages, the original white slips long turned yellow and curling, all the grades As. I turned the page and found football programs, mimeographed in blue ink on a sheet of paper, folded in half in the middle. The cover was just an image of a roaring lion in blue ink, with *Kenilworth High School Lions* written in an arch around the head, and underneath the head was a date and the name of an opponent. I opened one to find lists of both teams on the pages facing each other, coaches' names listed beneath the team, positions, height and weight and year for each player.

Uncle Jake was only five three and weighed one hundred twenty pounds when he was a freshman.

I'd been five three and weighed one hundred twenty pounds when I was a freshman.

On the back side was a list of cheerleaders, the band director, and a little ad from the Piggly Wiggly in Corinth.

I flipped through, feeling closer and closer to my uncle as I looked through the evidence of his long-forgotten life, a memory book he kept meticulously, taping pictures of his friends to the pages. There were some pictures from homecoming and prom, sometimes a picture of him posed with his older brother, Duncan a dead ringer for *his* nephew Kelly, maybe not as big and thick with muscle, but not small, either.

I reached the back and closed it.

I leaned back in the chair and close my eyes.

Cash.

There was only the one picture of him, and he was also the only person of color pictured in the entire book.

Why did I feel like he was important?

I can see it, the ruins standing out against the dark velvety green of the pine forest on every side of it. I'm safe here, no one ever comes here, no one will ever catch us here.

Why? Why am I worried—

I can hear something moving in the woods, not on the trail from the house, either. Someone or something is coming through the woods, heading this way. I hope it's Cash, and I feel my heart racing with excitement. I

don't get to see Cash as much anymore, now that they bus him into Corinth to go to school, now that they closed the Black high school out here.
And the hackles rise on the back on my neck.
It's not Cash.
Conflicting thoughts. I am aware of where I am, but at the same time, I don't know who I am, who these thoughts are coming from, why I am out here, who is Cash. Whatever is in the woods coming toward me—whoever—means to harm me.
But curiosity drives me.
Dunk says—Dunk has claimed that people are meeting out here at the ruins, trespassing, their intent toward us isn't bad, but they aren't good people.
Mama says—

I opened my eyes.
I blinked.
That didn't just happen.
Was I losing my mind?
Shaking, I stood up, dropping the scrapbook to the floor, pictures scattering. I sighed and knelt to pick them up with shaking hands. I typed into the laptop *Box of Jacob Donelson's clothes and personal things* before saving the document and picking up the scrapbook. I slipped it under my arm and carried my laptop in my other hand.
It was getting darker as I walked to the stairs. Thunder. Lightning.
Water pounding on the roof, harder than before.
I almost lost my balance twice on the stairs on the way down but finally got to the bottom. Lightning lit up the hallway as I headed to my room. My phone vibrated in my pocket. When I was safely back in my room with the door shut, I put the scrapbook and laptop on my bed and checked my phone.
It was a text from Mom. *Are you making that up? It's not funny. I'll call you later tonight.*
So she didn't know.
Did Dewey know?
So many secrets in this cursed house.
I wondered again who Cash was, or is. Just because Jacob was

gone didn't mean Cash was, too. Cash could still be alive, could still be here in Corinth County.

I took the picture and went downstairs. The rain was blasting down, the wind rattling windows and the walls, the whole house vibrating from the wind. This was a bad storm, much worse than any of the ones since I'd arrived.

Geneva came out of Miss Sarah's room and closed the door behind her. She looked worried. "There's a tornado warning in Tuscaloosa," she said quietly, glancing back over her shoulder at the door. "The weather seems to be heading this way. We don't get tornadoes up here in the hills much, but down on the flatlands…" She shook her head. "There was a bad one when I was a little girl."

"Do you need to go?" I asked.

"Nothing I can do down there, except get myself killed." She shook her head. "I do hope and pray everyone is safe."

"Do you know who this is?" I handed her the Polaroid.

"Lord, you sure do look like your uncle," she replied. "That's Cassius Porter and your uncle." She pronounced his name *cashes*. "He's a cousin of mine, second once removed or some such. I forgot they were buddies."

"Is he still alive?"

Geneva nodded. "Lives down on the Winfield road. His wife just passed last year."

"Do you think he'd mind if I stopped by sometime?"

She touched my cheek. "You're obsessed with finding out about your uncle, aren't you?" She smiled. "I don't think he'd mind. He'll probably have a heart attack when he sees you, though."

CHAPTER TWENTY-TWO

It took about an hour for the storm to finally pass, me checking the weather repeatedly on my phone. Each passing minute was torture. All I wanted to do was get in my car and go find Cash, find out whatever he knew about Uncle Jacob.

Had he been killed because he was friends with a Black kid?

That didn't make any sense, but I couldn't think why anyone would kill Jacob. He was only a kid. Sure, it was a human tendency to make the dead seem saintly, but I had yet to hear anyone say anything negative about him. Besides, nobody knew he was dead. I wasn't even completely sure, but at some point, Dr. Brady or the Alabama Bureau of Investigation would want a DNA sample from us to see if he was a Donelson.

But would they? It's not like the county sheriff wasn't a crook, and he might want to sweep it all under the rug.

When the rain finally let up, I knocked softly on Miss Sarah's door and then stuck my head in. She was asleep, drooling a bit, and Geneva looked up in surprise. She folded a corner of the page down in her book as I handed her my phone with the map app already open and whispered, "Can you drop a pin where Cash lives? I'm going to head over there and talk to him now that the storm's passed."

Geneva glanced at Miss Sarah before dropping the pin and handing my phone to me. "You be careful out there, with the roads wet and all," she whispered back. "And tell Cash I'll be calling him soon myself about the family reunion."

I nodded, closing the door gently and heading out to my car.

The air was still wet and cool outside, but it was starting to get humid again. I wiped sweat off my forehead and opened the car door. I slipped the keys into the ignition and started the car, leaning down to crank the air-conditioning up.

A dark brown car turned onto the dirt road. I watched as it went past. On the side in big black letters were the letters ATF. Alcohol, tobacco and firearms, I thought as it went down into the little hollow and then back up the other side, throwing up clods of muddy red dirt as it went over the ridge into Tucker Holler. That couldn't be good, I thought as I fastened my seat belt and put the car in reverse. Unless the Tuckers were paying them off the way they paid off the sheriff.

I didn't want to think about that.

I backed out and turned around, got on the county road, and started heading down the slope. It started sprinkling again as I headed down the initial slope leading to the sharp turn to the right, where the dirt road to the ruins heads through the woods on the left. I couldn't help but think about how beautiful and raw it was up here in the hills, with everything glistening and wet in the sunshine. It was a too remote for me—I couldn't ever live out in the country. But when I got to the scary parts of the road, where the flimsy guardrail was the only thing between me and a sheer drop of what appeared to be about a hundred feet or so, through pines and maples and other trees, I found myself clutching the steering wheel until my knuckles turned white and my shoulders tensed up. But the air smelled so fresh and clean—I could almost taste the green—and the sun was shining and the sky that lovely deep blue with just a few wisps of clouds drifting slowly across the canvas.

If not for the sprinkling and the wetness of the trees, you'd never guess a massive thunderstorm had just passed through.

"In half a mile, turn right on State Road 47," my phone instructed me.

Idly, I wondered why the Blackwoods had built their plantation house so high up in the hills. It didn't make sense. If they owned all the land around here, including the flatlands at the foot of this mountain, why didn't they build the house down there? When the roads weren't paved, getting up and down from Blackwood Hall would have been incredibly difficult.

I remembered Beau's story about the witch from New Orleans and smiled a bit. He'd say it was her idea.

What a family pedigree. A former soldier from North Carolina and a witch from New Orleans…

A witch. From New Orleans. In the 1820s.

What were the odds that a New Orleans witch from that time would be white? Didn't it make more sense that she'd be a voodoo priestess, which would mean—

Which would mean she was at least part Black.

Miss Sarah would love that. I'd love to see the look on her face if someone could prove that Madeleine Blackwood wasn't white. Maybe that was why they burned her.

"In one hundred yards, slow down and turn right on State Road 47," came the friendly female voice again.

I stopped at Four Corners. I turned right. I'd not driven this way before, and just past the abandoned corner store gas station was an unpaved road leading back into the woods, a mailbox at the end with its little red flag up. A barking dog came tearing down the road—which I assumed was a driveway—and ran alongside the car. But after a few minutes it fell behind and stopped. I could see it in the rearview mirror, trotting happily back to the driveway he'd come from. I passed a field with rows of watermelon vines, the big round green-striped melons resting in the dirt. Watermelons gave way to corn, to beans, to tomatoes and peppers.

"In a quarter mile, turn left onto State Road 178," my phone said pleasantly.

I crossed a little bridge, glancing over the side at the orangish-brown water, still and unmoving. A deer started to emerge from the woods, froze, and bounded back into the thickets. I came over a slight incline and saw the big sign up ahead, mounted alongside the road with a long arm about twenty feet above the pavement, with the big red letters STOP on it.

"Turn left onto State Road 178. In one mile and three quarters, turn left onto State Road 53."

I braked and allowed a filthy pickup truck to turn left in front of me before I turned myself.

It was just another country road, no different than the others, but along this road, houses were closer to the road than they were on the road where Miss Sarah's house sits. These were nicer houses, made of brick with porches supported by the antebellum columns, the yards carefully mowed and trimmed. A pasture, with cows contentedly munching grass as they moved around slowly in the heat of the early afternoon. A rusted truck, abandoned in a field, next to a black pond whose surface was still as glass. Fences, wooden or barbed wire, the occasional deserted barn rotting in the sun with a rusted tin roof. The road curved and rose again as I kept driving onward, waving back at drivers passing me in the other direction, all of whom waved at me as a polite courtesy—there was no way they knew who I was.

There was something to be said for rural Southern politeness.

"Turn left onto State Road 53."

I looked ahead but couldn't see a road, but as I continued up the rise, I saw a stop sign—State Road 53 apparently dead-ended into this road, and there was another abandoned corner store there, the wood rotting and the paint gone so it was just that rotting weathered gray. Two abandoned, rusty, red gas pumps sat amidst climbing weeds, and the abandoned station's sign still read *Gulf* on its skeletal post. I slowed and turned on my signal, watching to see if anyone came over the rise ahead of me, and swung the car into the turn. The road immediately started a downward slope, past a driveway and back through some woods. The car passed over a metal bridge, low to the water it forded, the rusted metal rumbling beneath my tires.

That bridge must flood regularly, I thought, looking back in the rearview mirror. There were no guardrails, nothing to stop a car from going off the side into the orange water maybe a foot or so below. I came out of the woods again and was surrounded by farmland, pastures and rows of corn, wheat, and various other vegetables. A woman in a tattered housedress was scattering feed to chickens pecking in the dirt by her wooden house. Like the drivers, she too raised her hand to wave at me.

"In half a mile, turn right onto State Road 117."

As I pulled up to the stop sign there, it was another dead end— State Road 53 only ran from where I turned off the other road to here. Left or right were my only options. There was a directional sign pointing to *Corinth 15* to the left, and *White's Chapel 7* to the right.

I wondered what White's Chapel was—maybe a segregated church? in this day and age?—before turning right. The ground was fairly flat here, the road twisting and turning through cornfields and pastures.

"You are half a mile from your final destination."

I passed yet another abandoned store, the roof and one of the walls collapsed, the sentry gasoline pumps standing vigil in the weeds.

"You are approaching your destination on the left."

I passed another brick house, and beyond the pasture I could see a battered-looking wooden house, with several enormous trees in the front, between two pastures. Across the street was a field with corn and other plants. But in the far corner of that field, I could see kudzu climbing over trees and spreading across flat land.

The kudzu will come through the window for you.

There was a mailbox alongside the road, and I could see the name on it before I even finish slowing down, my signal on. *Porter*, it said, and just as I read it the phone announced, "You have arrived at your destination."

I pulled into the gravel driveway and parked behind an enormous Ford pickup truck.

The house hadn't been painted in a while and was mostly bare gray wood exposed to the sun. It had a slanted roof with a vent in the corner where the roof met in the center. The columns supporting the porch roof were rusted iron. The driveway continued back to an enormous barn that looked even more battered than the house.

An older Black man came out onto the porch as I stepped on the stones placed as a makeshift walk to the front porch. There was a tire hanging from the lower branches of one of the enormous trees, swaying softly in the wind. It smelled like freshly cut grass—that wonderful green smell I couldn't get enough of since I arrived. He was wearing a plaid checked shirt underneath denim overalls that had faded and gotten soft from being washed so many times. He was wiping his hands on an oily reddish rag. "Can I help you, son? Are you lost?"

He held up a hand to shield his eyes from the sun and staggered back once he got a good look at me. He sat down hard on an old metal porch chair that rocked a bit under his weight.

"Cash Porter?" I asked, climbing up the cement stairs to the front porch.

He was staring at me, his worn face gone a little lighter. His big brown eyes were reddish and bloodshot, slightly yellowed, and I could see he was still a handsome man—when he was young he'd probably been breathtakingly handsome—and he looked fit and strong. "It can't be," he said, pushing himself up to his feet, not really talking to me but more to himself. "Ghosts don't drive, for one thing."

"I'm not a ghost," I said, holding out my right hand for him to shake. "My name's Jake Chapman. I'm Glynis Donelson's son."

He took my hand. His was calloused, warm, the grip strong. "I knew you had to have Donelson blood," he said, shaking his head. "I thought I'd seen a ghost."

"I look a lot like my uncle, don't I?"

"You do." He swallowed carefully, give his head another shake. "I never thought I'd see that face again. Can I get you something to drink? Some tea? Water? A Coke?"

"No, thank you." I sat down in the iron chair next to his. "I wanted to meet you. Your cousin Geneva—she's working for my grandmother now, taking care of her. She said you and my uncle were close when you were kids. I want to know about him."

"Your mother was just a child when he—" He cut himself off.

"Ran away?"

He looked at me. He said, "I heard y'all found a skeleton up there, near the ruins of the old house." He said it casually, leaning back in his chair, slapping at a mosquito on his neck. He blinked slowly. "I never believed for one minute that Jacob ran away."

"You think it's him we found?"

A corner of his mouth twitched. "I was supposed to run away with him." He stood back up. "I need some tea for this. You sure you don't want none?"

"Sure." The screen door slammed behind him, and my mind was racing. A wasp flew past my nose. The wind was starting to pick up a little bit, and I recognized the smell—more rain was coming.

I peered out, but the branches of the trees blocked out the sky in front of the little house. I looked off into the distance and saw a wave of roiling dark clouds, moving fast, heading in our direction. Great. I hoped I wouldn't have to drive back in that.

The screen door opened, and Mr. Porter handed me a mason jar filled with ice cubes and tea. I took a sip and hid the grimace. It was too sweet—I should have asked. But I swallowed it down.

"I'll be sixty next month," he said after a few moments and sipped from his own glass. "I've had a good life, Jake, I have. I have a daughter I love who lives in Birmingham, and her oldest is pert near ready for college. I had a long marriage with a woman I loved, and we made each other happy." His voice sounded hollow, like he was convincing himself, and I could see his free hand—the one not holding the tea glass—was gripping the arm of his chair so hard his knuckles were discolored. "I buried Lucille last year, right at the end of the summer. Cancer. She fought hard."

"I'm sorry."

"You didn't know her, but I thank you for your kindness." Cash Porter waved away my condolences. "We had a good life, me and Lucille. We've got a fine daughter, and now our grandkids…" His voice trailed off. "Nobody's asked me about your uncle in, oh, I don't know now, maybe forty years?"

"Your mother worked for Miss Sarah, didn't she?"

He nodded. He smiled, putting an unfiltered Camel between his lips. He lit it, inhaled with a sigh of relief, and said, "Never start smoking, son, it's a filthy habit, but it's the only one I got left now that I don't drink no more." He flicked ash. "Mama used to take me up to the Donelson house with her when she worked. Your uncle, now, he was about the same age as me, and so we used to play… all the games little boys play." His eyes stared off into the branches hanging low near the roof of the porch. "He was my best friend, but we couldn't go to the same schools back then, of course. He went to Kenilworth, I went to the colored school." There was no bitterness in his voice, his tone matter-of-fact. Segregation was wrong, but that's just how things were back then. "Must have been about when we were in junior high, Miss Sarah decided she didn't want her son having anything to do with me no more. She told Mama she couldn't bring me along with her no more. It just about broke my heart. I loved your uncle." He shook his head. "What fools we both were. We still saw each other, of course—we just had to be clever about it and sneak around a bit." He got a faraway look in his eyes. "Mama used to let me drive sometimes, and me and Jacob, we'd meet down at the ruins. He'd sneak out of the house and head down there, and..." He paused, as if lost in memory. "We were good friends. We thought maybe, if we ran away together, we could, you know, be friends and be together. But that ain't no way for a man to live."

"What isn't?"

His face twisted. "We were young and we...If you tell anyone I said this, I'll deny it. I don't even know why I am telling you any of this, but maybe it's because you look so much like him. I don't know. But I wasn't that way. I've thought about it a lot since then. I am not that way. After your uncle went away, I fell in love with Lucille, and we were happy. I'm not sorry I had a life with her."

It's not all or nothing, I wanted to say. *It's possible to love both men and women.*

"We made up our minds to run away that summer, when your uncle Duncan was killed in that car wreck." He made a tsking sound. "Duncan was always going to come out in a bad way, just a matter of time. He was like his daddy—he liked his moonshine, he liked to get drunk and act a fool. That wreck didn't surprise anyone in this county. Duncan was her favorite. He was the only one of them kids that mattered to Miss Sarah. After her husband died, Jacob used to tell me stories." He whistled. "Duncan was just like her, you know. Jacob, I don't know who he was like. Old Mr. Donelson was always out in the fields, didn't talk much, and of course he died when the kids were young. She grabbed on to Dunk like a life preserver. Jacob thought that was maybe why he turned out so wild. He was a racist, too, just like she was. Jacob didn't see difference. He was always happy, always laughing and smiling...unless *she* was around. That last summer, she got to be too much for Jacob. I don't know what happened or what she did, but we'd always talked about going away together. But you know, it was just two kids talking foolishness. We were supposed to meet at the ruins that night, were gonna take that beat-up old car of mine and head for the Birmingham bus station and head out to California. California..." He sighed. "I wasn't never meant to live in no California. But I went up there that night, to the ruins, and I waited for him. It was raining—a nasty night—but I wasn't about to take shelter and not meet him. I waited out there at the ruins till morning, and he never came." His jawline set. "And Miss Sarah, she told everybody he ran away, but I know that was a lie—he wouldn't have gone without me. He didn't have no way to run away without me. But who was going to listen to me?" He folded his arms. "I always thought she killed Jacob—you want to know the truth. I've always believed she figured out what we were up to, and she killed him."

"Did you say anything to the police?"

He looked at me like I'd gone crazy. "The police? You think a Black teenager was about to go to the police and tell them an important white lady in the county killed her son? Hell, son, she's a goddamned *Blackwood*. That name still means a lot around here. And back then? I'd be lucky they didn't throw me in jail." He shook his head again with a gentle laugh. "You sure ain't from here, that's for sure. I wouldn't go to the police now about something like that—for anything. The cops aren't there to help Black folk, son, and sure as hell not in Corinth County, Alabama, no sir. That wasn't the way things worked in Corinth County back then, and it sure as hell ain't the way it works up in here now. *Shee-it*, son, if y'all turned up his body, who do you think they'd string up for it?" He laughed. "It sure as hell wouldn't be a Blackwood. And him running away because he was so upset about Dunk getting himself killed? Pshaw." He leaned closer to me. "Jacob couldn't stand his brother—they'd never got along, even as boys—and the older they got and the more Dunk was like their mother, the less he liked him. Besides, the timing didn't make sense."

"What do you mean?" I looked at him. "Dunk was killed, and then Jacob ran away. Right?"

He shook his head. "No, son, that ain't right."

I could barely breathe. "So you're saying…"

"We planned to run away *before* Dunk was killed." He leaned back in his rocking chair and nodded, sipping his tea. "Jacob never showed at the ruins that night, and two days later Dunk got killed. Got drunk and smashed himself up and took Caleb McCallum to the grave with him. She said he ran away after Dunk died." He started rocking. "I never saw him again. I saw him that afternoon when we made our final plans to get to Birmingham. He never showed up. No one saw him again, and then she told everyone he'd run off, so upset about Dunk." He bit off the words angrily. "I can believe he changed his mind about running away with me. It would hurt, but I could believe that. But he never run away because of Dunk. He ran away because he liked boys, and she couldn't stand that—and neither could Dunk. I didn't tell anyone because no one would believe me, son. But that afternoon? When we met to make our plans? I'd never seen him like that before."

"And what was he like?"

His eyes narrowed. "He was terrified. He wouldn't say so, but he was scared to death."

CHAPTER TWENTY-THREE

I don't remember anything else we talked about—my heart was racing, and my mind was jumping all over the place. But we talked more, not about anything important.

I thanked him for the tea and hospitality. When I got up to go, he also stood up and took hold of my arm. "Now, son, everything I told you is just between us, understood? I don't want no trouble with that old woman."

I nodded and thanked him again, somehow managing to walk back out to my car on my shaky legs. I got into the car and waved at Cash Porter one more time, and he waved back before going back inside. I hoped he wasn't as shaken up as I was.

I loved him but it turns out I just wasn't that way after all.

I started the car. I looked up, and the dark clouds were getting closer, moving faster. The sun was lower in the sky than the clouds, so it was shining brightly underneath the dark clouds, casting the entire flatlands into an eerie light like nothing I'd ever seen before.

I queued up Taylor Swift's *Red* on my phone and turned the car around in the gravel.

When I reached the end of the driveway, I looked back in the rearview mirror. Cash was standing on the porch, watching me as I waited for a truck full of watermelons to go past so I could get out of here.

I heard his words in my head again.

Who was going to listen to a Black kid and believe him instead of the white lady? A Blackwood, at that?

Why had he told me? He'd been keeping his…friendship with Jacob a secret for over forty years. Must have been the shock of seeing the face of the boy he'd loved as a kid again. I remembered Miss Sarah's reaction to seeing me for the first time—she'd recoiled from me, like she'd seen a ghost. And if she killed her son, she must have thought I was an avenging spirit.

They were going to run away together. And the timeline—the one everyone believed, that Dunk had been killed in a car accident and Jacob ran away—was wrong. Of course she would lie if she'd killed him. What would she have done had Dunk not been killed? Would she have gotten away with the lie about him running away? No one was going to question her after she buried her eldest son.

She hadn't wanted her son to be friends with a Black kid. How would she have reacted to knowing that her son was in love with that Black kid?

She'd banned Cash from coming to the house when he was a child, hadn't she?

Maybe Jacob had told her he was leaving, and why.

My mother was one of the strongest people I knew, and she was still afraid of her mother.

There was no doubt in my mind now that the skeleton at the ruins was my uncle Jacob.

I pulled out onto the road and headed back the way I'd come, thoughts tumbling through my mind like runaway trains. My hands were shaking a little on the steering wheel, so I gripped it tighter.

The Klan mask and robe. Where had they come from? And what were those flashes I kept seeing in the woods? They'd led me to the Klan costume, and I'd only seen the flash once since then, hadn't I?

I'd never thought about ghosts before. New Orleans was supposedly one of the most haunted cities in the country—my landlord had even jokingly warned me that the house was haunted, but I'd never seen anything, had never felt anything, certainly not anything like I'd experienced since coming to Alabama.

If…maybe my uncle was trying to communicate with me, to tell me what happened to him. It couldn't be a coincidence that his skeleton had been found after I came here. I remembered those weird, disorienting feelings I'd experienced, the way the box had tipped over in the attic, so I would find the picture of Duncan and Jacob as children.

Had I not found that picture…

I shivered as I made the first turn on the way back.

For a brief moment I wished I was back at home in my apartment in New Orleans, happily FaceTiming or texting friends, trying to figure out ways to pass the free summer time. Would I have tried to make up with Tradd and his friends, had I not left New Orleans? Would I have kept on the downward spiral that put me in the hospital and on the road to Alabama?

This summer hadn't turned out the way I'd wanted. We'd made plans, hadn't we, Tradd and his friends and me? We were going to go to the beach a lot, get tanned, go to the gym, and go out every weekend, having fun, enjoying being young in one of the last summers we'd have before having to become adults.

Instead, we'd had that horrible fight, and I'd wound up in the hospital.

And here I was.

Dealing with ghosts and family secrets and murders that happened a long time ago.

I took the next turn and drove over that shuddering rusty metal bridge, so close to the muddy water, feeling it vibrate and shake. A vision of the bridge collapsing and my car plunging into the water flashed through my mind. A fat drop of water splatted against the windshield. I glanced up and saw the black clouds had caught up to me, and lightning flashed. I counted to myself—*one, two, three, four*—and the thunder roared, drowning out Taylor's voice through the speakers as I pressed the accelerator down. The road was curvy, and I could see the stop sign at the top of the hill ahead, the rotting old corner store on the left. I braked as more drops started hitting the car with loud thumps.

The rain was coming down hard now, the windshield wipers moving in double time across the glass, trying but not keeping up. I slowed the car down to a crawl, less than thirty miles per hour. I reached the crossroads where I needed to turn right—my phone informed me long before I could see the stop sign ahead—and I flipped on my signal.

I was afraid. I had the phone giving me directions. I had to be careful, watch what I was doing, and I'd be home before I knew it.

I remembered the roads got slick when they were wet.

My stomach was clenching, twisting into knots, my heart racing, my breathing fast and hard.

I was terrified, but why?

What did I have to be afraid of? Miss Sarah couldn't hurt me, and Kelly—well, Kelly…

If my uncle was reaching out to me from the other side of the grave, couldn't Dunk be doing the same with Kelly? He looked as much like Dunk as I did Jacob.

My grip on the steering wheel got tighter.

Beau said he was one of the good ones. So why was he so different with me?

If Duncan…

Chill, man, calm down it's okay you'll be okay you'll be home before you know it. You're imagining things because you've had some shocks. There's no such thing as ghosts and there's a perfectly logical explanation for everything that's been happening since you got here.

Wasn't there?

Home.

Miss Sarah's house was hardly that.

It hadn't been home for my uncle Jacob, either.

Mom might not be perfect, but I was so grateful she was my mother instead of someone like Miss Sarah.

A long-forgotten memory flashed through my mind.

I'm a child, walking through the woods behind my mom and Miss Sarah. Both are carrying buckets, and I remember we're looking for blackberries, ripened on wild bushes in the woods. We stop at a cluster of bushes and they both stand back and let me pick them, putting the firm blackberries into the bucket. They're talking as I ignore the ones that are still green and look for the plump, sweet black ones. I remember she's going to make jam from them, can them in the kitchen and store it for the winter because fresh is always better than store-bought, even after canning.

"Not that one, Jake," I hear my mom say as I put my hand on one that's still not quite ripe.

"I know, Mom," I say in my high-pitched child's squeak.

They're talking, but I'm not really listening to them. I'm focused on the berries and making sure none of those bees or horseflies land on me, sting me or bite me. I've gotten bee stung before and it hurt, oh, how it hurt, and I cried and cried, and ever since then I've made sure to give bees a wide berth. The bite of a horsefly also hurts, but nothing like a bee sting.

"He reminds me of my Jacob," I hear Miss Sarah saying, in her husky, deep-throated growl. "You'll have your work cut out for you making sure he doesn't go down that same path."

"There's nothing wrong with him." My mother's voice, her tone sharp and pointed. I know that tone—it means danger, be careful, or you'll be sorry.

Miss Sarah snorts. "You say that now. You'd be better off killing him now than trying to fix him later."

Mom didn't reply.

Instead, she grabbed my hand hard and yanked me away from the blackberry bushes. I yelled, and she started pulling me along behind her as she walked quickly through the forest, me crying, sobbing, because I wanted to keep picking blackberries. "I love blackberries. Mommy, let go, you're hurting me."

And she stopped when we reached the dirt road again, mosquitoes and gnats swarming around the small muddy stream, a frog leaping into the water from the road. She knelt down beside me and looked me in the face. "Jake, I love you. You're my son, and I will always love you, no matter what, do you understand that? I will never stop loving you."

Me, sniveling, my nose running and my face wet with tears, nodding.

She smiled at me, wiping the tears away with her hands and then wiping my nose with the bottom of her shirt. "Come on, let's go pack and go home."

I stopped at Fowler's Four Corners. The rain was lighter now, but the storm was coming up quickly behind me. There was an 18-wheeler stopped across the intersection from me. I flipped on the turn signal and waited for him before I turned.

My entire body was cold as ice.

Did she really tell Mom she'd be better off killing me?

No wonder I hadn't been back here since.

The heavy drops started falling again as I turned and started the initial climb, wanting to get back as quickly as I could before

I got caught in the onslaught I just drove through again—I didn't want to have to drive up that slope with those thin guardrails and sharp turns in the pouring rain.

But before I reached the top, it was pouring again.

Maybe that memory was the last time I was in Alabama before this summer.

"Siri, call Mom," I commanded, and Taylor stopped singing as my phone dialed my mother.

It went to voice mail immediately. She was two hours behind me, probably at work.

"Hey, Mom," I said, my voice shaking even as I tried to keep it steady, once the beep sounded, "I just had a really weird memory. Did Miss Sarah once tell you you'd be better off killing me than having me turn out like my namesake?"

I disconnected the call and slowed the car down again as the rain kept pouring down. I could barely see the road in front of me. I remembered those sheer drops. There was no surviving a crash through the guardrail, and another flash—but it couldn't be memory—went through my mind.

That was how Uncle Duncan died, wasn't it? Crashing through the guardrail? Driving drunk and too fast on one of these roads?

And I filled with sorrow, a sense of loss that pulled at my heart and filled my eyes with tears.

I shook it off, wondering if I was having a mental break of some kind.

I'd overdosed and almost died a few weeks ago. Maybe it rewired my brain, or scrambled things up there. Maybe that's what all of this was, something my damaged mind created.

Tradd's angry voice, bitterly sneering at me, *You're such a drama queen. It's always about attention for you, isn't it?*

My lower lip trembled. "Fuck you, Tradd. Fuck you to hell and back, okay? I am not losing my mind. This is all really happening."

The windshield wipers were pushing water off the glass as fast as they could but not fast enough, the windshield clearing for a moment before the heavy thick drops splattered over it again, but finally I reached that sharp ninety degree turn to the left that was the last slope up to the dirt road where Miss Sarah's old house was.

As I was turning onto the dirt road, my phone rang, interrupting Taylor yet again. The screen on the stereo said *Mom*.

I clicked the button on the steering wheel. "Hey, Mom, thanks for calling back so soon." I turned the car into the flat area alongside the house. Kelly's truck was sitting there, next to Geneva's car. I decided to sit in the car and wait for the rain to lessen before dashing for the house.

"Are you okay?" Mom said, her voice frantic. "What's all that noise?"

"I'm sitting in the car. It's pouring, and I'm waiting for a chance to make a break for the front porch. I take it you got my message?"

"Yes."

"Well?" I waited, listening to the rat-a-tat-tat of the rain on the car roof. I couldn't see anything through the windows, covered in water as they were, everything out there blurry and unclear. "Am I remembering that right?"

She was quiet for so long I worried the call dropped. She finally sighed and said, "Yes, you're remembering that correctly. Maybe. That's the gist of what she said, yes."

"Is that why you never brought me back here again, until now?" I prodded.

She was quiet again for a long time.

"Do you think she killed Uncle Jacob?"

"I don't know." She laughed bitterly. "Isn't that a terrible thing to say about your own mother? You'd think I'd be able to just say, right off, of course not, she could never do such a thing, you shouldn't say things like that about your grandmother." She laughed again, but there was no humor in it at all. "She scared me that day, Jake. I've always been a little bit afraid of her, but that day, the way she said it…" Her voice trailed off. "Before that day I never considered it, never occurred to me, never would have imagined such a thing could be possible. Jacob ran away. Duncan was killed in a car wreck. It all happened so fast, just a matter of days. I went from having two older brothers to having none." She choked off a sob. "I don't remember Duncan at all, and I've tried. I guess he didn't want much to do with a baby sister, you know? But Jacob…I loved him so much. He always had time for me, always took me along with him, never made me feel like…And when you were born, you were such a happy baby, and when they put you in my arms and you cooed at me and smiled, my first thought was *Jacob*, and that's what I named you." She cleared her throat. "She was furious with me for naming you that. Furious. Told me it was disrespectful to her to name my child after the child who'd betrayed her."

The child who'd betrayed her.

Lightning flashed and the call dropped.

I didn't have a chance to count *one* before deafening thunder shook the car.

I grabbed my phone and slipped it into my shorts pocket. I opened the door and ran for the front porch, my feet slipping on the wet stones, sinking into the thick red mud clay. I jumped onto the porch and slipped, falling backward, and I came down hard on the wet wood on my rear end. The shock jolted through my body, and my jaws snapped closed, and I sat there, water soaking through the seat of my shorts and into my underwear.

Gingerly I got to my feet, my back and legs aching, got out of the rain and away from the edge of the porch. I heard engines over the rain and looked at the road, just in time to see another row of cars with *ATF* stenciled on the sides, and some said *ABI*, streaming past on the road, muddy orange water coming up in a spray, and I realized the Tuckers were getting raided.

I went inside and slammed the front door closed behind me, then locked it.

They might not get all the Tuckers, and we were just on the other side of the slope from them.

They could come here.

My heart pounding, I reached for the light switch, but nothing happened when I flipped it, and I realized there were no lights on inside the house.

"Jake?" I looked up. Kelly was standing at the top of the stairs, holding a candle. "The power's out, and the generator didn't kick in." He sounded confused.

I didn't answer, just started groping my way down the hallway, my hand on the wall for support. Every so often as I walked, lightning briefly lit up the house, and I moved quickly before it faded to black again. I somehow reached my grandmother's door, but I heard Geneva's voice, measured and calm, reading.

I opened the door and saw her face, lit up by a candle. Geneva looked up at me and said, "Can you have Kelly go check on the generator? It should have kicked on by now." She glanced at my grandmother, whose hair was plastered with sweat to her skull. "She'll be fine, but the heat is making her uncomfortable."

I nodded and left the door open. I knew there were candles in the kitchen, and a hurricane lamp.

Kelly was in the kitchen lighting the hurricane lamp when I got there. He nodded at me. "I'm gonna have to go check the generator," he said as lightning flashed again. "I think it was turned off after the last time we had to use it, and maybe we forgot to turn it back on." He shook his head. "It was right around the time Miss Sarah had her strokes, so it got lost in the shuffle."

"Is it safe to mess with electricity in the rain?"

He laughed. "It's inside the pump house, so yeah." The hurricane lamp's wick took the flame, and the glow from the lamp cast bizarre shadows around the room. "I'll be back in a minute."

"Be careful," I said. "I think the Tuckers are being raided by ATF."

He didn't say anything, just went out through the mudroom, and I heard the screen door slam.

It was warm and clammy in the barely lit kitchen, and weirdly quiet without the ticking of the window unit. I glanced out the side window and saw Kelly's blurry form slipping and sliding through the mud as he tried to make it to the pump house.

Something drew me to the other window, the one over the sink, the one that looked out into the forest.

I saw a white flash in that place where I always saw it, where we found the Klan mask.

For a moment, the trees disappeared completely, gone, like they were never there. Instead, I saw a wide sloping expanse of lawn, green and glistening in the rain, a fountain bubbling despite the rain, and could see the spread of the big house in the distance, standing in the rain, lights glowing in one of the windows, like it had never burned, like it wasn't a wreck—

Like I was seeing into the past.

I shivered.

And I realized the flash of white that no one else could see was a signal of some kind, someone or something trying to warn me, to let me know I was in danger, that there were secrets that someone or something wanted me to know.

A rush of relief, a sigh of pleasure and happiness so intense I could almost hear it.

You understand at last.

Where did that come from?

The answer is in the woods, but you've always known that, haven't you?

The compulsion was so strong it carried me to the back door.

I stepped out into the mudroom just as the power came back on in the house, a television blaring somewhere inside, the air conditioners coming back to life from their silent sleep.

I stepped outside into the rain.

The light flashed again, but the woods were no longer there.

And even though I could feel the rain pelting my body, soaking my already wet clothes, the late afternoon sky was blue and free of clouds.

I headed for the path.

CHAPTER TWENTY-FOUR

Water was streaming down my face, a steady flow off my chin and down my arms and off my hands. My shirt and shorts were soaked through in no time, my shoes and socks as well. The water swirled around my ankles, cold and muddy, and my teeth were chattering.

But somehow, through the pouring rain and the darkness, I could also see a blue sky and felt the heat of the sun on my arms. But it blended into a night sky, velvety bluish black, with a full moon shining down onto the woods. The trees themselves seemed not real, somehow not tangible. I would blink and could see through them like they were clear, before they shimmered and became solid again.

You're losing your mind, Jake, get a hold of yourself, this isn't possible.
But it was somehow, it was all very real.
I'm not having a breakdown. I am not insane.

I could smell the green of the forest, but also there were new smells—honeysuckle and magnolia and sweet olive and jasmine.

Lightning flashed, and the illusion or whatever it was I'd been seeing was gone as everything went white for a moment. The thunder came almost as soon as the whiteness faded, so loud I could feel it in my nerves, my teeth rattling and the horrific smell of ozone and everything was as it should be, as it was, but then everything shifted again.

I heard splashing and turned to see Kelly slogging through the water toward me, his mouth moving, but I couldn't hear what he was saying. He leaned toward me and said into my ear, his breath tickling my skin, "Are you okay?"

"I don't know," I shouted back, staring around me in wonder.

It looked—it looked like a weird Photoshop experiment, where someone took pictures of the exact same location at different times and layered them over each other, so things didn't seem solid or real, and the more you looked, the more things changed. The rain was constant, though—even when it was the moonlit night, the rain kept coming down, as it did when I could see the sunny afternoon...

When the trees weren't there.

"What the hell is happening?" I heard Kelly shout and felt him take my hand in his and squeeze it.

It took me a few moments to realize what he was saying. "You see it, too?"

Relief flooded through me. I couldn't be going crazy if he was seeing it, too.

Impulse drove me forward, Kelly walking along beside me, still hanging on to my hand. I crazily thought, for a moment, so much for him being a homophobe because he sure didn't seem to mind holding my hand. We kept walking, splashing, having to pull our feet free from the gripping mud and water to keep going, sometimes slipping. I almost fell once, but Kelly grabbed me in his strong hands and kept me from going down. As his hands gripped my arms an image flashed through my head—

I was running through the house, someone right behind me, someone who wanted to hurt me, someone who was terribly angry and wanted to punish me, and I had to get away, I had to, I had to save myself because Cash was going to be waiting for me, and my bag was already hidden down at the ruins, and we'd get into his old car and drive to Birmingham and take the first bus to New Orleans and get away from here. We'd be together and that's all that mattered but somehow she found out—

And I knew *she* was Miss Sarah.

My own mother wanted to kill me.
But that wasn't her chasing me. I ran down the hall to the stairs to

the attic, not thinking, just trying to stay ahead of him. He has a baseball bat—he's always hated me, has always tortured me, and now he is going to kill me. I remember the time we were kids and he deliberately broke my arm and claimed it was an accident, and Mom always believed him instead of me. She gave him license to make me miserable, and that was part of the reason why I wanted to get away—

Kelly's grip on my hand tightened.

"No!" he shouted into the night, into the rain, as we reached the tree line, the path to the ruins. He dropped my hand and pressed the heels of his hands against his forehead. "No, I won't do it—you can't make me do it!"

And it faded out of my mind, and we were on the path, water running past us on its way down to the creek at the bottom of the gully, and Kelly turned and looked at me. He looked stricken, apologetic, scared.

I heard someone calling my name from behind me, behind us, but it was faint and distant, lost in the wind and the rain. I couldn't recognize the voice, either, but I wasn't controlling myself anymore. Instinct and impulse were moving the both of us forward, that we both were meant to see whatever it was we were going to see, and this was happening for a reason.

This was why I came here—I knew that now. My summer trip to Alabama was already written, was meant to happen. This was why I met Tradd, and why everything went so wrong, because I had to overdo it, I had to overdose, so I would have to come here and be here, on this land, in this state, on this night, in this storm.

This was what had to happen, what I was meant to experience, to see.

What was meant to be.

Somehow, I knew. This was the anniversary of the night Dunk was killed, the same date the Lost Boys had died.

And even as those words went through my mind, I felt a shuddering sigh of relief pass through me, and heard a ghostly echo in my ears: *Yes, yes.*

Only you can set us free.

And I realized, finally, what everything meant. He'd been

trying—*they'd* been trying—to make me see, to get me to understand, ever since I got here.

Uncle Jacob. He was trying to let me know, to understand, what happened to him.

But it wasn't just him, either. There was another presence there, too, not as strong as him, not coming through as clearly.

Three Jacobs.

I lost my footing on the slick, slippery path and went down before Kelly could grab hold of me. I went down face-first into the cold muddy water, getting up onto my hands and knees, coughing and spitting muddy water out of my mouth.

Over the rain, over the wind, over the trees moving and rustling against each other in the storm, I could hear other things, too—shouts and screams and the sound of someone running through the woods—

Oh my God they mean to kill me I have to keep running oh my God in heaven please help me don't let them catch me don't let them hurt me.

—and then it, too, was gone as quickly as it had come, and yet I could still hear noises. Something was crashing through the woods from the direction of Tucker Holler, but still I kept walking even as I heard popping sounds in the distance—

Is that gunfire? Surely the Yankees aren't coming up here—there's no reason for them to come here. They burned Tuscaloosa, but why would they come here? There's nothing for them here unless they just want to burn everything and steal and—

I shook my head, which was starting to ache a little bit, a pressure point of pain right directly between my eyes, and I pinched the bridge of my nose between my thumb and forefinger. Mom always did that and said it helped with headache pain and pressure, and I felt like…

Like I had to get to the ruins, I needed to be there for some reason, and Kelly beside me was muttering something I could barely hear. "This is happening, this is happening, this is happening. I'm not imagining this. It's real—this is all real, and it's always been real, and I'm not crazy even though this can't be happening…"

And I knew, somehow, that I hadn't been alone with my dreams and weird feelings—he'd been going through the same thing, and if only we'd compared notes…

I heard my name being shouted again in the distance, like the person calling was far away from me, but it wasn't calling *me*, that had nothing to do with me, like it's coming…

From across the centuries.

My arm—something grabbed my arm with a grip so hard I cried out, and I was spun around, and there was Kelly, but *not* Kelly, somehow at the same time. Again that strange sense of another image being Photoshopped and layered over his face and body, a body that was not as big and developed as Kelly, and the face was slightly wrong and different, the two faces shimmering underneath each other, one trying to take precedence over the other. He dropped my arm and cried out, putting both hands to his face, and said, shouted, screamed, "What's happening?" and he was terrified. I could sense it, and so I reached out into that weird shimmery whatever it was and grabbed his arm this time.

I was oddly grateful to feel hot skin, muscle, flesh, hair, could feel his pulse.

He was substantial.

Real.

Which was a relief because I was not sure what was real anymore and what wasn't.

And not sure I cared.

"It's okay, Duncan," I heard myself saying. "This is meant to be. We're supposed to find out."

Duncan?

And I saw Kelly nodding in agreement, his hair plastered to his scalp, the water cascading off his chin and down his body. He clasped his big hand over mine where it rested on his forearm, and he whispered, "I'm so sorry, Jacob."

He moved my hand down his arm to his hand, and he gripped mine, hard. I could feel the slick wetness from the rain and the calluses from weights, and yet at the same time it also felt softer and drier and less warm, and for a moment I had to repress the urge to scream, to start screaming and run as far away from him as I could because—

He's going to kill me he hates me oh my God why

—but it passed, and again everything felt like it was somehow meant to be, it was meant to happen this way, the story was written a long time ago, and it had played out, over and over again, time after time after time, and we were always brought back to this place, to this time, to repair something, to fix what needed to be fixed and—

I felt the terror, the shock, the wonder, and then I saw it, again through the haze, the house standing there, wooden walls painted white and the marble columns gleaming in the fading sunlight. Those columns had cost a fortune—Grandpa Abraham special-ordered them from Italy. It's Carrera marble, and a wonder people from all over the county, from this part of the state, would come to look at and marvel—Abraham's beautiful farmhouse with its classic columns and high-ceiling rooms—and he built it up here as a showplace, with the entire flatland of the small valley the Sipsey River carved out between the hills spread out as a breathtaking view from the front porch, shaded from the sun by that high roof and the second floor gallery, and I heard a horse, the sound of clopping hooves drawing near. Someone was coming, on horseback, and I felt a sudden rush of fear—

And then the shining house in the dying light of the afternoon was gone again, and all I could see, through the darkness and the rain, were the ruins in front of me, in front of us, because Kelly was just as big a part of this as I was.

And someone was coming through the woods from the direction of Tucker Holler. I could hear them crashing through the underbrush, splashing and smashing and running, trying to get away.

Fear tickled the bottom of my spine.

"Someone's coming," Kelly whispered, and I could hear the fright in his voice, great big two-hundred-plus-pounds-of-solid-muscle Kelly was terrified, more terrified than he'd ever been in his life. "Who's riding a horse through the woods?"

I realized Kelly wasn't, for some reason, hearing the present but was hearing the past—someone coming toward us on horseback—and he wasn't seeing everything I was seeing, and as I stared at the ruins, everything shimmered, and the big house was there again, and the front door opened, and I saw a woman coming out. She looked tired and thin and hungry, and I felt my heart lurch—

Mother, that's Mother, do you see her, Duncan?

—and Kelly's grip on my hand tightened until it hurt, and he whispered, barely loud enough for me to hear, "What the hell is going on around here?"

And he dropped my hand just as the horse came into view, and the man on the horse was wearing a filthy uniform, but it was not a blue uniform but rather a gray one—

It wasn't a Yankee, but a Confederate deserter. The *story* was true, but it had the details wrong. It wasn't a Yankee but someone on the same side their kinfolk were fighting on.

And I saw them, filmy and not fully formed, just like the woman. Somehow, Kelly and I had traveled back through time, and we were witnessing, actually witnessing, what happened to the Lost Boys over a hundred and fifty years ago.

This can't be possible this can't be possible what is happening.

Yes, there were two teenagers, wearing the clothes of a long-forgotten time, clothes no one would wear today, and they had our faces, Kelly's and mine, and the clothes were dirty and patched—

Jacob and Duncan, their names were Jacob and Duncan just like my uncles.

And the Confederate deserter was swinging down from the horse, the two boys standing at the corner of the house, their mother on the porch, and he approached the front steps, and she was rejecting him. I saw her mouth moving, but she wasn't saying anything I could hear, but I knew what she was saying because I witnessed it happen the first time. I was there, and somehow, somehow I was seeing through time and space and dimension and seeing it all happen again, playing out in front of me like a movie being projected on a screen that was transparent because I could also see the ruins through the glimmering flickering images. She was saying they had no food, but whatever he can forage from the fields he's welcome to, and she can't offer him a bed for the night because the enslaved people had all run away, and it wouldn't be proper to have a strange man under her roof, and he agreed with her gallantly, and then he grabbed her, forced himself on her, and the two boys came running around the house, and he pulled his revolver and shoved her. She fell off the porch, and her neck snapped. You could see it happening as she hit the ground, her body lifeless and limp, and he fired and a flower of red exploded on young Jacob's chest and I winced—

I could feel it—it was like I was punched in the chest and now it was buzzing and painful and numb and everything was going gray for me and I lost my balance and fell to my knees.

Now Duncan was on him, and they were fighting over the gun, and the deserter knocked him into one of the columns, and Duncan slid to the ground as the deserter moved inside. And I could smell smoke, flames—and Duncan was just lying there on the ground as the deserter came back out, climbed up onto his horse, and rode back away as Duncan slowly got to his feet, but the house was burning, burning, burning, and there was nothing he could do about it...

I heard Kelly whimpering and realized he could see it, too.

And then it all faded away, like it never happened, and somehow, *somehow* I knew that Duncan buried his mother and brother, never stopped feeling guilty about not being able to protect them or save them or save the house, and he left, went west, disappeared into the West but never ever forgave himself for it.

And now it was dark, the rain still coming down hard, and someone was coming through the woods, and I felt it, felt everything he was feeling—

I have to get to Cash. I have to get out of here—oh my God, they're going to kill me. I never thought, I never thought they would turn on me and do this to me. Oh my God, why do they hate me so?

And I knew this time it was my uncle, running through the woods to get away from Miss Sarah's, to get away from his mother and his brother and his life, his terrible life here that was a lie, always a lie, everything about it a lie, and he and Cash were going to run away together to California where they could live openly and honestly and be together, and I could feel the love he had for Cash, the love he had deep inside, a love he wasn't going to be able to turn away from or ignore. He'd rather be dead than live that horrible lie.

But he never dreamed that Duncan would be the one to kill him.

I knew, I felt it.

It was Duncan coming after him, Duncan with his baseball bat, Duncan ready to kill him, herding him back out of the woods to the house, because of the abomination, the sin, not just for loving another boy, for being in love with another boy—maybe he could have forgiven and gotten past that, maybe someday he'd come to understand his brother—but Duncan could not forgive or forget it was a *Black* boy, bad enough that his brother was a pervert but a—

I wouldn't let that thought finish.

Cain and Abel, the mark of Cain.

I remembered my Bible class at St. Sebastian's, remembered the verse perfectly:

> *And Cain said to his brother Abel, "Let us go outside." And when they were in the field, Cain rose up against his brother Abel, and he put him to death. And the Lord said to Cain, "Where is your brother Abel?" And he responded: "I do not know. Am I my brother's keeper?" And he said to him: "What have you done? The voice of your brother's blood cries out to me from the land. Now, therefore, you will be cursed upon the land, which opened its mouth and received the blood of your brother at your hand…"*

And I knew, knew as the verse came back to me and went through my mind, I knew the truth.

Miss Sarah knew. She'd always known. She was the one who set Duncan on his brother, played on his bigotry, played on his emotions, until he was in a murderous rage.

And I could see it, feel it, the terror, the running, the stitch in the side every time I/he tried to breathe, the agony with every step, the gradual slowing, and the knowing that Duncan was coming up behind me/him, that he was going to kill me, and the tears, the sad tears because I/he'd always believed, always, that his/my brother loved me, and I tripped, went down to my knees and I looked up into his eyes and—

They softened. The eyes softened and I knew, I knew he wasn't going to kill me.

Kelly was muttering, "I won't do it I won't do it I won't do it."

And the sense of relief was so strong, and I struggled to my feet and everything went dark.

Everything faded.

Everything was gone.

We were back in front of the ruins, in the pouring rain, and someone was coming through the woods toward us, someone running away from Tucker Holler. Kelly's eyes were glazed over—he didn't seem to have snapped back into the present from wherever it was we were—and I grabbed his arm again, but he yanked it away from me like it burned him, and his eyes widened, and I could see the dirty man, tall and skinny with the look of a Tucker, coming through the trees at us, and he had a gun, his eyes were wild and he raised it and pointed it at me.

Kelly stepped in front of me as he pulled the trigger.

The gunshot exploded inside my head, and then my shoulder jerked and suddenly felt like it was on fire.

But I didn't have time to process that because Kelly had fallen back into me, and his body was limp and deadweight, and I collapsed beneath it as my arm and shoulder began buzzing, and I screamed as the pain reached my brain through the nerves, and scream and scream and scream, trying to get out from under Kelly, but my right arm wouldn't move—it was less than worthless—and I used my left to push on his deadweight, and I could smell blood everywhere, and then finally I'm out from under and holding my right arm with my left. I didn't see the Tucker anywhere, and I was running, running screaming through the woods back to the house, and I realized I've been shot and Kelly was probably dead...

I had to get help. Kelly saved my life. And I slammed up the steps and into the mudroom and into the kitchen, and Geneva was there, staring at me, her eyes wide, and I realized she was holding the telephone, and I shouted at her, "Kelly's been shot and he needs help. I need help," and she nodded at me strangely, and I couldn't understand why she was just standing there.

And I looked into my grandmother's bedroom and knew.

Miss Sarah had finally died.

Chapter Twenty-five

We buried Miss Sarah in the little cemetery at Crossroads Baptist, next to her husband and her two sons. Yes, we delayed the funeral until the DNA tests came back to positively identify the skeleton in the woods as Uncle Jacob.

It was the least we could do.

Afterward, Mom, Dewey, Kelly, and I went back to the house. Like me, Kelly had been shot in the shoulder. The same bullet he tried to take for me went right through his shoulder and into mine, where it lodged and had to be removed surgically at Corinth County Medical. He'd have to miss a few weeks of working out, but it was better, as he said, than dying.

Depending on how his shoulder healed, he might not be able to play football again.

"She told me everything," Dewey admitted after Mom had poured all of us a belt of whiskey. "When the skeleton was found, she confessed." His reddish-pink face gleamed with sweat, his scarce hairs plastered across his scalp. "Jacob never ran away. He intended to—that was his plan—but she found out." He tossed back the whiskey and grimaced. "So much dirty laundry…"

It was even worse than I'd imagined. Both Paw Paw Donelson and Miss Sarah had been heavily involved in the Klan—Dewey suspected Paw Paw had been the local Grand Wizard but couldn't be sure. It was the desegregation of the schools that brought the Klan back, but Paw Paw himself had died before they could burn any crosses or lynch any Black children. He'd been the driving force behind it all, and once he was gone…well, Miss Sarah had tried to keep it going, but even though she was a force that people feared, she was still a woman, and no Klansman worth his dark soul would take orders from a woman. The Tuckers had been in the Klan, too—that was part of the bond between Miss Sarah and Ma Tucker. It was Ma Tucker who originally told Miss Sarah that her second son was spending an awful lot of time with Cash Porter, and that it seemed, well, unnatural.

She'd been grooming Duncan all along to revive the Klan when he was old enough to take charge, and he and Jacob hadn't ever been close. She'd always pitted them against each other. But her dark poison didn't take root in Jacob somehow, which was one of the reasons she turned on her own son. After Ma Tucker told her what Jacob was up to, she did a little snooping of her own and found out just how deeply involved with Cash Jacob actually was.

"She called him a pervert," Dewey said, his voice shaking. "All these years later, and she still couldn't forgive or love her son. He had it coming, she said, and so she got Duncan to do it for her."

"Duncan didn't kill Jacob," I interrupted, looking over at Kelly, who smiled back at me.

"I'm just telling you what she said," Dewey replied tersely.

Kelly shook his head slightly, and I nodded. He was right—we'd already talked about it. We knew Miss Sarah was the one who killed him when Duncan couldn't do it. Duncan had chased him back toward the house from the ruins. Jacob had slipped and fallen to his knees. Duncan raised the bat but couldn't do it. Miss Sarah must have taken the bat and chased him into the house and up to the attic. He had gone out onto the balcony and, with nowhere else to go, had gone over the railing. His neck broke when he hit the ground, and the last thing he saw before he died was his mother, leaning over the railing, looking down at him with a grim look of satisfaction. Duncan had helped her bury him back by the ruins, and two nights later he got so drunk he drove off the side of the mountain and died.

"She lied to you." Mom threw back her own whiskey and poured herself another shot. "Jacob died from a broken neck, not being hit in the head with a baseball bat."

"I'm just telling you what she told me," Dewey replied.

"She told everyone that Jacob ran away after Dunk died. No one questioned it. He was planning on running away, after all."

I knew Mom was right. I remembered running across the attic, heading out onto the balcony, my head hurting so bad from the blow in the woods, and they were behind me…

He'd gone over the balcony railing and broken his neck.

"So, you shut down the dig," I said softly.

"I didn't know what to do," he replied. "If I'd known, I would have never given them permission to dig out there. How was I supposed to know that was where she'd buried him?"

"It's why she was so against letting them excavate." Mom held up her glass and studied the whiskey. "All these years…I wonder how many times I walked over his grave and didn't even know it?" She shivered. "Poor Jacob. Rest in peace, my darling big brother." She took another drink and wiped at her eyes. She looked at me. "And to think, I sent you here for the summer to keep you out of trouble."

"I think I can handle New Orleans now." I smiled back at her. There was no doubt about that at all in my mind. I mean, if my biggest problem was dealing with the end of a toxic relationship, I'd be just fine. At least my brother and my mother weren't trying to kill me.

And succeeding.

Cash Porter had come by to see me, once the word got out that the skeleton was Jacob. The story Dewey put out there was that Miss Sarah had confessed that Dunk had killed Jacob accidentally, and they covered it up. An old tragedy, and a sad one, too—and one that people would readily believe. No one needed to know the truth, and no one needed to know Kelly and I had been seeing ghosts, either.

"So I was right—he didn't run off and leave me," the old man said, once we were alone. His eyes filled with tears. "I never wanted to believe it, you know? All this time, he was out there in the woods." He wiped at his eyes.

"Trust me, he loved you," I said. "Don't ask me how I know, but I do. He loved you more than anything, and he wanted to go away and make a life with you somewhere else. He died loving you."

Cash just nodded, wiped his eyes one more time, and then stood up. He shook my hand. "Sometimes things work out for the best," he said softly. "I had a great marriage, and I love my child and grandchildren. It's been a good life. But every so often, I'd wonder how different things would have been. Ah, well. Thank you, Jake, for letting me know."

"It's what he would have wanted."

Kelly and I had also finally compared notes. I'd been right—I was getting flashes of memory from Jacob, and he was getting them from Dunk. That was why he'd been so strange with me, a weird combination of anger and guilt. I'd like to believe Dunk felt remorse for what happened, and maybe it was the guilt that led him to drink so much a few nights after Jacob's death.

We also decided not to tell anyone what we'd experienced, especially about the Lost Boys. "No sense in everyone thinking we're crazy," I'd said, but had also tipped off Beau. Sometime after I'd gone home to New Orleans he would *discover* where Duncan had buried his mother and his brother. The story of the Lost Boys would finally have an ending.

Beau was right—Kelly *was* one of the good guys. He took a bullet for me.

As for me and Beau? Well, I didn't want to transfer and neither did he. But it was only about a six-hour drive between Tuscaloosa and New Orleans. We might be seeing a lot of each other, and we would figure out if we had a future.

Mom and Dewey hadn't decided what to do about the old house, but they were talking about letting Dr. Brady's team use it as a permanent base. The house needed a lot of work, but that wasn't my problem.

I was kind of looking forward to going back to New Orleans and taking up my life again. It was going to be different from now on. Never again would I let a guy isolate me from friends or stay with someone who didn't treat me right. I certainly was never going to overdose over some guy, that was for sure.

I had too much to live for—and in a way, I felt like I owed it to the other two Jacobs, whose lives were cut so sadly short, to live as full and rewarding a life as I can.

It was about time a Jacob with Blackwood blood died of old age in a warm bed.

About the Author

Greg Herren is a New Orleans–based author and editor. He is a co-founder of the Saints and Sinners Literary Festival, which takes place in New Orleans every spring. He is the author of thirty-three novels, including the Lambda Literary Award winning *Murder in the Rue Chartres*, called by the *New Orleans Times-Picayune* "the most honest depiction of life in post-Katrina New Orleans published thus far." He co-edited *Love, Bourbon Street: Reflections on New Orleans*, which also won the Lambda Literary Award. His young adult novel *Sleeping Angel* won the Moonbeam Gold Medal for Excellence in Young Adult Mystery/Horror, and *Lake Thirteen* won the silver. He co-edited *Night Shadows: Queer Horror*, which was shortlisted for the Shirley Jackson Award.

He has published over fifty short stories in markets as varied as *Ellery Queen's Mystery Magazine* to the critically acclaimed anthology *New Orleans Noir* to various websites, literary magazines, and anthologies. He has worked as an editor for Bella Books, Harrington Park Press, and now Bold Strokes Books.

A longtime resident of New Orleans, Greg was a fitness columnist and book reviewer for Window Media for over four years, publishing in the LGBT newspapers *IMPACT News*, *Southern Voice*, and *Houston Voice*. He served a term on the Board of Directors for the National Stonewall Democrats, and served on the founding committee of the Louisiana Stonewall Democrats. He is currently employed as a public health researcher for the NO/AIDS Task Force and served four years on the board of directors for the Mystery Writers of America.

Visit Greg at his blog, http://scottynola.livejournal.com/ or his website, http://gregherren.com.

Soliloquy Titles From Bold Strokes Books

Bury Me in Shadows by Greg Herren. College student Jake Chapman is forced to spend the summer at his dying grandmother's home and soon finds danger from long-buried family secrets. (978-1-63555-993-4)

I Am Chris by R Kent. There's one saving grace to losing everything and moving away. Nobody knows her as Chrissy Taylor. Now Chris can live who he truly is. (978-1-63555-904-0)

The Dubious Gift of Dragon Blood by J. Marshall Freeman. One day Crispin is a lonely high school student—the next he is fighting a war in a land ruled by dragons, his otherworldly boyfriend at his side. (978-1-63555-725-1)

Jellicle Girl by Stevie Mikayne. One dark summer night, Beth and Jackie go out to the canoe dock. Two years later, Beth is still carrying the weight of what happened to Jackie. (978-1-63555-691-9)

All the Worlds Between Us by Morgan Lee Miller. High school senior Quinn Hughes discovers that a broken friendship is actually a door propped open for an unexpected romance. (978-1-63555-457-1)

Exit Plans for Teenage Freaks by 'Nathan Burgoine. Cole always has a plan—especially for escaping his small-town reputation as "that kid who was kidnapped when he was four"—but when he teleports to a museum, it's time to face facts: it's possible he's a total freak after all. (978-1-163555-098-6)

Rocks and Stars by Sam Ledel. Kyle's struggle to own who she is and what she really wants may end up landing her on the bench and without the woman of her dreams. (978-1-63555-156-3)